Copyright © 2021 Lauren Landish.

All rights r

Cover desig..

Cover Model: Luke Pearce.
Photography by Randy Sewell.

No part of this book may be reproduced in any form or by any electronic or mechanical means, including information storage and retrieval systems, without written permission from the author, except for the use of brief quotations in a book review.

This book is a work of fiction. Names, characters, places, and incidents are either the product of the author's imagination or are used fictitiously, and any resemblance to actual persons, living or dead, events, or locales is entirely coincidental.

The following story contains mature themes, strong language, and sexual situations. It is intended for mature readers.

All characters are 18+ years of age and are non-blood related, and all sexual acts are consensual.

Table of Contents
Alpha's Baby 4
A Look Ahead 5
Chapter 1 6
Chapter 2 15
Chapter 3 27
Chapter 4 31
Chapter 5 35
Chapter 6 38
Chapter 7 47
Chapter 8 49
Chapter 9 60
Chapter 10 69
Chapter 11 73
Chapter 12 78
Chapter 13 88
Chapter 14 96
Chapter 15 107
Chapter 16 118
Chapter 17 128

Chapter 18...137
Chapter 19...146
Chapter 20 150
Chapter 21...167
Chapter 22 176
Chapter 23 180
Chapter 24 186
Chapter 25 190
Chapter 26 198
Chapter 27 203
Chapter 28 211
Chapter 29 215
Chapter 30 226
Chapter 31...231
Chapter 32 236
Chapter 33 245
Chapter 34 255
Chapter 35 263
Chapter 36 268
Chapter 37 278
Chapter 38 287
Chapter 39 292
Chapter 40 297
Chapter 41...307

Alpha's Baby
by Lauren Landish

I've always had a crush on my ridiculously handsome stepbrother, Stefan. For years, he's always been there, at my side. We've played together, laughed together, and even cried together. But then our relationship turned weird.

Anytime he was near, I found myself filled with lustful thoughts, and when he touched me, it felt like I would burst into flames. Soon, just being in his presence became too much to bear. I started avoiding him at all costs, and when I did encounter Stefan, I would act like a cold-hearted bitch to him so he would never suspect my true feelings.

But sometimes, the things you hide have a way of coming to light . . . when you least expect them.

A Look Ahead
Bella

The masked gladiator led me to a back room. Inside, it was dark with very dim lighting. The bass of the loud music faded in the background as he closed the door, but it still shook the walls.

Though it was dark, I could still see his silhouette as he slowly approached me. My legs trembled beneath me. I thought, and not for the first time that night, what was I doing here again?

Those thoughts fell away as the Gladiator reached me. The heat from the closeness of his body made me shiver. He reached out and placed a hand on my shoulder and I shuddered again.

I looked up at him, and even in the darkness, I could see the intensity in his eyes—eyes that seemed incredibly familiar—but for some reason, I didn't dwell on it.

I just knew right then, without a doubt, that I was going to let him fuck me. And though no words had been spoken since he'd led me into the room, I'm sure he already knew that I was his.

Chapter 1
Bella

For as long as I can remember, I've always had a crush on my ridiculously handsome stepbrother, Stefan. For years, he'd always been there at my side. We've played together, laughed together, and even cried together. But our relationship turned weird when I started to realize just how different boys and girls are and how amazing that can be. I think the first time I noticed was when I went to one of his lacrosse practices. When it was over and he peeled off his gear and his t-shirt, it was like a light shone down from above and a voice said, *This is who you're meant for*.

Suddenly attracted to him, I could no longer be around him without feeling like a perv. The simple things we used to do with each other, like watching movies together and even doing homework, became incredibly awkward.

Anytime he was near, I found myself filled with lustful thoughts, and when he touched me, it felt like I would burst into flames. Soon, just being in his presence became too much to bear. I started avoiding him at all costs, and when I did encounter Stefan, I would act like a cold-hearted bitch to him so he would never suspect my true feelings.

Naturally, Stefan was confused by my sudden change in behavior. He couldn't understand how I'd suddenly gone from his best friend to this frosty ice queen. Though it hurt me to treat him that way, I couldn't tell him that I was doing this for the greater good, that I had thoughts no sister should have about her brother. I couldn't tell him that I yearned for his lips pressed against mine and to run my fingers through his silky blond hair.

I couldn't tell him that I wanted him.

You see, I knew that our relationship could never be, would never be. We were siblings, not by blood but by our parents' marriage. My fantasy of being with Stefan was just that, a fantasy.

It was during this time that Stefan began dating. He'd bring home girls when my parents weren't home and have wild and crazy sex with them, all within my earshot. Even through the walls, you could hear them, and the girls sounded like they were going through a life-changing experience, even the ones I knew were total sluts and Stefan wasn't their first rodeo.

It just pissed me off all the more. Sometimes, I would listen and get all hot and bothered, and often, I had to relieve myself. I would masturbate and pretend I was one of the girls he was fucking, but that became old after a while. I didn't want to pretend anymore. I wanted the real thing.

Eventually, I grew very jealous of the string of girls he would bring back home and found it quite easy to continue being a major bitch to him whenever we interacted. I swore that every scream they made, every moan, every time they made the sounds I wanted to make, it was his fault, that he was taunting me with their cries of passion.

When it came time to graduate high school and move on to college, I was greatly relieved. I had gotten accepted into a prestigious school called North State University, and for the first time in a long time, I was happy.

I was finally going to be free.

I would no longer be burdened by my attraction to my stepbrother or have to listen to him fuck random chicks every weekend. Since I made sure we wouldn't be attending the same university, I knew that I would only see Stefan on holidays, something that was acceptable to me because I knew I would only have to bear his presence for a short time before we were out of each other's life again.

Meanwhile, I would be joining the hottest sorority on North State's campus, Kappa Beta. As a member of this prestigious sorority, I knew I would most likely get hooked up with some popular, hot frat guy and would soon forget all about Stefan and his hot body.

Or so I thought.

* * *

"Come on, girls, swallow that dick!" some chick in the background yelled.

I tried to drown out all the cheering from my wild sorority sisters who stood crowded around the table, watching me and my opponent shove big, fat dildos down our throats, and concentrate.

Had I known that dick-guzzling contests were a part of the Kappa Beta's long line of second-semester traditions, I would have never signed up for it, hottest sorority or not. I thought that the stupid shit stopped after Rush Week and first semester. Apparently, I was wrong.

Be that as it may, I had signed up and had been

accepted. And once I committed to something, that was it. I was going to stay with Kappa and prove to all of these girls that I had what it took to be one of the best of the best, too. But as one of the freshmen, I was automatically looked down upon, and because of this, I had to prove myself.

Hence, the dildo sucking contest. I mean, every girl wants to win one of those, right?

The rules were simple: Head to head—no pun intended. Whoever gagged on their respective dildo first, lost. And this wasn't your average dildo. Oh, no. They're fucking scary.

I had already beaten out eight other girls, and now only one remained: Veronica George. Veronica was a major bitch, a junior with long, blonde hair, green eyes, and pouty lips that were currently wrapped around the shaft of her dildo. She was hugely popular and was thought to have the hottest boyfriend on campus, though I thought he was nothing special. A typical tanned and oiled gym jock, in my opinion.

Veronica eyed me with challenge as she pushed her dildo down a half-inch. She was three-fourths down the shaft and I was likewise. So far, it was the furthest anyone had gotten the whole contest. But I could tell that I was going to have to go all the way down to the ball sack to win this one, because apparently, Veronica really knew how to suck a mean dick.

The trouble was, I was really close to gagging.

I gripped the rubbery flesh and pushed it down slowly, hoping I didn't gag. I could feel it encroaching upon my tonsils and I struggled to keep the dreaded reflex at bay.

What if this were Stefan's cock?

I had no idea where that thought came from, but it was a bad omen. Suddenly, all I could think about was Stefan gripping me by the sides of my head and throat fucking me for all I was worth.

The thought, while a huge turn-on for me, was terribly distracting, and along with all the yelling in the background, I found my focus slipping.

Still eying me, Veronica pushed the dildo even further down, causing a large bulge to appear in her throat. I began to panic. There was not much left for Veronica to take down. One more push and she would have downed the entire length of the 8-inch cock, winning the contest.

I had to act fast or it was over.

Eying her with defiance, I gathered my courage and tried to force the rest of the entire shaft down my throat. That's when I nearly lost all of my lunch.

Shit!

The crowd around the table went wild as I wrenched the cock out of my mouth and gasped for air, hacking and coughing.

Across the table, Veronica jumped up, removed the giant dildo from her throat with ease, slapped it down on the table, and squealed in delight. "I win!"

Her words and joyous laughter felt like a knife in my heart. I'll let you know now that I am very competitive and don't like losing . . . even a dumb ass dick-sucking contest.

Who had made up such a contest, anyway?

"It's okay," I muttered under the noise of the crowd as I wiped spittle from my lips with the back of my hand and regained my composure. "It's a stupid contest anyway."

I tossed the fat dick on the table beside Veronica's saliva-covered one, glad to be rid of it. The rubbery flesh had left a nasty taste in my mouth, and I would be glad when I could go rinse with a minty mouthwash.

"Everyone, quiet!" yelled a voice, getting results. It was Hanna Jones, Kappa's president, standing in the center of the room beside the table.

With long, dark hair that she wore in a girly ponytail and sultry, dark eyes, Hanna was dressed in a pink skirt and a white blouse that was tied in a knot to show off her tanned, flat midriff. Pink and white were our sorority's colors, and I had been wearing more of it than I was used to, hopefully something that would taper off once my freshman year was over.

When the room finally quieted down, Hanna smiled at me. "Nice try, Bella. I was impressed. I never saw a new girl get so far before."

"Thanks," I mumbled. I still couldn't believe I had just participated in the contest. And even worse, I had lost.

"You should be proud," Hanna continued. "You defeated eight other girls and nearly beat Veronica, our undefeated champion."

"She wasn't even close!" Veronica scoffed, folding her arms across her chest. "And you know it."

"She came closer than any girl ever has to beating you," Hanna pointed out. "You have to admit that."

Veronica rolled her eyes. "Whatever you say."

"Isn't it time to choose the Sacrifice now?" one of the sorority sisters asked Hanna with breathless excitement.

I quirked an eyebrow in confusion. What was this? Were the girls not content with just holding a cock-gagging contest? Now they were into satanic rituals too?

"What's a Sacrifice?" one of the other freshmen, Sara Delaney, asked. When I first joined the sorority, Sara and I had become fast friends, mainly out of necessity. Even within a sorority, there were cliques within cliques, so that meant new girls had to stick together.

Hanna's eyes sparkled with mischief. "As most of our senior members here know, every once in a while, we honor a deal we have with our brother fraternity, Alpha Gamma."

"And what deal is this?" Sara asked suspiciously.

A grin spread across Hanna's face. She seemed to be enjoying this. "Just like we receive new sisters who must prove themselves, Alpha Gamma receives new brothers who must prove themselves as well. Every so often, an Alpha gets challenged by an upstart. If that upstart wins, he wins a special offering from Kappa Beta for one night."

Sara glared. "Am I understanding you right? Are you saying that the Sacrifice is one of us contest losers?"

Hanna's grin nearly split her face. "Correct."

"That's such bullshit!" Sara raged. She looked around at her gathered sisters. "C'mon, guys, a dildo-sucking contest is ridiculous enough as it is, but our bodies being offered to some dumb, iron pumping jock? That's absolutely nuts!"

"You gave an oath when you joined this sorority that you would do anything for your sisters," Hanna pointed out.

"Yeah, I did, but I didn't agree to prostitution."

"It's not prostitution," Hanna argued.

Sara looked unconvinced. "Yeah? Then what is it?"

"It's called 'taking one for the team'."

"Oh give me a break—"

"Anyway," Hanna cut in loudly, turning away from Sara like she was old news, and I suspected that when it was time for us freshman to have a chance to live in the house, Sara wouldn't be invited. "I'm going to try something new this year."

"What?" someone in the crowd asked.

Hanna's eyes roved over the contest losers. "Usually, the one who was knocked out of the contest first would be the Sacrifice. This year, I'm going to let Veronica pull a name out of a hat. Whatever name she pulls is the Sacrifice."

The crowd broke off into excited murmuring.

Hanna gestured to one of the girls in the crowd. "Get the hat, Ashley."

While the crowd murmured excitedly, Ashley scurried off and then returned a few minutes later with a NSU hat and slips of paper that she had scribbled all of our names on. Meanwhile, I was still trying to wrap my mind around it all. One of the losers of the contest would be giving her body to a total stranger?

What the hell had I gotten myself into?

Hanna grabbed the hat from Ashley and the crowd quieted. "Veronica."

Veronica stepped forward eagerly. I could tell she was enjoying this too much.

"No peeking," Hanna warned, holding out the hat to Veronica. "Reach in there without looking."

Veronica turned away and blindly reached into the hat. She dug around for a moment while everyone whispered amongst each other. Several of the losers looked anxious while they watched Veronica, probably worrying that their name would be pulled out of the hat while others looked excited. Let's face it. We'd been busy doing sorority stuff, so some of us hadn't been getting any action in a while.

Sara scowled at Veronica, who was still blindly shuffling through the hat. "There is no way in hell I'm agreeing to this if she pulls my name out of that hat. They will just have to kick me out."

Sara's comments made me think to myself, what if Veronica pulls my name?

She isn't, I told myself. *There's no way she'll chose me. There are eight other girls' names in there.*

Veronica finally grabbed a folded piece of paper out of the hat and opened it. She gave a dramatic pause as she stared at the paper.

We all waited with bated breath.

"Well?" Hanna demanded impatiently. "Who is it?"

Veronica tore her eyes away from the paper and my heart began to pound as her gaze centered on me like a hawk. "Bella James."

Chapter 2
Stefan

I could never understand my attraction to my stepsister. Sure, she was hot, but so were many other girls around my age. I guess there was something very special about Bella. Maybe it was her sparkling green eyes, her sensual mouth, or her long, flowing, dark brown hair that always seemed to blow in the wind behind her like a banner. Or maybe it was the way she looked at me or the way she said my name softly that seemed to say that she wanted me.

Whatever the case, I found myself slowly falling in love with her over the years. It'd started in high school when one day, I just noticed that more than being my stepsister and best friend, she was a very beautiful girl too.

It was hard not letting my true feelings show whenever she was close. Not to mention the excitement that plagued me whenever we were in the same room. Sometimes, I would have to excuse myself to keep her from seeing my boner.

Because of this hypersensitivity to her presence, physical contact with her became incredibly difficult. It was at this time that I began to avoid her. My hormones were raging out of control and I feared that if I continued being in her presence, something awful would happen.

Eventually, I got a girlfriend, a pretty girl named Mindy. Mindy was pretty hot, with blonde hair, blue eyes, and big tits. Still, whenever I was with her, I could only fantasize about Bella and her pretty face.

Our relationship didn't last long. I found myself quickly losing interest in Mindy. She just couldn't compare to my stepsister's beauty, and she was quite the airhead.

That's when I went on a dating spree, looking for someone who could make me forget about my desire for Bella. At the time, I was a very popular guy in high school, being a star athlete and all, and there was no shortage of girls that wanted me.

I'd bring them home, fuck 'em, and then leave them when I got tired of them. I know it sounds shitty, but I was looking to fill a hole inside me. I couldn't have Bella, so I needed to continually release that pent-up sexual frustration that she caused.

This was about the time when Bella began to treat me like utter shit, and I assumed it was because of all the girls I was bringing back home. She was probably thinking I was such a misogynistic douchebag.

From a certain point of view, she was right, but I wasn't trying to be a douche. I wanted badly to tell her that I was doing it for the benefit of us both, on the grounds of our being stepbrother and stepsister. Our relationship could never be, and the quicker I could get over her, the better. And with each girl, I prayed that she would be the one who could make me forget Bella. Each time, it didn't happen, and I was left frustrated as, just at the moment of climax, it was Bella's face I saw in my mind, regardless of who was in bed with me. It was shitty for me to use them like that, but I can't change it now.

Soon, I began to feel her hatred of me was for the best. It kept me away from her and reinforced the idea that we couldn't be together.

Once it was time to go off to college, I knew that I would finally kick my secret obsession of Bella. Just like in high school, I'd be popular at college and would be able to fuck as many hot chicks as I wanted. I was happy because I'd finally be able to forget about Bella's pretty face and gorgeous body.

Boy, was I wrong.

* * *

"Fuck 'em up, Craig!" yelled someone within the rowdy crowd.

"Yeah, Craig! Don't let that pussy upstart beat you!" yelled another.

Drowning out the taunts of my brothers, I growled as a line of sweat rolled down the side of my face, the veins standing out on my forearm. I refused to be baited, though I would have been happy to show those punks what a real 'pussy' was if I weren't so engaged in defeating my opponent.

After all, I didn't run three miles every day and work out in the gym five days a week for nothing.

At six-foot-two, I was built like a superhero with well-defined muscles all over my body. I was born an athlete, a star player. And like any star player, I was in it to win.

"Shit," my opponent, Craig Parker, growled, sweat lining his face as we grappled with each other. Shirtless and covered with a sheen of perspiration, we were sitting at a table in the middle of the Alpha Gamma living room, engaged in a fierce arm-wrestling match. I had the upper hand, with Craig's arm almost touching the table.

Craig was a worthy opponent, with muscles almost as well-defined as mine. But he lacked mental focus, and that was a weakness that I exploited to perfection. Victory begins in the mind, and I knew I had Craig beat there.

I maintained eye contact with him, willing him to believe that his efforts were futile. He couldn't win. I was stronger, mentally and physically, and he was the shit under the sole of my shoe.

Craig clenched his jaw, straining with all his might, and sweat poured down the sides of his face. He managed to move my arm back a fraction of an inch and a surge of adrenaline rolled through me. It was what I'd been waiting for. It gave me the angle I needed.

Roaring, I smashed his hand into the table and jumped up, pounding my chest in victory.

The room erupted in jeers and cheers with several of Craig's fan-boys booing me. I didn't give a fuck. They were all just mad because I had beaten every single Alpha Gamma hotshot thus far and was on my way to being crowned top Alpha for the Second Semester Arm Wrestling Tournament. After transferring to NSU, I hadn't been forced to go through Rush Week, but I still had to prove myself to the guys, and the tournament was it.

"Fuck, man!" Craig cried, jumping up from the table and shaking his wrist. "I want a re-match!"

I shook my head. "You kidding me, bro? I beat you fair and square."

Craig stepped up to me, his face red with rage,

and he shoved me.

"Enough!" Todd James, president of Alpha Gamma, snapped. He quickly stepped between us, saving Craig from getting his face rearranged. "Stefan beat you fair and square, Craig. If you want to arm-wrestle him again, you'll have to wait until the next competition."

Craig looked like he wanted to argue, but then he backed down. "Total bullshit, man." He walked back into the crowd to nurse his wounded pride, shaking his head.

Todd looked after Craig for a moment and then turned and looked at me. "You're doing good, Livingston. Better than I thought. Looks like the rumors about you being the best jock at South State were true."

Todd was referring to my being a new transfer to NSU. Back at South State, I had been the top player on the lacrosse team. One of my teammates, Jared Stroing, another freshman hotshot, couldn't handle all the attention I was getting, so he started taking shots at me.

Naturally, I responded by letting him know in no uncertain terms that I was the top dog, and any attempt to get in my way would result in his ass getting kicked.

Well, Jared didn't seem to get the memo and continued taking cheap shots at me during games, nearly causing us to lose and making me look bad in the process. Finally, I had enough and got into a fight with him in the middle of one of our very important matches against a rival team.

The fight ended up costing us the game and Jared suffered a broken nose. For punishment, I was forced to apologize and was suspended from the lacrosse team.

But that wasn't enough for Jared's parents, who

had watched me ruthlessly pummel their pussy son into the ground, and they wanted to press charges.

Eventually, after much back and forth between our legal representatives, our family lawyer hammered out a deal. I was to leave South State, and in return, the Stroing family would drop all charges against me.

My parents immediately wanted me to agree to this deal. After all, it would save them a whole lot of money and spare the school a scandal. I fought against them for a while. I didn't want to give Jared what he wanted from the beginning—to be head of the lacrosse team. Fuck that. I'd kicked his ass, and South State was my territory now.

In the end, though, I gave in. It wasn't worth the time, money, and stress my parents and I were likely to go through if we got embroiled in a drawn-out legal battle. Besides, everyone at the game had seen me totally wreck Jared's face, and I would be hard-pressed convincing a bunch of jurors that Jared had been the one who had started it.

So I packed up and went to the nearest university that would take me, which happened to be NSU, actually transferring in without losing any credits. I'd even gotten into Alpha right away, since they had a partner chapter at SSU that I'd been friendly with. In a lot of ways, I couldn't have had it any easier.

The one thing that bothered me about the whole affair, though, is that I did not receive one call of support from Bella. She had to have known what happened with me, with her and my stepmom keeping in contact, but she didn't care.

I guess she was still in bitch mode. Still, it pissed

me off. We were close at one time, and she didn't even have the decency to pick up her phone and call me when I was down.

To make matters worse, I still had no idea what university she was attending. For some reason or another, Bella had lied about what school she would be going to when she left home, telling me that she was going to Guilford, which turned out to be bullshit when I looked like a total asshole poking around campus in my South State team gear trying to find her, only to be told there was no Bella James at Guilford. I had no idea why she lied, but it hurt.

"Stefan?"

I tore myself out of my reverie and shrugged, looking at Todd. "What can I say? I play to win." I looked around the room in a lazy, cocky manner that I was sure would piss a lot of people off. I'm not always that way, but these guys expected it. "I bet my left nut sack that I can beat anyone here."

"You sure about that?" asked a deep voice. Jace Randall, dressed in just grey sweats, his chiseled abs on display, stepped into the middle of the room and eyed me with challenge. Jace, a pretty boy with looks that got him into more panties than he could count, was rumored to be the biggest badass in the entire school and was the last contestant I had yet to beat.

Judging by his ripped abs and cut arms, I had finally met a worthy opponent. My body thrummed with excitement as I coolly studied him. I had been anticipating this from the moment I began the challenge, top dog against top dog.

Even though I had only been at NSU a short time,

I knew Jace to be a major prick who thought he was better than everyone. Then again, if the cheap ass tin foil trophy on the mantle with his name scribbled on it was to be taken seriously, he had a good reason to think that way.

I also knew that if I defeated Jace, I would become the undisputed alpha of Alpha Gamma.

Nothing would make me happier.

"Yup," I said in a nonchalant manner that I knew would have Jace's blood boiling. "Beating you will be like a walk in the park."

Jace's jawline bulged as he clenched his jaw and I laughed inwardly. I was already getting under his skin.

"Let's go," he growled, heading over to the table and sitting down with a grunt. Jace began flexing his arm and slapping himself on his bicep.

"Sure," I said with a smile and a wink, walking over to the table with a confident swagger and sitting down. I rolled my shoulders back and shook out my wrists as Jace eyed me with hatred.

Having just participated in a bunch of arm-wrestling matches, my wrists were sore and my arm felt swollen, pumped to the edge of exhaustion. Jace had participated in none since he was the reigning champion, and he would be facing me with full energy.

It wasn't exactly fair, but that was the point of the game. A true alpha had to prove his strength by defeating a string of his opponents back-to-back.

"Last match," Todd said, enjoying the silent aggression between us both. He wasn't a physical type. He was more the mental type, but I liked him anyway. "Whoever wins is top Alpha and wins the prize from

Kappa. Ready yourselves."

Jace and I both placed our right elbows on the table and clasped hands. I noted the strength behind Jace's grip and begrudgingly admitted to myself that this would not be an easy match.

"You're dead meat, Livingston," Jace growled at me with confidence.

I tightened my grip on his hand, letting him know that I wasn't afraid in the least.

We scowled at each other as the room around us began to clamor with excitement at the upcoming match. Adrenaline rolled through me, and the weariness I felt melted away. I was ready to do this.

"On your mark . . ." said Todd, "set . . . go!"

Immediately, I let out a grunt as the full force of Jace's strength pressed down against my arm and I lost a few inches to his advance.

The room became loud as our brothers began shouting for which one of us they wanted to win. Most of the shouts were for Jace, since I was the new guy and he was the school's hotshot, but I didn't let that distract me.

Jace growled, pushing my hand down a little further toward the table. Panic threatened to overwhelm me, but I remained calm. Due to my previous matches, I had less energy than I thought, and the adrenaline that had been pumping through me moments before was fading away, leaving me with fatigue.

Sweat rolled down my jaw as I fought back, my hand inching closer to the table from Jace's brutal onslaught. Around us, the crowd only roared louder, anticipating my defeat.

Across the table, Jace's eyes blazed with triumph

as he sensed my growing weariness and doubled his efforts to put me down. It was all I could do to stay afloat, twisting my side to keep my hand from slamming into the table, growling and grunting.

I had to hand it to Jace. He was one tough bastard, and I was slowly beginning to realize that even if I hadn't been tired, he would have been no easy opponent.

As my hand drifted down toward my defeat, I began to wonder if it was worth it. The prize? My name on a tinfoil trophy and some slut from one of the top sororities from NSU who could end up being an absolute dog. I knew it wasn't beyond a frat like Alpha Gamma to play cruel pranks on new members by dangling a sweet prize in front of their faces and making them go through a ton of work to get it, only to find out it wasn't worth the effort in the end.

But then, for some reason or another, Bella and her pretty little mouth and sexy body entered my mind. I imagined that she was the prize I would be winning and that it was her body that I would be ravaging.

A fire grew in my stomach as I imagined my body pressed against hers and ravaging her with passionate kisses. Soon, the fire roiled into a raging inferno and a sudden flood of strength flowed through my weary limbs.

With a roar of confidence, I began pushing back against Jace. My hand, which had been an inch away from the table, rose back up several inches.

In response, Jace pushed back furiously, hoping to slam my hand down onto the table with brutal force. I pushed him back further, our hands falling into the neutral position, and then slowly, I began pushing his hand back toward the table.

The crowd went wild at the turn in events, with many gawking in disbelief at my comeback.

Panic showed in Jace's eyes as his face twisted with effort. I knew he couldn't believe it. How could I, after all those matches, possibly have the strength to beat him?

I clenched my teeth, pushing with all the strength I had left in my body. I had to win this. Jace, as hot as he thought he was, wasn't shit in comparison to me. Beating him would show him that.

"Fuck," Jace cried, overcome with panic as he frantically tried to regain ground against my determined advance.

Once I heard the panic in his voice, I knew I had him. With cool, determined confidence, I looked him straight in the eye while I pushed him further toward his defeat.

Poor Jace. He tried everything, twisting his body, huffing and puffing, and he even almost cheated by using his other arm for leverage. It all did him no good.

I slammed his hand down against the cool wood a second later. The room around us went absolutely crazy, with many not being able to believe my turnaround victory. I wrenched my hand away from Jace's and jumped up from the table with my wrist feeling like it had been run over by a semi and my limbs sore and exhausted.

Thanks, Bella, I thought as I exulted in my victory.

Todd came over and clasped me on the shoulder,

respect showing in his eyes. "Congrats, Livingston. You are the new top Alpha."

Around the room, everyone was chattering with each other and eyeing me with that same respect. Several of Jace's buddies went over to question and comfort him, but he pushed them away, jumped up from the table, and glared at me. His wrist and hand were a bright red and his chest and cheeks were flushed, his body covered in a sheen of sweat. "You're lucky, Livingston," he growled at me. "I didn't eat breakfast this morning."

I held back a laugh. "Sure," I said. "A bowl of Wheaties would have made all the difference."

For a moment, it seemed as if Jace would rush me, and I tensed my body in preparation. But then he turned away, swearing all the while, and left the dorm living room with several of his buddies on his heels.

"He's never going to live that one down," Todd said as we watched them leave and several of our frat brothers gathered around to congratulate me on my crazy win.

"Good," I replied, filled with satisfaction at my victory and my mind on the upcoming prize. "I don't want him to."

After all the congratulations and pats on my back, my brothers began to tell me all about the anonymous hot chick I would most likely get to bang from Kappa.

I was assured that she would be a perfect ten and that I would be pleased. I was even told that I would probably become a pussy magnet after I fucked her, with every slut on campus wanting my dick.

I was pleased by all the hype. This would be just

what I needed—a bunch of hot chicks that would make me forget about my unhealthy obsession with my stepsister.

Bella will be old news by next week, I thought as I daydreamed about all the girls that'd be fawning over me before the year was over. Hell, I'd work my way through the entire Greek alphabet if I had the chance.

But as I sat there being bombarded with lewd jokes and envious salutations, a small voice at the back of my mind was telling me that nothing could be further from the truth.

Chapter 3
Bella

"This costume is so you, Bella!" Hanna cried eagerly, almost hopping up and down.

I wasn't so sure. I was standing in an adult costume store located several blocks away from NSU with Hanna, trying to choose what I would wear for my upcoming special night.

I eyed the skimpy costume, a two-piece white bra and panties, complete with wings and a halo. I thought it looked ridiculously absurd, some tramp's version of Halloween five minutes before getting fucked. Oh, wait. I *would* be getting fucked.

I thought about walking out of the store right then and there. And I would have if I weren't being courted by the head of Kappa. As it were, I felt obligated to go along with the proceedings or risk being kicked out of my sorority.

"I don't know," I said, fingering the outfit. "I don't think that mask will hide most of my features."

"Are you kidding?" snorted Hanna. She grabbed the flimsy costume off the rack and pressed it against me, sizing me up. "It will more than do its job. Plus, you're still new here at NSU. No one will even know who you are."

I bit my lower lip to hold back a nasty retort. It was easy for Hanna to be so nonchalant about my concerns when she wasn't the one who was being offered as a sacrifice to some drunken jock.

"Are you sure about that?" I dared ask. "All the Kappa girls know I'm going to be the Sacrifice. How do I know they won't just disclose my identity to one of the Alpha boys whenever they think I've slighted them?"

Hanna looked up from the costume and rolled her eyes. "Seriously, Bella? Do you have no faith in your sisters? No one is going to tell on you. We all took an oath when we joined this sorority. No one, and I mean no one, rats on a fellow sister."

"But what if they do?" I persisted. "You can't honestly guarantee that no one will tell. I'm just saying, Hanna . . . you're cool, but shit happens."

Hanna let out an exasperated sigh. "Look, if someone reveals your identity, they will be kicked out of the sorority, stripped of all their titles, and humiliated for the duration of their stay at NSU. Do you honestly think that any of those bitches wants to risk that?"

"No," I said after a moment. "But—"

"Okay then," Hanna snapped, handing out the costume to me. "Stop being such a baby and go try this on."

I stared at it. What was I doing here? Did I really want to go through with having sex with a total stranger just to prove to myself that I could get over Stefan?

And was it really worth the chance of possibly being exposed as a slut after it was all over? Despite Hanna's assurances, I was no fool. I knew at some point that my identity would be found out, whether through one of the sisters telling on me or the guy himself eventually recognizing me.

While I would probably be humiliated and called names, the Alpha I slept with would likely be celebrated and hailed as some sort of sexual hero.

Such was the way of the campus I lived on. Even funnier, I'd signed a 'morals pledge' when I enrolled, a joke on paper if I ever saw one.

"Bella?" Hanna asked impatiently. "Are you going to try this damn costume on or not?"

I was tempted to tell Hanna to take the costume and go wipe her ass with it. Was there really any point to going through with this whole ordeal? I mean, honestly, what was in it for me?

I get to screw some hot jock and pretend it's Stefan, I thought. *And release all that sexual frustration I've been holding in.*

"If you are having second thoughts and are backing out of this, tell me now," Hanna said, her voice going cold. "I need to know if you're not going to be part of the team."

Hanna really had her nerve.

After a long moment of standing there, I snatched the costume out of her hands. "I'm in."

I turned and walked off to the dressing room. I had to admit one thing, at least.

I would look hot in it.

Chapter 4
Stefan

"I'm going to go with this one," I said, grabbing up the gladiator costume that consisted of an elaborate loincloth, a mask, and a headdress.

The costume didn't do much to cover up most of my body. My chest, abs, and even some of my ass would be on display wearing it, but that's the way I wanted it. The gladiator totally fit in with my personality, the huge competitor and show-off that I was.

I was at an adult costume store with several of my frat buddies, Todd, Craig, and Jace. Since the arm-wrestling match, both Craig and Jace had made an effort to befriend me.

I was okay with kicking it with them because I was new and needed friends at NSU.

All three of the guys eyed the costume, laughing. "Dude, that is so you!"

I grinned and began heading toward the dressing room.

Five minutes later, I examined myself in the dressing room mirror. I have to say that I looked like Spartacus himself, with everything I had worked hard for on display.

The loincloth did little to hide the fact that I was well-endowed, something that I wasn't ashamed to show off.

"I could totally see chicks digging this," I whispered, flexing my muscles.

After I was done preening, I grabbed the mask/headdress and slipped it on. Then I grabbed the clothes that I'd been wearing when I came into the store—some blue jeans and a t-shirt—and I stepped out of the dressing room, intending to walk out of the store dressed in the costume for kicks.

I was walking out of the male dressing room area, not watching where I was going, when I felt something soft slam into my chest.

I heard a small cry and a light thud. Startled, I looked down. There, sprawled on the floor was a sexy, masked angel. She had long, dark hair that lay across her mask like a shawl, a shapely figure, and killer legs. Something about her seemed familiar, but I couldn't put my finger on it.

"I'm sorry," I said, quickly offering my hand to the mysterious vixen. "I wasn't watching where I was going."

The masked angel glanced up at me for a moment and looked away quickly as if she was afraid to check out my body.

"Neither was I," she mumbled underneath her breath, making me strain to understand her.

"Let me help you up."

"That's ok, I'm fine." The angel quickly scrambled to her feet and without a second glance my way, hurried away.

"Hey, wait up!" I called.

The masked angel continued on, nearly breaking into a sprint. I quickly made my way after her, easing through aisles, when I heard a sharp whistle, laughs, and giggles.

"Oh, my God, what a hot gladiator!" A group of

three college girls were pointing at me and whispering amongst each other, their eyes lit up.

"Thanks, ladies." I grinned at them briefly and glanced at where the angel had run off to. She was nowhere in sight.

"Do you have a name?" one of the girls asked.

I looked around the store for several more moments before turning to the girls and grinning. "Spartacus," I said.

After a little flirting with the three girls, I found Jace, Craig, and Todd near the counter.

"Did any of you see a hot angel run through here?"

"Yeah," Craig replied.

"Where'd she go?" I asked.

Craig nodded at my loincloth. "Looks like in your crotch."

The fellas had a good laugh at that. I could laugh right along with them. I knew I had nothing to be ashamed of.

When it came time to pay for the costume, Todd was adamant that I pay for it. I slapped my jeans on the counter and my wallet fell out of the pockets before I could grab it.

Jace was the one to pick it up. "Dude, who's this chick in your billfold?"

I didn't even have to look to know who he was referring to. "That's Bella, my stepsister."

Craig and Todd crowded around Jace to get a better look at what he was staring at.

Jace's face was a little pale. "That's your stepsister?"

I nodded.

"Fuck, she's hot."

"Yeah," Craig chimed in. "I'd totally smash that."

Anger surged through me. "None of you dickwads would have any chance with her. She doesn't go for dumb jocks."

In reality, what did I know about Bella's actual taste in guys? She had never confided in me what kind of guys she liked, and I kind of assumed that she wouldn't like the dumb athlete.

Whatever the case, the way my frat brothers were salivating over her was pissing me off.

"How would you know?" Jace asked, feeling his balls drop a little again, it seemed.

I just didn't want to kick his ass with half of my ass hanging out of a loincloth. I snatched my wallet from his hands and pulled out a wad of cash to pay for my costume. "Because she told me. End of discussion."

Chapter 5
Bella

"Are you ready, Bella?"

It was the night of the Sacrifice. I was standing before the Kappa living room mirror with several of my sorority sisters surrounding me, making sure my costume was absolutely perfect and that the mask hid most of my features.

The entire room was filled with excited chatter, making me even more anxious than I already was.

Apparently, the guy I would be sacrificed to was a new student on campus and no one knew his identity. And supposedly, no one from the Alpha fraternity knew mine either, but I had to wonder if that would change after tonight.

Both sides claimed that they had taken an oath not to reveal the identity of either participant. I was filled with anxiety that it was all just a lie.

But that wasn't the only thing that was on my mind.

Back in the costume shop, I had run into a masked gladiator. My God, did he have a beautiful body—just as beautiful as Stefan's, and that was saying something.

I had run away from him though, for some stupid damn reason.

"Yes," I said finally. "Let's rock."

Twenty minutes later, I was stepping into the Alpha fraternity building with my sisters. I looked around, a little frightened. There were jocks all around and loud music playing. All of them had beer in their hands and were eyeing me lewdly.

Anxiety threatened to overwhelm me. My breathing became heavy and ragged. I couldn't go through with this. What had I been thinking? This whole thing was going to wind up ruining my reputation at the school. I had to get out.

I looked around frantically, seeking a way out.

That's when I saw him.

No fucking way.

Stefan

My mouth went dry when the angel from the store stepped into the Alpha frat house. Though she was surrounded by a group of very hot sorority girls, my eyes were only on her.

After a moment, I walked over and stood before her. I watched as she looked me up and down. This was the first time I could get a good look at her. There was something familiar about her features beneath the mask, but I couldn't place it.

"What are you waiting for?" Todd asked from the sidelines. "Take her in the back and show her what a gladiator you are."

The room broke out into lewd cheers and loud whistles. I looked back to the girl. The poor thing was trembling, her hands and knees shaking. For a moment, I wondered if she would back out of her commitment as I extended my hand to her.

The roaring of the crowd grew louder, and the angel looked down at my hand like it was a snake. Sweat began to beat my brow and I feared that she would lose heart and turn and run from the room.

That's when she grabbed ahold of my hand. There was something about that grip, about those fingers, and I felt myself get carried away.

Chapter 6
Bella

I couldn't believe it. I was about to fuck a total stranger.

The masked gladiator led me to a back room. Inside, it was dark with very dim lighting. The bass of the loud music faded in the background as he closed the door, but it still shook the walls.

Though it was dark, I could still see his silhouette as he slowly approached me. My legs trembled beneath me. I thought, and not for the first time that night, what was I doing here again?

Those thoughts fell away as he reached me. The heat from the closeness of his body made me shiver. He reached out and placed a hand on my shoulder. I shuddered again, but it wasn't just because of fear, but also a deep, animal desire.

I looked up at him, and even in the darkness, I could see the intensity in his eyes, eyes that seemed incredibly familiar—but for some reason, I didn't dwell on this.

I just knew right then, without a doubt, that I was going to let him fuck me. And though no words had been spoken since he'd led me into the room, I'm sure he already knew that I was his.

Without warning, he pulled me against his hard body, eliciting a gasp from me. Then his lips smashed into mine with passionate urgency, his hands roving over my curves. I moaned as I parted my lips and let his tongue inside, and he began swirling it around, tasting every inch of my mouth.

After a minute of swapping spit, he suddenly picked me up and carried me over to the bed, laying me down gently.

With no warning, he began ravaging my neck, his lips burning into my flesh. A soft sigh escaped my lips as jolts of electricity wracked my limbs. God, he knew how to set me on fire.

Slowly, he kissed his way down to my chest. He removed my bra and then brought his lips against my erect nipple, licking it.

I moaned, my fingers finding a place in his hair.

He bit into my flesh gently, kneading my nipple with his teeth. I clenched a handful of his hair and let out a soft cry. He was amazing.

The masked gladiator kissed his way down my stomach until he was between my legs. Removing my white panties, he put his lips on my wet mound. A louder cry escaped my lips at the incredible sensation.

He began sucking and slurping on my pussy like it was his last meal. My thighs shaking, I arched my back and reached down and grabbed him by the sides of his head.

He shook his head wildly as he sucked on my lips, kneading them with his teeth. While it felt good, his mask was chafing against my thighs and irritating me. I resisted the urge to pull it off, not wanting to interrupt him. I didn't want to break the magic spell he was somehow casting over me.

Then, while sucking my clit, he slid two fingers inside. I gripped the sides of his head tightly, arching my back even more, crying out at the ceiling.

I had never felt so good in my entire life. If this was what sex with a total stranger was always like, I never wanted it to end.

He rammed his two fingers deep inside me, sucking and slurping while he looked up at me. I was taken by the intensity in his eyes—eyes that seemed more and more familiar to me—and a growing inferno blazed inside my stomach.

A few more seconds were all I could take. I let out a wild scream at the ceiling, a scream so loud that I thought they would hear me over the loud music playing in the living room, as my body was rocked with explosion after explosion.

When it was over, he was suddenly on his knees in front of me. My breath caught in my throat at the huge bulge that was imprinted against his loincloth. His cock must have been enormous.

Even though I had just come, desire coursed through me as I gazed at the impressive bulge. This specimen before me was like a god, and I wanted to serve him.

My mouth watering, I quickly undid the loincloth and pulled it halfway down his chiseled ass cheeks. His big, fat cock flopped out, nearly slapping me in the face. I salivated even more. It was beautiful, with a large mushroom head and a thick, luscious shaft.

Looks like that dildo sucking contest is going to come in handy, I thought.

Moving forward, I opened my mouth wide and

eagerly wrapped my lips around his fat cock. Immediately, my masked gladiator threw back his head and moaned. His skin felt warm in my mouth and I could feel his cock throbbing.

A sense of déjà vu coursed through me at the sound of his moan. I don't know why the feeling came over me, but I was too busy to pay attention to it.

I slowly bobbed my head back and forth down his shaft, taking as much as I could.

"Fuck," he moaned, and again, in my mind, I felt a little tickle, like I knew that voice.

I gripped the shaft of his cock as he moved his hips in tandem. It wasn't long before he gripped both sides of my head and began guiding me down his shaft.

Slowly, he picked up speed, and before long, he was bucking inside my mouth like a raging bull. I placed my hands on his ass and squeezed, guiding him forward with each thrust. I did my best to take his cock without gagging. Luckily, it wasn't long before he cried out. I gagged as a sea of salty load blasted down my throat. He held me in place, forcing me take every last drop of his cream. All the while, I could feel every contraction of his big dick in my mouth.

When it was over, I pulled away choking and gagging, struggling to keep down his load.

But Mr. Gladiator wasn't done with me. He threw me down on the bed and then pulled me onto all fours. I heard him grab something off the nightstand next to the bed and heard the rustling of plastic. A condom.

His breathing was ragged as he put it on. I was amazed that his cock was still rock hard. I must have really turned him on.

He mounted me, and when he plunged his cock into me, I let out a shocked gasp. He felt so enormous inside me, spreading my hole as wide as it could go.

He began humping me, going balls deep, slowly at first to allow me to adjust, but then he began to pick up speed.

I cried out as he penetrated the depths of my insides. I felt his strong hands wrap around my neck as he lightly choked me. He brought his lips to my neck, kissing and nibbling passionately as he pounded my pussy.

The bed was shaking, rumbling like thunder, mixing in with the bass music in the background. Sweat formed over my body, mixing with his.

He growled softly in my ear as our flesh clapped together. Even while the fire grew inside my stomach, there was a growing sense of familiarity that began to overtake me.

His chiseled thighs slammed into my ass, making music to my ears. My thighs began to tremble violently, my insides quivering from his vicious assault.

After one last brutal thrust, he let out a strangled cry as he blasted his seed inside me, thankfully within the condom.

Like earlier, my body was rocked with nuclear blasts, my stomach expanding and contracting rapidly, my limbs shuddering.

He collapsed onto the bed next to me, his breathing ragged, his powerful chest covered in a sheen of sweat.

"That was insane," he said, his first full sentence since he took me into the room.

The sudden realization hit me like a freight train. I thought I knew that voice. I stared at him in horror as I recognized that chiseled jawline and proud nose, seemingly for the first time, the pieces falling into place.

My hands shaking, I snatched the gladiator mask from his face and gasped.

"Stefan?" I asked breathlessly with disbelief.

Stefan sat up in the bed, his face as white as a ghost. "Bella?" Shock laced his deep voice. "What are you doing here? I thought you were going to Guilford."

I sat there in a daze, not responding. How could we have been so clueless? Here we were, two childhood step-siblings, and we hadn't recognized each other because of simple costumes? The masks weren't even all that damn good.

"Bella?"

"I lied," I whispered. "I told you I was going to Guilford so you wouldn't know where I was."

Stefan's handsome face twisted in confusion, and it took effort for me not to stroke his powerful jawline. "Why?"

"The real question is why are you here?"

Stefan stared at me, his eyes briefly falling to my chest. I felt sort of self-conscious in front of him with my tits in front of his face, even though we'd just had sex. What was the use of covering up when he had just ravaged me?

Either way, I folded my arms across my breasts and scowled at him expectantly.

Stefan scratched at his neck. "I got in a huge fight back at South State. Broke a guy's nose. His family threatened to press charges if I didn't transfer schools."

He stared at me, a hurt expression in his eyes. "I don't know why you never called me to cheer me up."

I looked away from his gaze. "I never knew anything about it," I replied.

"You didn't?"

"Nope. Since I came here, I've kept my conversations with Mom very brief. She... I didn't want to explain everything to her."

Stefan made a face. "That's news to me."

I became quiet as the bass from the music outside the room filled the silence.

"Stefan," I said quietly.

"Yeah?"

"What have we done?"

Stefan seemed to understand immediately. "Let's not lie about it anymore, Bella. We did what we have wanted to do for a long time."

The answer hit me like a sledgehammer. This whole time, I had been somewhat unsure if Stefan truly wanted me. Now, I knew without a doubt.

"There's no way we didn't recognize each other through these costumes," Stefan continued, placing a gentle hand on my arm. "I think, on a subconscious level, we both ignored the obvious because we wanted so badly to be together."

It was probably true. As I had pondered before, how could we not have known? The answer was simple: because we didn't want to.

As I thought about what we had just done, a horrible sense of shame began to descend upon me.

"This was wrong," I whispered. "Horribly wrong."

"Why? We both wanted it and are two consenting

adults."

I felt afraid because what Stefan was saying was true.

"What do you think would happen if your dad or my mom knew about this?"

Stefan took a while to respond. "Who cares what they think?" He stared at me with an intensity that made my skin prickle. "What matters to me is . . . what do you think?"

In that moment, I was more scared than I had ever been in my life. The way he was looking at me, he didn't want this to be a one-time thing, and what scared me more than anything else was . . . I didn't want it to be a one-time thing either.

"I have to go," I mumbled, jumping up from the bed and slipping back into my skimpy costume, making sure to put my mask back on. "I've got to get out of here."

Stefan jumped up from the bed, reaching out to me. It was hard not to stare at his magnificent body. "Bella, please don't do this."

I slapped his hand away and made my way to the door. "Sorry, Stefan, but this can never be."

Stefan scrambled to pull on his loincloth. I must say, if I weren't in such a frantic state, I would have enjoyed watching him slip it on.

"Bella, wait!" he cried. "Don't go out there. The fellas, they've all seen your picture and they know . . ."

His words were lost in the blast of bass as I swung open the door. I ran down the hall, hoping I would be able to run out of the frat house without any of the party-goers noticing.

Halfway to the dorm living room, I ran into a hard wall and my mask tumbled from my face. I looked up into the eyes of some jock whom I didn't recognize, but he seemed to recognize me.

"Holy shit," he exclaimed loudly over the music. "You're Stefan Livingston's stepsister."

I started in shock. Stefan was a new transfer at NSU. How did his buddies already know who I was?

The jock was shaking his head. "I can't believe it. The fellas are not going to believe this."

Horror washed over me as I realized what was to come. "Move out of my way, dickwad!"

I shoved him aside and ran from the dorm house, tears of shame flowing down my cheeks.

Chapter 7
Stefan

I stumbled out into the hallway, my loincloth barely covering my bottom half, but that was the last thing on my mind.

"Bella!"

I froze when I saw Bella run into Craig at the end of the hallway and her mask slip from her face. Surprise registered on Craig's features and I saw their lips moving as they exchanged words, and then Bella shoved Craig aside and sprinted from the hallway.

"Shit," I hissed. I had exaggerated a little that all of the guys knew who she was, but she just had to run into one of the ones who did.

I couldn't believe my bad luck. Somehow, against all odds, I had wound up at the same school as Bella, won a contest, and subsequently, her as a fuck buddy.

Craig was about to turn away to chase after Bella, but then he saw me and his eyes lit up. I groaned as he quickly began making his way toward me.

"Dude," he said, his voice filled with mirth as he got closer. I could already hear the rumors now. "You got balls. Your own stepsister?"

"If you know what's best for you, you'll leave right now," I growled at Craig, my fist balling by my side.

Craig laughed, unperturbed by my threat. "Was her pussy as good as I think it is?"

I didn't even think about my next move. It just happened. I lashed out at Craig with my fist and it collided against his jaw with a loud crack. Craig's head snapped back and his eyes glazed over as he fell against the wall, crumpling to the floor.

Without a second glance, I stomped my way through the house, ignoring the curious glances the partygoers threw my way, all the girls pointing at my half-naked body, and the giggles.

I didn't care about any of it. I had only one thing on my mind—finding Bella and telling her that I was in love with her.

I had no idea what sort of shit storm we were about to walk into.

Chapter 8
Bella

"I have been hearing some disturbing rumors, Miss James," said the Dean of the school, Howard Sturm. A distinguished man in his sixties, Howard had a mop of pepper-colored hair, bushy eyebrows, and a large belly, and he looked every bit the distinguished educator. "Rumors involving someone who is perhaps related to you."

He was dressed in an expensive, executive business suit and was eyeing me like a hawk as I sat across from him in his office. He'd called me in after my last class, his face cloudy from the moment I walked in. And the forecast hadn't improved. "Please tell me they're not true."

I clenched the armrest of my chair, my nails digging into the wood. "They're not, sir," I said as confidently as I could manage. "They are all lies, made up by people who are out to get me."

The fallout for my tryst with Stefan had been awful. When everyone had gotten wind that Stefan was my stepbrother and that we had slept together, I became the brunt of cruel jokes and threats. I don't know who broke the news first, and I didn't really care. I just knew that my life had gone to hell almost overnight.

Since then, I'd gone into hiding, only going to certain classes that I thought were safe. Most of all, I avoided Stefan like the plague. He seemed hell-bent on trying to talk to me. He'd been blowing up my email and cellphone constantly, but I don't know why he was bothering. We were already in enough trouble as it was.

I'd also moved out of the sorority house and into a vacant dorm room of my own. I couldn't stand to be around those worthless, two-faced bitches who had helped spread the rumors about my sleeping with Stefan.

So much for Sisterhood, I thought sourly. *And blood oaths.*

Howard studied me closely. "Well, I hope what you're saying is true."

"Or?" I asked, my pulse racing. I dreaded the answer. If there was no lid put on the matter soon, this had the potential to blow up into something that would result in my being banned from the university. North State was one of those that had a 'morality clause' in your paperwork, which most people treated like a total joke, but obviously, it could come to bite me in the ass here. Everyone had treated it like a joke all last semester, but now . . . now I was scared.

"Or there will be repercussions."

I heard the note of doom in Howard's voice and my limbs trembled.

"There will be an official investigation launched into this matter. If you are found guilty, you and your stepbrother will be expelled from this school."

My hands began to shake violently. This could cost me everything.

"Do I make myself clear, Miss James?"

It was a long time before I could reply. "Yes," I choked. "Totally."

Howard nodded. "Good. You are dismissed."

* * *

I ran into my dorm bathroom and retched into the toilet. After several dry heaves, I pulled back and wiped my lips with the back of my hands. For the past few days, I had been nauseated as hell.

I had mostly attributed it to the ongoing investigation and scandal surrounding my fraternity-sponsored liaison with Stefan.

"Whatever the hell has gotten into me," I muttered, holding back another dry heave, "I hope it passes soon. I can't keep these people off my back if I'm trying to hold in the contents of my stomach."

I flushed the toilet and stood up. As I was walking back to my room, someone pounded on the front door. I froze, not knowing what I should do. My first thought was that it was someone from the school's newspaper again, looking to interview me.

Finally, I decided I wouldn't answer and continued on to my room. The pounding only got louder. Sighing, I turned and walked to the front door, angrily swinging it open and twisting my face into a scowl.

"Look, I already gave you your God damned interview, and I'm not giving you another one—"

"Bella."

There was Stefan, standing there in his gym sweats, his t-shirt plastered to his powerful chest. He had never looked so damned good in my entire life.

"What are you doing here, Stefan?" I hissed, trying to put on a strong front. "After what happened, you should have known better than to come here!"

Stefan gazed at me, his eyes intense. "Bella, I had to see you."

I glanced around, hoping no one was watching. Around this time, most classes had been done for the day, but it still wasn't too late for someone to be lurking about—but I saw no one.

"What for?" I demanded. I felt a light flutter in my stomach staring at Stefan's chiseled jawline. He looked so handsome with his hair plastered to the sides of his face that it almost hurt. "Haven't you done enough damage? Now you want to make sure we get expelled from this school too?"

Stefan scowled. "Fuck this school," he growled with an intensity that had me taking a step back. "I don't give a shit about it."

I shook my head. "Please stop, Stefan. We can't do this here."

"We can," Stefan rejected. "And we will."

"No," I said weakly.

"Yes," he insisted. He stepped up close to me, and the warmth of his powerful body immediately enveloped me. "Bella, I've been meaning to do this for a long time."

"Stefan, please leave," I pleaded. "I can't deal with this."

"I've just never had the courage."

"Stefan, I'm going to close the door and go back to my room now. And you're going to return to your room and forget about me." I began to close the door, but Stefan nudged his foot in the jamb, stopping it cold.

"I love you, Bella."

I froze, my pulse suddenly pounding between my ears. "What did you just say?"

He looked at me earnestly and my heart nearly jumped out of my chest. "I love you."

In that moment, I understood that he meant that he loved me, not as a stepsister, but as a lover.

"You can't mean that," I finally whispered.

"I do. I've been in love with you for a long damn time." Without a word, he pulled me into his arms, smashing his lips into mine. Immediately, my body felt like it would burst into flames as desire roared through the pit of my stomach.

I don't know how long we stood there embraced in a kiss, but it felt like an eternity.

Finally, he pulled away and I let out a gasp, gulping down air. Looking down at me, Stefan gently caressed my face. "I'll protect you from here on out, Bella," he said softly. "You don't have to worry about the school's stupid investigation. We're going to be okay."

The feeling of nausea began to return, and I wondered if it was the stress of all of this or if it was the same nagging sickness that had been plaguing me for the past few days.

"We're going to ditch this dumb ass school and transfer to a different campus where no one knows us, and then . . ." Stefan paused, his face twisted in concern as he studied me. "Bella, are you okay?"

I pressed my hands to my stomach as a feeling of horror washed over me. Suddenly, I knew why I had been sick the past few days.

It shouldn't be possible, I thought to myself. *No fucking way. We were safe!*

"Stefan," I said weakly, holding back the urge to throw up on his toes.

"Yeah?" The concern in Stefan's eyes touched me. "What is it, Bella? You look really sick."

I took a deep breath. "I think I'm pregnant."

* * *

"Wait one damn second . . . how could this have had happened?" Stefan demanded as he paced the living room floor of my dorm. I was sitting on the small couch, cross-legged, watching him, my mind awash with thoughts of doom. "I took every precaution. I mean, I had a fucking condom on!"

Fresh from outside, my hot stepbrother was still soaking wet from the rain, his t-shirt plastered to his washboard abs. His hair was a wet mess and he had fresh stubble shading his powerful jawline. He had never looked hotter to me in that moment, but for once, I wasn't being overrun by my raging hormones for him because of our present dilemma.

"I don't know," I replied, my voice shaking. "I really have no idea."

"Fuck," he hissed, turning on his heel and walking in the opposite direction, only to turn back around and walk back the other way.

Tears slid down my cheeks. This was all my fault. Had I not agreed to go along with the stupid Sacrifice just to prove myself to the sorority, this would have never happened. Never mind the fact that I had also gone along with it just to prove to myself that I could forget about Stefan. Guess I was wrong.

"We must have been so into it that the condom broke."

"I guess." The theory seemed to be the only plausible one.

Stefan nodded and replied, "Unless . . ."

"Unless what?"

"Unless you've been with someone else."

The flash of jealousy and anger that appeared in Stefan's eyes was frightening, and I found myself rearing back against the couch.

"No," I said quickly, my pulse pounding in my ears. "I swear, I haven't."

The only guy I've ever wanted to be with is you, I thought to myself. *It's part of the sick reason I did the Sacrifice anyway . . . to forget about you.*

I was thinking these words, but I couldn't find the nerve to actually say them to Stefan. Frankly, I was still embarrassed over the entire ordeal. It seemed so unbelievable. We should've recognized each other behind the costumes.

Stefan was probably right. Deep down, we had known but chose to ignore it. We were in a fantasy and went along with it. I was having a hard time swallowing this notion. Of course, I was always attracted to him, but I didn't think I'd ever act on it.

"How am I supposed to believe that?" Stefan demanded. "When you were willing to sleep with me before even knowing who I was?"

I wrapped my arms around my chest and looked down at my legs in shame. I had the response, but it was hard to speak through the lump inside my throat.

Stefan resumed his pacing. "Speaking of which, I can't believe that you were willing to sleep with a total stranger. I really thought you were above such behavior, Bella." There was bitter anger in Stefan's voice, and the sound of it stung my skin like a wasp.

"I don't see why you're bringing this up now," I said weakly. I wanted to be angry, but with the way my stomach felt and everything else, I just felt pounded, destroyed . . . helpless. "You didn't seem to have a problem with it after you found out."

"Well, I haven't been able to speak to you since that night." Stefan stopped pacing again to stare at me. "With everything happening so fast, there was little time to process. And at the time, I was just happy to be with you."

"And I was happy to be with you too," I whispered.

"If that's true, why were you willing to sleep with a total stranger then?"

I sucked in a deep breath. "Because . . . it was the only way I could think of to take my mind off you. You're not the only one who's had feelings for the other."

A blanket of silence descended over the dorm living room. Outside, I could hear the pitter-patter of rain and I felt a twinge of anxiety. Sara Delaney, the girl I had become friends with while at Kappa, would be back any moment from her study group.

Sara, who had been sympathetic to my plight and angry about the whole Sacrifice deal, had followed me, leaving Kappa in a pretty epic rant that ended on the front lawn of the house, the campus police waiting to step in if things got any more heated.

I told her she didn't have to, but she shrugged it off.

"I don't like those bitches anyway," she said at the time. "They're all so slutty and stuck up. Bunch of hypocrites. Fuck it. I'd rather be with the real people."

I felt a little uneasy with the words, considering I was the one who agreed to go through with the Sacrifice.

But I knew she didn't mean anything by it. So, we had moved in together, and surprisingly, we even became close friends.

Stefan was still staring at me, but I was surprised to see understanding in his eyes. "So, you weren't on the pill?" he asked, changing the subject back to the matter at hand. His deep, sexy voice was more subdued now, much softer. "I just kinda figured . . ."

I thought back for a moment. "I was, but I recently stopped taking it because it made me so sick to my stomach and caused me to break out all over my face. And I wasn't getting any action anyway." I began shaking my head, feeling panic course through my body as the cold realization of my actions set in. "My God, Stefan, what are we going to do?"

Stefan quickly walked over to the couch and sat down beside me. He placed a calming hand on my trembling thigh and I immediately felt a jolt run through my skin. Almost immediately, I was taken back to the night he fucked me, and I could almost feel his hands roaming all over my body. "Calm down, Bella. I think we're getting a little ahead of ourselves. Let's think rationally about this for a minute. We have no evidence that you're actually pregnant besides your feeling sick." He rubbed his hand up and down my thigh, causing my internal heat to raise several notches and thoughts of him devouring my neck to flash through my mind. "How long have you felt sick, anyway?"

"I've felt nauseated for almost a week, worse in the mornings . . . and when I think about it, I missed my period." I began to shake, my sinful thoughts momentarily forgotten as I began to wail. "Mother is going to kill me!"

Stefan wrapped his arms around me and gently rocked me, softly cooing, "It's okay, baby, it's okay. Stop panicking. Let's at least get a test done before we jump headfirst into hysteria."

Sniffing and trying to get ahold of myself, I parted my lips to reply, but the sound of a pop tune interrupted me. It was my cell, lying on the nightstand next to the couch. I picked it up and checked the caller ID.

"It's Mom," I breathed, my anxiety rising.

I hadn't spoken to either of my parents since that night. I'd been avoiding them like the plague, but eventually, I knew I was going to have to answer if I didn't want them coming all the way down to NSU to find me.

"Don't answer it," Stefan urged immediately.

I looked at him. "Why not? I haven't talked to Mom since this all happened. I'm sure she's wondering what the hell is going on."

Stefan pried the phone from my hands and silenced the ringtone. "Because I said so." There was a firm tone of authority in his voice that gave me pause. "I've been ignoring their calls too. We can't talk to them without getting our story straight. For all we know, they might have heard rumors about what happened here. We have to play this smart, Bella."

Stefan's ringtone went off then. He placed my phone back onto the nightstand and dug into the pocket of his sweatpants.

"It's Dad," he muttered after a quick glance. He turned the cell off and stuffed it back in his pocket. "They're probably going to continue to bug the shit out of us until we answer."

I glanced at my phone. The screen was lit up again. Mom wasn't going to give up easily. "I don't know how long you think we can just ignore them, Stefan. We're going to have to answer to them sooner or later."

"We just have to stall long enough to figure out what we're going to do," Stefan said, jumping to his feet and holding his hands out to me. "Give me your car keys." He nodded toward my dorm bedroom. "And go get dressed for the weather. We're going to take a little ride."

I peered at him. "What for?"

His next words filled with me dread. "Rite-Aid. I'm taking you to get a pregnancy test."

Chapter 9
Stefan

I couldn't believe it. I had possibly impregnated my step sister. The likelihood was extremely difficult to wrap my mind around and I was hoping that it wasn't true. I mean, how does one process something like that?

Several blocks from the university, I slowly brought Bella's white Honda Civic to a halt at a red light on a small cross street, the sound of rain softly pattering against the hood of the car.

"How could I have been so stupid?" Bella asked from the passenger seat. She had come out of her dorm dressed in jeans and an NSU hoodie to shield herself from the rain. But even dressed down like a plain Jane, she was beautiful to me. The sound of a country music tune, ironically about a surprise pregnancy, played quietly in the background. "Had I not gone along with such a stupid tradition, this would never have happened."

Her soft voice sounded afraid, and my immediate urge was to reach across the space between us and comfort her, but every time I thought about doing it, my thoughts went back to how soft and intoxicating her skin had felt on the night of the Sacrifice, and I feared I would lose control.

I wanted her. God, I fucking wanted her. But Bella seemed to be in a fragile state, and I didn't want her to think I was trying to take advantage of her, given the circumstances.

I impatiently tapped my fingers against the steering wheel and peered into the rearview mirror, trying to push my lust-filled thoughts from my mind. There were several cars behind me, but traffic didn't seem that bad. "Don't beat yourself up over this, Bella. I'm just as much to blame for this as you are. You know, it takes two to tango."

After all, I had been just as willing to fuck an unknown slut as Bella was to fuck some unknown, moronic frat jock, so who was I to judge? Actually, I felt a little bit ashamed and like a hypocrite for trying to come down on Bella about it back at her dorm. I hadn't been able to help myself, though. The thought of Bella wanting to fuck someone else made me see red. I just wasn't sure how I could explain it without coming off sounding like a jackass.

Bella shook her head, her face twisted with worry. "The school is going to have our heads for this. The Dean warned me today about it."

I turned to look at her. Her cheeks were wet with a mixture of rain and tears, and her eyes had bags under them. Still, she had never looked so beautiful to me, and if we weren't so wrapped up in a colossal shit storm, I would have pulled over onto the side of the road and fucked her right then and there.

"He's blowing smoke. The school can't do shit to us," I assured her, resisting the urge to wipe the tears away from her cheeks. The light was about to turn green and I needed to keep my eyes on the road. "The last I checked, having sex with someone who has no blood relation to you is not illegal. So what if our parents are married?"

Bella gave me a look. "Come on now, Stefan. You know what we did is considered forbidden."

And that's why I liked it even more, I thought.

"So?"

Bella gaped at me like I was insane. "So? Look at the rumors that are spreading around campus. I mean, I have to practically skip half of my classes because I don't want to become the brunt of stupid jokes."

The light turned green and I floored the gas. "Look, Bella, who cares what those idiots say? People are always going to talk, no matter what. It was an accident, plain and simple. The only people who even knew you were my stepsister were my frat brothers." I clenched my teeth, bulging my jaw. "And I wish I could beat the fuck out of the one who told everyone."

After I had slugged Craig for daring to ask me about how tight Bella was, he went and told several other members. From there, it spread like wildfire, and there was no taking the story back.

At first, everyone had been talking shit about what Bella and I had done, but that quickly changed when the school launched an investigation into the activities of both the Alpha fraternity and the Kappa sorority, specifically about 'lewd competitions with sexual prizes.' Both chapters were facing being disbanded.

Everything had changed then, and everyone suddenly had my back. Ironically, the investigation had caused it to be in the best interest for both institutions to deny what happened the night of the Sacrifice and to protect the reputations of Bella and myself.

"The most that's going to happen is they will

disband Alpha and Kappa." I snorted. I had so wanted to join a frat, and now, I didn't give two shits about it. "And from my point of view, that's not really a bad thing."

Bella let out a sigh as I turned a corner and Rite-Aid came into view. "I really hope you're right, Stefan."

"Trust me," I said with more confidence than I felt in order to reassure her. "I am."

A minute later, I pulled into the parking lot and quickly took a vacant parking space in front of the store. I turned off the engine and looked over at Bella.

Bella pulled up her hoodie, undid her seat belt, and opened her door. I could see her hands shaking. She was scared shitless. I couldn't blame her. It hurt that I had partly caused her anxiety.

I placed a comforting hand on her arm before she could climb out of the vehicle. "Bella?"

Bella sniffed, taking the back of her hand and wiping at her cheek. I almost pulled her into my arms. "Yeah?"

"Don't worry about any of this, okay? No matter what happens, everything is going to be all right. I'm going to be here for you, whatever the result."

Gratitude briefly replaced the worry in her eyes. "Thank you, Stefan," she replied softly. "That really means a lot." It was kind of strange, Bella being so fragile. In a way, I kind of liked it, given the circumstances. She'd always been a bitch to me, and now, I was the one she was going to have to look to for support. I was now Bella's protector.

Bella began to climb out of the car, but I called her again.

"Bella."

"Yeah?"

I wiped at the sweat that had begun to bead my brow. "Hold on, would you? I'll come in with you."

Bella shook her head, waving me off. "It'll be easier if I do it alone. I'll be right back."

Bella

Pulling the stuffy hoodie off my head, I strolled into the pharmacy, feeling weak in the knees, my pulse increasing by the second. It was all so surreal. Here I was, going to buy a pregnancy kit to find out if I was pregnant with my stepbrother's baby.

"You need any help, Miss?" asked a deep voice as I neared the female hygiene aisle.

I looked up into the eyes of a handsome employee. He looked around my age, and in a way, he reminded me of Stefan with his dirty-blond hair and blue eyes. Dressed in jeans and a t-shirt covered by an apron, he had a smile plastered on his face that showed off a pair of dimples and straight, white teeth.

Oh, hell, I thought in exasperation. *Not now.*

"No, I'm fine," I muttered. "Thanks for asking."

He peered at me closely, refusing to take the hint. "Is everything all right? You look kind of pale."

"I'm fine," I repeated. "It's just the weather. I hate rainy days."

The blond continued to look at me. "Hey, do you go to NSU?"

"No," I lied. I nervously cast a glance out the store

window and wondered if Stefan could see me talking to the guy. With how jealous Stefan seemed to get at the thought of me wanting to sleep with another guy, the last thing I needed was him seeing a cute guy chatting it up with me.

The worker's features twisted into a thoughtful expression. "I could have sworn that I've seen you around somewhere. Hey, I know where I saw you. You're that chick who—"

I began moving away. "Sorry, gotta go. My grandma is stuck at home, sick with severe constipation. I need to get her an enema and get back to her fast!"

That will make him leave me alone, I thought as I quickly rushed past him and made my way to the opposite side of the store. Once I was sure the nosy fellow had gone off helping another costumer, I made my way back to the feminine hygiene aisle.

Each step I took toward the pregnancy tests felt heavier than the last. By the time I stood in front of all the choices, my heart was pounding within my chest like a smith's hammer. I stood there, transfixed, almost overwhelmed by a range of products. Eventually, I settled on a box labeled *First Response.*

I paid quickly and walked into the tiny bathroom, closing the door behind me and locking it. The sound of the clicking lock sounded like my doom.

I walked over to the sink and opened the box. Two lines for positive, one line for negative.

After I was done, I waited anxiously, my limbs trembling. Three minutes. The box had said to wait for three minutes.

The time seemed to tick by very slowly, each

second seeming like an eternity. When it was time, I closed my eyes, willing the test to be negative. After praying desperately for another minute, I popped open my eyes and stared at the test.

A shocked gasp escaped my throat, and then a sound that I didn't even know was possible, a sound that reminded me of my soon to be destroyed life.

Two lines.

Stefan

I knew the results the minute Bella walked out of the pharmacy with an expression that said she was about to have a nervous breakdown.

Positive.

I let out a groan and rested my head on Bella's steering wheel.

I lifted my head back up as Bella reached the car. She didn't even get into the passenger side all the way before she began sobbing—great, big hiccups that quickly morphed into full-blown wailing.

"Oh, God," Bella wailed. "Oh, God."

"It's okay," I soothed, pulling her into my arms. Even though she was wet, she felt extremely warm, and under normal circumstances, I would have probably gotten excited. But right now, that wasn't at the forefront of my thoughts. "It's okay. I'm here. I'm here." While I held Bella, I could see people entering the store turning to stare at us. I knew it was bad for us to be seen together so close to the school, but this couldn't be helped.

"I just can't believe it, Stefan," Bella cried into my chest, her tears staining my shirt. "I can't."

I can, I thought. *Honestly . . . I kinda like it.*

"We'll get through this," I said softly, rubbing her back. Both of our worlds had been turned upside down, and the shit was about to hit the fan. But I would deal with it somehow. "I just want you to stop beating yourself up about it."

"My life is over," Bella sobbed. "Finished."

"Don't say that," I growled to her angrily. "We're going to make the best of this, Bella James."

I held Bella for the next few minutes, rocking her, massaging her shoulders, and giving her soft kisses on the cheek, telling her that everything was going to be okay. I knew it was going to get tough, but she needed me to be positive.

When she finally calmed down, she pulled away from me and wiped at her wet face with both hands. She stared at me, her eyes red from crying. "What are we going to do now?" She sniffed.

I immediately knew what she was asking, and I already knew the answer.

"We're keeping it," I said firmly. "No matter the cost. We have to."

"I can't believe you're saying that," she said softly, studying my face. "What about our parents, Stefan? Telling them is going to be a nightmare."

I gritted my teeth. One question, and she had opened up a whole can of worms. I knew we had quite a challenging road ahead of us. "Let me handle them."

Bella was shaking her head. "You can't just blow

everything off with macho assertions, Stefan. They are going to find out, someway, somehow."

"Maybe," I said in denial. "But it'll be okay. I'll make sure of that."

Bella stared at me for a long time before responding, and the sound of the rain hitting the roof of the car filled the silence. "You can't promise that."

"Watch me."

Bella rolled her eyes, and I felt a little jolt of happiness. Some of her spunk was coming back. "Please. And what about the investigation that the school is launching, huh? What are we going to do about—"

I placed my index finger against her lips. "Shh. One thing at time." I twisted my torso and pulled my seatbelt on, snapping it in place. Bella followed suit a second later. If nothing else, we were both safety conscious. Funny, huh? This coming from two siblings who had just wound up with an unplanned pregnancy.

I fired up the engine and began backing out of the parking spot. "Don't worry about the investigation. I'm going to have a word with the dean. You have nothing to worry about."

"You promise?" asked Bella skeptically.

I looked over at her and gave her a confident grin. Was I full of shit? Of course I was. But right now, being full of shit was better than the alternative. "Just wait and see."

Chapter 10
Stefan

"What can I help you with today, Mr. Livingston?" asked Howard Sturm, the big-bellied Dean of NSU. A mug of steaming coffee sat in front of him.

After the long day of dealing with an emotional Bella, I had made an appointment to speak with him. I figured if he was calling Bella into his office, I wasn't long to be called myself, and I wanted to take control of the situation. And since my name was fast spreading across the campus, it hadn't been hard or taken long to gain access to the powerful man.

I studied the dean for several moments, concealing my contempt for him. Being an athlete, I didn't too much care for people who let themselves go. I get it, he didn't need to run marathons, but really . . . the man needed to start taking care of himself before he ended up having a heart attack.

I sat back in my chair and looked at the Dean as if he were my equal. Never let your opponent sense weakness—another rule I'd lived by in sports, and it seemed to fit here too. "These rumors flying around campus," I said, gesturing in a nondescript manner, "about me and Bella. None of them are true."

Howard studied me for a moment, appearing irritated by my cocky demeanor, before chuckling. "Well, I would certainly hope not, Mr. Livingston. That would be quite . . . disturbing if they were," he said with a frown.

"Well, something should be done about it," I said. "People shouldn't be allowed to go around spreading those rumors about something that never happened. I have a valuable reputation as a star athlete. Ultimately, this thing could follow me long after I'm gone from NSU. And while pro lacrosse isn't exactly the same as pro football, it could hurt my potential future earnings . . . something that the university could be liable for."

If it were up to me, I'd get people to stop talking by the way of physical intimidation. But of course, that would only make matters worse. I felt like an idiot for trying to use some half-baked *Law & Order* bullshit lawyer speak with the dean.

Howard folded his hands in front him and sat back in his chair. "I wouldn't be concerned from the university's perspective, Mr. Livingston. After all, several witnesses say it did happen, and I already spoke with the school's legal team on the law on slander, so your threat is just hot air. But back to the witnesses. So you're saying they're all lying?"

I nodded. "That's exactly what they're doing. There are a lot of guys out there who are jealous of my All-Star athlete status, and just as many girls are jealous of Bella."

An amused grin broke out on Howard's chubby face, and I must admit, it made me want to slug him in his gut. "Whatever the source of these rumors, and whatever the veracity of these claims, it's not exactly you or your sister who is being investigated here, Mr. Livingston. Rather, it's the Alpha fraternity and the Kappa sorority as a whole. You see, I know all about the wild traditions that you young kids indulge in. As much as some of the things you kids do is frowned upon, I can totally relate. Believe it or not, I was young once too. But there is a limit to what we can allow."

He continued on, not noticing my expression of derision. "But, when things get out of hand and disturbing rumors can damage the school's reputation, my office demands that I take action. If the panel finds any evidence, both Kappa and Alpha will be disbanded. Some students may even be expelled." He stared directly into my eyes to drive his point home.

I leaned forward in my chair, challenging Howard's gaze. "I really don't think you will find anything, sir. In fact, I think it would be best for you to call off your little investigation. I mean, think about it for a minute: There's no solid proof that either institution broke any school laws with traditions that have been going on practically since the school was founded. I would think a scandal of this magnitude being revealed would hurt the school's image."

Howard chuckled. "Well, that's exactly why you're not Dean of this school, my boy. Such logic is not only corrupt, but weak as well." He shifted in his seat. "But let's say I indulge your idea for a moment. Why would I want to just sweep this whole thing under the rug, despite all the things we've heard from the students around campus?"

I checked the urge to lean across the table and grab Howard by the collar. That was one bad thing about myself I wish I could fix—my temper. Sometimes, I let people get under my skin far too easily. I'd like to think that some of it was because I was a young, competitive athlete who had too much testosterone raging through his blood. "Because, Sir, Alpha Gamma is one of the most talked about fraternities in the whole state. Shutting it down will not only tarnish its name, but it'll weaken the school's popularity."

Howard let out a pig-like snort. "You obviously don't keep up with the news too well. After Baylor, Harvard, and a bunch of others, choosing to ignore this could have far worse ramifications if it turned out to be true." He glared at me. "Don't you see what position I am in, Mr. Livingston? What would that say about my character and leadership if I turn a blind eye to the . . . immoral actions that are happening beneath my nose?"

Howard sucked in a deep breath, closing his eyes. He opened them a second later, not allowing me to respond, and said quietly, "I think we have just about exhausted the possibilities of this conversation, Mr. Livingston, and I think I've wasted enough of my valuable time on this issue. The investigation will continue, and if the rumors are verified, all guilty parties shall be dealt with." He nodded at the door. "That is all."

"Look," I insisted, refusing to just walk away. "I apologize if I came across as disrespectful, but you have to consider everything—"

"That is enough, Stefan," the Dean interrupted. "You've said your piece. Don't make it worse on yourself."

"Fine," I growled. "Bella and I won't have any part in all of this ridiculousness."

"I'd advise you not to do anything rash, Stefan," Howard warned. "And that's the final warning I will give you."

I walked out and slammed the door behind me. It

wasn't too productive, but I did gain some information.

Chapter 11
Bella

For the first few days after finding out I was pregnant, I walked around in a zombie-like daze. The unexpected events still stunned me—I had my stepbrother's baby inside me. It was both a blessing and a curse. The thought of having his baby brought joy to me, but having to explain it to everyone would be dreadful.

In the meantime, Stefan and I had agreed to avoid each other for a while until the rumors and jokes died down. I was to go to my classes, acting as if everything were normal. But ignoring some of the jerks poking fun at me wasn't going to be easy.

Meanwhile, the school's investigation against Alpha and Kappa was heating up, and it was only a matter of time before both Stefan and I would be further pulled into the quagmire.

When I was done with classes for the day, I was approached by the president of Kappa, Hanna Jones, and her faithful sidekick, she of dildo sucking fame, Veronica George, while making my way across campus to my dorm room.

I'd heard that they wanted to speak with me, but I had nothing to say to them. I don't know if it was Kappa or Alpha that started the rumors, but it didn't matter. Kappa certainly hadn't helped things until they realized they could be in trouble too.

Both girls fell into step on either side of me.

Hanna was carrying a bunch of books with her hands folded around them while Veronica had nothing. Hanna was the first to speak. "I heard the Dean had a talk with you."

"Yes," I said succinctly, not bothering to hide my displeasure at being approached by them. "And?"

Veronica scowled. "So? Did you say anything about how girls gain entry to our chapter or anything about hazing?"

Irritation flowed through my body. "No. Why would I? I have just as much reason to lie as the rest of you. Maybe even more so, considering—" I stopped short of saying the words.

"You swear you didn't say anything about me or about our deal with Alpha?" Hanna demanded. "Cause if you did—"

I hissed in exasperation. "I didn't say crap! I don't understand why you two are bugging me right now. Shouldn't you be back at the house, making sure everyone has their story straight?"

Veronica shook her head angrily. "I really can't believe your bitchy attitude, Bella. You should be kissing the ground we walk on for letting you join our sorority. You have some nerve treating your sisters like this."

"You aren't, and never were, my sister," I said tersely. "Because it was either a Kappa or an Alpha who opened their fucking mouth the first time. Let's get that straight right now."

"You see that, Hanna? You see how ungrateful she is?" Veronica snarled. "I warned you to never to let this chick in. Now we're forced to lie on her behalf just to defend ourselves, all because she wanted to screw her brother."

I stopped in my tracks. "That is not true!" I half-yelled.

Several students in the area stopped to stare at the confrontation.

"It's not?" Veronica hissed, her eyes darting to the onlookers then back to me. "Who do you think you're kidding? Do you really expect us to believe that you didn't know the guy behind the gladiator mask was your brother or that he didn't know who you were either?" She rolled her eyes at the sky. "Please."

"Shut up, Veronica," I growled. "No one cares what you think . . . unless it's about winning dick-sucking contests."

Veronica's faced twisted with rage and she got in my face. "You dirty brother fucker—"

Shifting the books into the nook of her arm, Hanna pushed Veronica away from me. "Stop it, V. We already have enough problems on our hands." She looked at me. "Actually, we didn't follow you here to quiz you on what you said to the dean."

I glared at Veronica, who was scowling at me with hatred, and crossed my arms over my breasts. "Why are you here, then?"

Hanna took a deep breath. "I've come up with a plan to protect both Alpha and Kappa."

I studied her warily. "And what plan is this?" I really didn't trust any plan that Hanna or Veronica could come up with. After all, it was their silly Sacrifice tradition with Alpha that had us all mixed up in this mess in the first place. Any plan that they came up with certainly wouldn't have my best interest in mind.

"I had a long talk with Jace Randall today," Hanna began.

I let out a groan. Great, dumb meets dumber. Jace might have been one of the most popular guys on NSU's campus, but he was a total douchebag.

"And he believes," Hanna continued, ignoring my glare, "that it would be in the best interests of us all if you pretend to be his girlfriend for a while. Going around together, making a show of it, will do much to quell the rumors about what happened the night of your Sacrifice."

"No," I was saying immediately, shaking my head. "I refuse." I have to be honest, I was a little taken aback at how they were all banding together to save their own skins.

Hanna stared at me like I was crazy. "Why not? Have you seen Jace? He's hot as hell."

I glowered. I didn't mention how he or one of the other members of the frat were probably some of the assholes who started the rumor mill that had us all in this fucking mess. I'd already stated that fact. More than anything else, though, I just didn't trust him. "Jace is an absolute douchebag."

"Seriously?" Veronica asked in disbelief. "One of the hottest guys in the school wants you to be his girl and you turn him down? What's the matter with you? You claim you didn't mean to sleep with your stepbrother. Here's your chance to prove to everyone that you didn't. Not to mention, it's just pretend anyway."

"Yeah," added Hanna. "Don't you want to try to squash the rumors?"

"No," I said flatly. "I'm not pretending to be Jace's whore."

Hanna's eyes flashed dangerously. "You made an oath when you joined Kappa—"

"An oath that became null and void when I left," I cut in.

Hanna ignored me, continuing on. "And you are honor-bound to help your sisters, just like we're trying to help you now."

I laughed inside. Hanna and Veronica didn't give a damn if I dropped dead right then. They just wanted me to go along with their plans because their precious sorority was in danger.

"I'm sorry," I said after a moment. "I can't help you guys. Besides, whoring myself out got us all into this mess. I don't think more whoring is going to get us out."

Veronica stepped toward me, but Hanna reached out and stopped her. "Well, you had better start thinking about the consequences if you don't," she said, "because I can guarantee you this—if Kappa falls, so will you."

Chapter 12
Stefan

I sat in English class, my thoughts consumed by Bella. I still couldn't believe that she was pregnant. She was carrying our child. The very thought seemed alien to me. It was crazy how I'd come to NSU for a brand-new beginning and wound up with just that, an absolute, life-changing one.

Whatever the case, I was going to do whatever I could do to minimize the damage I'd done and make sure Bella was taken care of during her pregnancy. The problem was, I had limited options.

It was clear to me that Bella would only be able to finish out the semester at most. After that, we'd both probably have to put school on hold for a while.

Fleeing back home wasn't an attractive option. Our parents would wonder why we were not finishing out our degrees, and once Bella started to show, the questions would really start to fly.

"What's on your mind, handsome?" asked a sultry voice.

I started and looked over to my right. It was a chick named Veronica George. With giant hoop earrings and lush, dick-sucking lips, she was dressed in a skin-tight halter dress that made her obvious implants stand out and some shiny black heels. She didn't look like she was carrying any books, but when you were that hot, why study when you could blow the professor for an A+?

Still, with all that going for her, Veronica was as

fake as Barbie, and she couldn't hold a candle to Bella. I'm sure some guys dig that fake shit though.

She probably lies there like a dead fish in the sack anyway, I thought, sizing her up. *Stuck-up girls who think they are hot like her always do.*

"Hey," I said in a casual manner that said I didn't think Veronica was anything special, not letting my eyes linger too long on her body so she wouldn't get the wrong idea.

"It's a shame what's happening with the investigation and all," she said, leaning forward in her seat. "You know, for all of us."

Got it. She's a Kappa. I ignored her. There was no point in engaging in conversation with someone from Kappa about the night of the Sacrifice.

"Hey, do you hear me talking to you?" she hissed when I didn't respond.

I looked up from my work and gave her a blank stare. "I thought you Kappa chicks were good at taking dicks—I mean, hints."

Veronica's eyes flashed dangerously, and I could instantly tell that she was one to watch. "That was a really low blow."

"I'm sorry," I said with false sincerity, "but seriously, I don't want to talk about it."

Veronica became silent for a moment. "I don't see how you both can claim you didn't recognize each other."

I clenched my teeth, jutting out my jawline. "We didn't."

Veronica's look turned soft. "Tell me how. I'll listen."

I wondered briefly if it was worth my time engaging her. She obviously had ulterior motives, and the way she presented herself made me feel that she couldn't be trusted. Either way, I decided there was no harm giving her a little bit of the truth. And maybe I just needed someone to hear the truth about that night.

Talking quietly as to not disturb the class, I told her all about my starting at South State as an All-Star, in-demand athlete, my fight with a fellow teammate, and then my subsequent transfer to NSU.

"And so, that's how I wound up here," I said when I was done with the story. "I had no idea Bella was enrolled at this school. I thought she was going to a different school, which is why I didn't believe that the Sacrifice could be her."

"I see," Veronica said softly, her expression fraudulently empathetic. "I can see how that could make your eyes lie to you."

I sighed inwardly. I could tell that she was lying and that she didn't believe one word I said, but it didn't matter. None of these people mattered.

Instead of continuing the conversation, I went back my work and ignored Veronica for the rest of the class. I'm sure it drove her crazy, but I didn't care. In fact, I took enjoyment that my snub would bring her estimation of her hotness down a notch or two.

When class was called and I was gathering my books, Veronica stepped up to my side.

I was immediately hit by a bubblegum-type fragrance that made me think Veronica George was cheap.

"We should totally hang out sometime," Veronica

suggested hopefully, placing a hand on my shoulder. I knew what she was offering—a good time and sex—which was surprising, all things considered. She wasn't my type even before Bella, and now . . . I eyed her wearily, and decided that she needed to be knocked down another peg or two. "Sorry," I said with a wide, mocking grin. "Your mouth isn't wide enough for my dick."

Dusting her hand off my shoulder like it was an annoying insect, I let out an amused chuckle and walked off, leaving Veronica standing there with her mouth wide open in shock. I probably shouldn't have, but from what Bella told me about her, she deserved it.

* * *

After a long day of classes, I walked back to the Alpha fraternity house. Unlike Bella, I hadn't moved out after the night of the Sacrifice. I was seen as somewhat of a hero. The guys had all been willing to cut me slack about what happened, especially because of Bella's smoldering looks, and some even thought better of me because of it.

I didn't think it was fair, but little did I know that I was about to get my first dose of criticism from a bunch of enraged feminists.

On the manicured lawn in front of the Alpha frat house, I encountered a small group of female protesters holding up signs. I figured they were part of a religious chapter of NSU, given the signs of protest they carried. Huh, religious feminists. That was a new one to me.

I found it amusing there was not one guy among their group. For a moment, I debated on ignoring them and continuing on inside the frat house. But then I thought I needed a laugh and walked over. As I approached, the majority quieted down, seemingly surprised that I had the balls to confront them.

"Is all of this really necessary?" I growled menacingly at the girls, walking up with faux anger. I stopped in front of the group and assumed a stance of authority, placing my hands on my waist and glaring at them.

"We are protesting the sin that goes on in this house," a protester said. "It is a filthy affront to the decent students who go to this school with all the drinking, partying, and sex that goes on in there. Not to mention members like you, who exploit your position."

I didn't bother to respond. There really was no arguing. They'd get tired soon enough.

Inside the frat house, it was a hub of activity. There were groups of my brothers sitting around the dorm living room, engaged in conversation with serious-looking school officials. I lowered my head and quickly walked through the room, not wanting to be called over and badgered with questions.

Someone had contacted me earlier in the day with a note stating that Todd James wanted to talk to me. I thought now was as good a time as ever to get the conversation out of the way.

Since the night of the Sacrifice, Todd was one of the ones who had treated me with even more respect, which was surprising given the fact that he was Alpha's president. I figured he was the political type and would have been covering his ass as hard as humanly possible.

After several moments, the door swung open. Todd was standing there shirtless and wearing gym sweats, a grin on his face. "Stefan, my man," he greeted me cheerily. "Come on in."

I stepped into the room and Todd shut the door behind me. Being the president of Alpha, he had the best room in the dorm, but it wasn't saying much. His room was a mess, littered with clothing on his bed and floor and several sets of dumbbells scattered all around. Posters of hot supermodels hung on his wall. Nearby, his laptop was open on his desk, the screensaver set to an eye-catching photo shoot of Kate Upton.

"What's all that out in the living room?" I asked, staring at the screen. "I thought they were supposed to be interviewing us individually."

Todd made a face. "The school decided they wanted to question a group of us all at once, as if that was going to change our story. So far, everyone has been sticking with the same storyline—nothing really happened that night, and the Sacrifice is just a game of destroying your most-prized possession for the fraternity." He gave me a look. "Of course, we know what the Sacrifice really is, but we can't let those assholes know that."

I still thought it funny that Bella and I were being protected by our peers only because none of them wanted to see their chapter fall. I also found it amazing that no one had cracked and told the school administrators what really happened. They were loyal—I have to give them that.

I suppose I should have been relieved, all things considered.

"There's just one problem," Todd said slowly.

I tore my eyes away from the laptop's screen saver

and looked at him. "What's that?"

"Craig Parker. He's not happy about having to cover for you after you hit him."

I let out a derisive grunt. "Fuck that dude, seriously. He deserved exactly what I gave him," I growled. The words that Craig said to me that night still made my blood boil. "All he had to do was keep his fucking mouth shut, so I shut it for him."

Todd scratched at his armpit. "Come on, man, do you really have to be that way? Everyone is covering for you and your sis, and you should be on your knees counting your lucky stars. All you have to do is apologize to him and it will help smooth things over."

"Never gonna happen." I said, shaking my head.

Todd stared at me for a long time before seeming to give up. "We can talk about Craig later." He scratched at his hair nervously. "There's actually something else I wanted to talk to you about."

I raised a questioning eyebrow.

Before Todd could answer, the door swung open and in walked Jace Randall with a cocky grin on his face that I immediately wanted to punch off. Since the night of the Sacrifice, he'd gone from being one of my biggest ass kissers to being so passive-aggressive that I wanted to kick his ass pretty frequently.

"'Sup, Livingston." He nodded at me as he closed the door behind him. He walked over next to Todd and crossed his arms over his chest, still giving me that fucked-up grin.

I looked to Todd. "What the hell is this?"

Todd took a deep breath. "Everyone is going around saying you banged your sister and that we're running some kind of prostitution ring, offering the sorority sisters to our brothers."

"And?" I asked. Judging by Todd's nervous expression, I could tell I wasn't going to like where he was going with this. "We already know what they're saying. And those are just rumors until someone admits to it and can prove it."

Todd looked to Jace, who just nodded at him, his annoying grin growing wider. "So, uh, yeah. Jace wants to pretend to be your sister's boyfriend. He thinks if he's seen around campus with Bella, it would quiet all the rumors about your sleeping with your stepsister and help our damaged image."

"I ain't gonna lie, Livingston," Jace chimed in. "I've wanted to hit that ever since I saw her sexy ass picture in your billfold."

My pulse pounded in my head and I instantly saw red. "You son of a bitch!" I rushed Jace with every intention of breaking every bone in his face, but Todd sprang in between us, holding me back and probably saving Jace's life.

"Hey, man!" Todd cried in a hushed voice as he struggled to hold me back. "There are school officials out there, for fuck's sake! If you guys start fighting in here and they hear it, that's probably the end."

"The hell with this frat," I snapped, straining against Todd, who was using his entire body weight to keep me from murdering Jace.

Jace grinned from the safety of being behind Todd. "What's the matter, Livingston? Why so mad? Are the rumors actually true that you're in love with your sister? Because I don't see what it matters to you one way or the other if I go out with her to help save your ass."

I didn't realize that, in my anger, I was probably giving the vibe that I cared about Bella in a far more intimate way than should be proper.

I took a deep breath to calm my anger and pushed Todd away from me, resigned to keeping my anger in check from there on out. "That's because I don't want her to go out with such a douchebag. She's still my stepsister, you fucking jackass."

Jace laughed. "Is that the real reason? Or is really because you just want to keep it all in the family?"

"Dude, Jace," complained Todd. "Stop fucking instigating and trying to get Stefan all riled up. This is serious shit we are in, and we don't need infighting tearing us down." Todd turned to me and gave me an imploring look. "Come on, Stefan, you're not thinking rationally. Your cooperation affects us all, and it ultimately benefits you and Bella. I mean, look at how politically correct the world is nowadays. Frats get shut down because of people making racist jokes. What the hell do you think is going to happen when people are going around saying Alpha promotes prostitution?"

I clenched my jaw angrily, my blood pressure rising. I had to admit, Todd's words had merit. I just didn't want to go along with the scheme for obvious reasons. But if I didn't go along with it, it would definitely confirm to Jace and even Todd that there was something more going on between me and Bella than just an accidental one-night stand.

"Fine," I grated finally. I glared at Jace menacingly. "But I want to make one thing clear—you're not to lay a hand on Bella while this is going on, you understand?"

Jace snorted. "How the hell do you expect people to believe she's my girl if I'm not banging her?"

I swallowed back the rage that rose in my stomach, not willing to be baited anymore. "Not one fucking hand," I growled. "Or else you lose that hand."

Todd stepped in between us again, as if anticipating me to lose control any moment, but he needn't bother. I was done with the conversation. I turned to leave the room, but I paused when Jace called my name.

"Yo, Livingston."

I paused with my hand on the doorknob, my back to my two frat brothers.

"What if she puts a hand on me? She's kind of too hot to resist." Jace was testing me, but I'd already had enough.

I walked out and closed the door behind me.

Chapter 13
Bella

I had no idea what to do. Hanna and Veronica's plan was absolutely idiotic, and I felt cheaper even thinking about the whole thing. I was still not sure if I should tell Stefan or not.

I also feared the stress that the whole situation was putting on my body. My mom had told me long ago that stress in her life had caused her a miscarriage. I wasn't going to let that happen to me. Not our baby.

I walked into my dorm room, exhausted after being hounded by Hanna and Veronica. The rumors appeared to be getting worse, and there was talk of Kappa being disbanded.

I didn't care one way or the other what happened. I just wanted to be left alone because I had more important things to worry about.

The aroma of pastries greeted me as I closed the door. Sara, who had cut one of her classes, must have been cooking her cupcakes again.

Cooking was her favorite pastime, and I must admit, her cupcakes were damned good. She 'd been trying to get me to learn how to bake, explaining to me that it would help relieve some of the stress that I'd been going through.

Sure enough, I saw her behind the counter as I set my books down on the couch.

"Hey, Bella," she greeted me cheerfully. Sara had her hair pulled back in a bun and was wearing a pink apron over her blue jeans and white t-shirt. "How was your day?"

"Do you have to even ask?" I muttered. "It was horrible."

She frowned. "I'm sorry to hear that."

"What is that you're making?" I asked, changing the subject. "It smells absolutely wonderful."

I wasn't really a pastry eater—I usually ate like a bird to maintain my figure, but my stressful day had me absolutely ravenous.

And it must be the baby inside me, I thought.

"It had better smell wonderful," joked Sara. "Otherwise, the cooking classes I'm taking would be an utter waste of time." She looked at me closely. "Do you really want some? You're usually always complaining about how you want to keep your figure and hate eating bad food."

"Yes," I growled. "Like now."

Sara grinned at me. "Those assholes must have really gotten to you. You sound like you're ready to pig out. But, bad news—they won't be done for another fifteen minutes."

Fifteen minutes? Damn woman, what was she trying to do to me? "Okay, I'll go get washed up then, and when I come back, they'd better be ready."

Sara chuckled. "Okay, Mistress Bella."

I left the living room and went into my bedroom to get a change of outfit. I took a quick shower, even managing not to fantasize about Stefan while in it. After, I was blow drying my hair when my cell rang. I walked over and grabbed it off the bed, swiping the touch screen.

My mother's smiling mug popped up, underscored by a *Call from Evelyn Livingston*.

I stared at it while the cell continued to ring. I was tempted to answer—boy, was I tempted.

After an intense internal struggle, I let out a sigh and silenced the phone. Stefan and I were in this mess together, and I wanted to be on the same page with him, so that meant I was going to do whatever he told me to do, no questions asked.

Several minutes later, I was sitting at the living room table, stuffing my face with delicious chocolate cupcakes.

"Gosh, Bella," Sara said, watching me eat. "I've never seen you so ravenous."

"I'm stressed the hell out," I said over a mouthful of creamy cupcake. I was going to have to get Sara to teach me how to make them. They were damned good. "And you've got skills. This is fucking delicious. What do you expect?"

I saw sympathy flash in Sara eyes, and she slowly reached out and placed a hand on top of my hand that wasn't holding the cupcake. "You know what, Bella? I can't pretend to understand what you're going through, but I know a good person when I see one . . . and I honestly believe you about the . . . mistake you made."

I nearly choked on my cupcake, not because of

Sara's empathy, but because she was absolutely wrong about me and Stefan. Even had I known that Stefan was behind the gladiator costume—and I was not yet convinced that I hadn't known on some subconscious level—I would still have screwed him willingly, eagerly letting him ravage my body for everything it was worth.

Before I could finish chowing down the cupcake and reply, there was a loud knock at the door.

Sara rose to her feet, looking at the door. "I wonder who it is?"

I quickly swallowed down the rest of the cupcake. "Don't answer that," I gasped breathlessly, almost choking on crumbs. "It's probably one of those stupid school officials, here to ask more questions."

Sara bit her lower lip and stared at the door. "They're going to know we're here, Bella."

"So?" I whispered. "We don't have to answer if we don't want to."

I was wasting my time trying to tell Sara not to answer. She was too much of a goody-two-shoes.

"I'm going to answer it," she said finally. "If it winds up being one of those investigators, I'll tell them that we don't want to talk."

"Whatever," I said.

"Don't worry, Bella. I've got your back."

Sara walked over to the door, peeked through the peephole, and then cracked it open so whoever was outside could not look in.

I started with surprise when she said, "Hey, Stefan, what a surprise to see you here."

"Hey, Sara, is Bella here?" I heard Stefan ask, my heart quickening a few beats.

"Um . . . she's . . ." Sara sounded flustered, and I took pity on her.

I jumped up from the table and ran to the door, pushing Sara out of the way.

"What are you doing here, Stefan?" I demanded. My heart fluttered at seeing him. He was so sexy, dressed casually in jeans and a black shirt that fit his cut torso like a glove. His hair was slicked to the side, but what really got me is that he looked extra pissed off. "I thought we agreed to . . ." I glanced at Sara quickly and bit my lower lip.

"I came to talk to you," he replied, his voice urgent. "And it couldn't wait."

He pushed past me without asking to come inside, and I closed the door, my pulse racing.

Stefan looked over at Sara, who was staring at Stefan like he was a piece of meat. It made me jealous, and I wanted to tell Sara to back off and find her own man. Stefan read my expression, though, and turned to my roommate. "Sara, can you give us a moment alone, please?" Stefan could be the absolute gentleman when he wanted to.

"Sure," Sara said after a short pause. She lingered for a moment before walking out of the room.

Stefan gestured at the couch. "Have a seat."

Back at home, I would have told Stefan to kiss my ass for ordering me about, but now that I was his, I felt an odd sense of acquiescence in his presence. I walked over to the couch and sat down, and almost immediately, Stefan began pacing.

Then he stopped and centered his gaze on me. The look of anger in his eyes made me shiver. "You're not going to like what I'm about to say."

"What is it?" I asked. I wondered if I should tell him about Jace's offer.

"My frat bros have been pressuring me. They think it's in our best interests if you are seen around campus with another guy until this investigation thing blows over." He snorted. "And they couldn't have chosen a worse guy to set you up with. They want you to go out with Jace Randall."

I almost told Stefan about Hanna and Veronica approaching me, but for some reason, I held it back. Something told me if I told Stefan about it, he would go berserk.

"I don't want to do that, Stefan," I said truthfully. "I mean, what's the point? When you really look at it, what's so bad about what we did? We're not even related!"

"Yeah, I know that, but look what's already going around campus. You don't need all this stress right now." Stefan sighed. "Look, I almost beat the fuck out of Jace for even proposing such a deal, and I don't want this thing happening any more than you do, but I made sure that if you agreed to it, he's not to lay a finger on you. Alpha and Kappa are determined to do damage control, and if we don't help them, we'll both pay for it."

I let out a disgusted sound. He agreed to this? Why? What's so wrong with this, anyway? "I can't stand this," I whined, tears coming to my eyes.

Stefan rushed over to the couch and sat down beside me, wrapping a powerful arm around my shoulder. "Don't cry, baby. I can't stand it any more than you can. But let's just go along with this for a little while until we figure out what we're going to do about our situation, okay? And if Jace harasses you in any way, let me know. Though that shouldn't be an issue since you guys are only supposed to hang out in public, where other people can see you."

"Okay," I agreed weakly after a drawn-out silence. I didn't like it, but to save our reps, to help Stefan . . . Thinking about him, I became even more aware of his touch on my arm. The heat from Stefan's body felt like it would set me on fire. "Fine. I'll do whatever to help us get out of this mess."

"Thanks, baby." Stefan kissed me gently on the cheek. Sitting so close to him, I could smell his scent, a masculine fragrance that had my ovaries heating up. I began to feel a warm glow in my stomach and I couldn't help myself. I returned his kiss. Next thing I knew, his tongue was in my mouth, swirling around like an eel. Eagerly, I wrapped my arms around his neck as he sucked on my tongue. Our kissing quickly became extremely passionate, and we began to roll all over the couch, groping one another all over. Stefan's hands were all over my body, causing sparks of electricity wherever they went.

"God, you make me so crazy," Stefan whispered in my ear, his hot breath burning my throat.

He rolled over on top of me, kissing me like a madman, and I could feel his big, hard cock pressing against my stomach. I wanted it so badly and would have grabbed it if he didn't have me in a submissive position. But when his hands went down to the button on my pants, I suddenly realized where we were and what we were doing, and I pushed him back with a gasp.

"We can't do this, Stefan," I panted. "Sara is in the next room."

Disappointment showed in Stefan's beautiful eyes, which had been filled with lust moments earlier, as he pulled back off my body. "You're right."

"I also think we shouldn't . . . you know . . . until we're gone from here."

Stefan bit his lower lip. "That's going to be a hard rule to follow."

"But it's for the best . . . for both of us."

My heart nearly broke at the look of hunger in Stefan's eyes. He wanted me, and I could tell it took everything he had to resist. "I know."

"But as soon as we're gone and away from here . . ." I said mischievously, trying to cheer him up.

"I'm going to fucking knock the bottom out," Stefan growled lustfully.

Laughing, I gave him a quick peck on the lips. "You sure about that?"

Stefan's eyes were filled with a certainty that was almost palpable. "I'd bet my aching left nut."

Chapter 14
Bella

I spent the next two weeks of hell pretending to be Jace's girlfriend. I made sure that we were always in a very public place when we were seen together, because I was afraid to be alone with him.

Still, Jace repeatedly tried to make out with me and get me to go back to his frat room, and I would have to remind him that our relationship was just for show.

Unfortunately, that only made him try harder.

He'd argue that our relationship would seem fake if we were never even seen kissing once. I knew he would never stop there, and I told him to keep dreaming.

To get back at me, Jace began parading me in front of all of his fraternity brothers, who, not surprisingly, were almost as obnoxious as him.

Luckily for me, the school was supposedly bringing the investigation to a close, so my faux relationship with Jace was fast coming to an end. Jace also realized that I would be ditching him soon, so his attempts at getting me in the sack became a bit more desperate.

Every day when classes were over, Jace would invite me back to the Alpha frat house for a drink and to just 'hang out', and every day, I would decline.

The main reason he wanted to sleep with me was for bragging rights and to get back at Stefan in some weird, sick way. Of course, if I went back to the Alpha frat house with him, Stefan would surely see us both together, which is what Jace probably wanted. He wanted to retake his position as alpha in the house, and triggering a fight with Stefan would be the easiest way to do it. I didn't want to give him that chance.

Still, I'd wind up in serious trouble if I wasn't careful. Because of his desperation, Jace was dangerous. He'd already shown he could be forceful. I didn't know how much longer he would keep taking no for an answer before deciding that he would just take what he wanted.

I'm sure he thought that once I agreed to pretend to be his girlfriend, it would have been easy to get me to sleep with him.

The fact that I wouldn't simply give in to Jace's crass advances was a major blow to his enormous ego. It killed him that I didn't just fall on the floor and spread my legs wide for him like I'm sure most other girls did. His bitterness at my rejection showed in every conversation we had. All he could ever talk about was how I could sleep with my stepbrother, but I couldn't give a nice, honest guy a chance. He didn't seem to get the clue that by constantly bringing it up, he was being anything but a nice, honest guy.

Whatever the case, there was no way I was going to sleep with Jace Randall, no matter how hard he tried. Even if Jace were the sweetest guy on earth, I wouldn't sleep with him. Scratch that—even if he possessed the last dick on earth, I wouldn't sleep with him. I had a baby and Stefan to worry about. Of course, Jace didn't know about the baby part, thank God, but that didn't matter.

All that mattered to me was getting through the

semester without someone getting hurt and then figuring out what to do with my life.

Unfortunately, that wasn't going to be easy.

* * *

I was walking alongside Jace in the hallways of NSU's science building to my next class, telling myself that in only a few days, it would be all over. I was ecstatic that I would be free, and if the school found that both Kappa and Alpha should be eliminated despite everyone's efforts to conceal wrongdoing, so be it.

I glanced over at Jace, who was wearing form-fitting blue jeans that hugged his firm ass, a white t-shirt, and his NSU jacket, his hair gelled and spiked. Just looking at him made my stomach turn. I should have been flattered that one of the hottest guys on campus wanted to fuck me, but he was a major douchebag and a complete turn-off.

Besides, I had to admit to myself now that I was in love with Stefan.

Jace glanced back at me and grinned, his eyes straying down my outfit, flashing with lust.

I knew I shouldn't have tried to look extra cute today, I thought with disgust, looking away from Jace's crude leer. *But who knows how long it'll be before I can't fit into any of my clothing? I'm already dreading having to go up in sizes.*

A size two my whole life, I wanted to dress as girly as possible before I blew up like a balloon.

So, keeping with tradition, I was wearing a black skirt and white blouse, complete with strapped heels with faux encrusted diamonds, my hair pulled up in a side ponytail. My makeup had me looking extra vivacious, with a colorful eye shadow that made my eyes pop, barely-there pink blush, and a soft lip-gloss on my lips.

Due to Jace's lustful gazes, I kept trying to put a little distance between me and him by walking a few feet apart, but every time I did, he would casually wrap his arm around my waist and pull me back in.

The passive-aggressive move was working my last nerve, which I'm sure Jace was perfectly aware of, but I let him do it because we were supposed to be boyfriend and girlfriend.

Just a few more days, I told myself repeatedly. *And this will all be over.*

A group of Alpha Gamma jocks were gathered in a group down the hall ahead of us, talking and laughing with one another. I recognized a few of them and groaned because I knew Jace would stop to talk to them.

"I'm going to go ahead to class," I informed Jace, pulling away from his grip. "I have some work that I didn't finish last night that I need to turn in."

Jace grabbed hold of my arm before I could walk away, his eyes ahead on the pack of jerks. "It can wait for a minute. Come say hi to the fellas with me."

"Actually, it can't." I tried to pull away, but he was too strong. "I'm on the verge of falling a grade if I don't get this assignment turned in on time." Of course I was lying. Surprisingly enough, and despite my situation, I was actually excelling in all of my classes, sitting on an A minus average. "Please let go of me."

Jace grinned at me and tugged me along, ignoring my request. "Stop whining. It will only be a minute. We have to make a show of our relationship, remember?"

"Making a show and enduring harassment are two different things," I replied. "Your frat brothers are complete assholes. I don't want to talk to them."

"No, they're not," Jace said. "They're cool. You should learn to lighten up a little."

"And you should learn that no means no," I growled.

Rather than respond, Jace pulled me down the hallway to his friends.

"'Sup, Jace?" one of the guys asked. Like Jace, he was a gym rat. All of the guys were. In fact, there was so much testosterone surrounding me that I was afraid I might grow balls. But their bulging muscles didn't impress me. Whenever I looked at a guy at NSU, I compared him to Stefan, and so far, no one had matched up to him.

"What's up, dude?" Jace replied, clasping hands with the guy and then with the rest of the group. I fidgeted nervously as all of their eyes fell on me, feeling like a piece of meat surrounded by a pack of hungry wolves. "What are you punks up to?"

"Nothing much. Just hoping that dumb ass investigation shit is finally over." The brunette nodded at me. "You hit that yet?"

Grinning, Jace draped his arm around my shoulder and pulled me close. "Nope. She won't put out."

"That's a shame," said one of the other guys. "She's such a hot piece of ass."

To supposedly want to save their fraternity, they sure had a terrible way of showing it. I guess they knew I had to endure it, and as long as no one else heard them, they were going to berate me.

Crossing my arms angrily across my breasts, I averted my gaze, my cheeks burning, uncomfortable from all the lewd stares. This was exactly the crap I was fed up with.

"What's up with that?" the cut, dark-haired jock asked me directly. "There's not a chick I know who wouldn't want to be Jace's girl."

That's because they're all sluts without an iota of self-worth, I thought.

When I remained silent, he added, "Maybe you should get your dad to marry her mom and then she'll sleep with you."

An angry lump formed in my throat and I found it hard to swallow back a biting comeback. There was nothing to be gained by saying anything to these guys.

Jace laughed and sneered at me. "Maybe I should. What do you say about that, Bella, huh? If I become your bro, will you want to fuck me then?"

"You know what?" I hissed, finally fed up, my hands trembling from rage. "Fuck you. Fuck all of you! I hope your fucking frat house gets shut down and you all go to hell!"

All the guys burst out in laughter, but I was done caring. I jerked away from Jace and began to move away. Then Jace tried to grab me but I broke into a sprint.

"Get back here, Bella!"

"Fuck off!" I yelled, hoping he didn't give chase as I tried to keep my balance in my heels. Even in normal shoes, I wouldn't have had a chance of outrunning him, but damn it if I wasn't going to try.

I couldn't bear another moment in that asshole's presence.

My heart pounding in my ears, I rushed down the hallway, not daring to look back. People were stopping and staring at me as I stumbled down the hall in my heels, but I didn't care. I just wanted to get away—away from Jace and his buddies, away from all the drama.

I rounded a corner and gasped as I ran into hard flesh.

"Stefan," I sobbed, filled with relief, tears streaming down my cheeks. "I can't take it anymore."

Stefan wrapped his arms around me and I immediately felt a sense of solace. I was in the arms of my protector. If Jace followed me down the hall, I knew that Stefan would deal with him. "Calm down, Bella. What's wrong? Did Jace put his hands on you?" Stefan's eyes burned with a dark, murderous rage.

"No," I sniffed, trying to get ahold of myself. "Though I think he would have eventually. He's been trying to get me to go back to his dorm with him from the moment this all started." I shook my head. "I'm sorry, Stefan. I can't do this anymore. I don't care what happens. I'll go crazy if I have to spend one more second with that asshole."

I told Stefan about all the verbal abuse I had been suffering at the hands of Jace and his frat brothers and Jace's constant attempts at getting me to sleep with him. As he listened, Stefan's jaw bulged out as he clenched his teeth in rage.

When I was done, Stefan placed his chin on top of my head. "Shh. It's okay. You don't have to pretend any longer. I should have never let those fuckers pressure me into making you go along with their plan. I made a mistake." Stefan pulled back and hooked a finger under my chin, tilting my head for me to look up at him. "Can you forgive me?"

"Only if you take me away from here," I said, my voice aching with need.

Stefan stared into my eyes. "Okay," he said huskily after a moment. He grabbed me by the hand and led me down the hallway. As we walked past other students, they stared. But Stefan didn't give a fuck, and neither did I.

He led me to a deserted hallway and to an unmarked door. Glancing around to make sure no one was about, he opened the door and led me inside. It was hot and stuffy when I stepped into the small room, the faint smell of bleach assaulting my nose. The room had a very small walkway surrounded by stacked boxes, and a mop and bucket sat in the corner. Above, the shelves were filled with all sorts of cleaning products.

Stefan gently closed the door behind him, plunging us into darkness.

I squinted at him through the dim lighting as my eyes started to adjust. There was a window at the back that brought in some light. "Stefan? Why'd you bring us here? When I said take me away, I didn't mean to take me inside a smelly janitor's closet—"

"Shh." Suddenly, I felt Stefan's body pressed up against mine. "I think you know why I brought you here." His voice was heavy with lust.

"I thought we agreed that we weren't going to do this until the semester was over," I whispered. My limbs were trembling. I couldn't tell if it was from fear or need or both.

"I lied," Stefan said. "You know you need this as much as I do."

Stefan ran his hands up my arm and to my neck, gently caressing it before pulling me into a hungry kiss. I melted in his arms, surrendering to the fire within. Our tongues swirled in each other's mouth, and I reached up and wrapped my arms around Stefan's neck.

Stefan tilted me back slightly, passionately kissing me and dominating my mouth with his tongue. He continued, moving me back inch by inch, until I bumped up against one of the boxes.

Still kissing me passionately, he hefted me up into his arms and set me atop one of the boxes. He broke away from me then, leaving me breathless, moving his hands up my thighs until he had pushed my skirt up to my waist, exposing my panties.

He lowered himself and began kissing his way up my thighs until he got to my soaked panties. He rose up slightly, lifting me up off the box several inches so he could slide my panties off.

I threw back my head and moaned as Stefan dove into my pussy, his mouth gobbling up my clit. He sucked and slurped my juices like a hungry man, causing my thighs to tremble around his neck. Soon, he stuck two fingers inside and slid them in and out as he sucked my clit, my eyes rolling into the back of my head from the pleasure.

Stefan continued to work me like an instrument. When he bore down on my clit with his teeth, it was all I could take, and I let out a strangled cry as I came.

He held me there in place while my body was

rocked with powerful spasms, sucking in all my juices like it was the sweetest nectar on earth.

"God, that felt so good," I breathed when it was over, my thighs weak.

"I'm not done with you yet," Stefan growled. He climbed to his feet, my juices still on his chin. He grabbed his shirt by the bottom and pulled it over his head, revealing his washboard abs in the dim light. Tossing his shirt to the side, he undid the button of his jeans and pulled them halfway down his powerful thighs.

I gaped in awe at the big, fat cock that flopped out, hard and ready for me. I reached forward and ran my finger down his powerful chest, awed by the power of his masculinity, and then I ran my hand all the way down his happy trail to his cock. When my hand gripped his hardness, he pushed me back onto the box, making me lose my grip, and grabbed me by the waist with both hands.

He lined his hard body up with mine and entered with one powerful thrust. I gasped as he filled me up.

I was about to say something about a condom, but did it even matter? I was already pregnant, and he was the father.

I actually liked the feel of his big dick inside me without the condom. I felt more connected to him without the flimsy barrier between our flesh.

Slowly, he thrust his cock deep inside me, allowing me to adjust to his size. Then he began picking up speed, his powerful thighs slamming into me. The smack of our flesh and my pleasured cries filled the room.

I reached down and dug my nails into his chiseled ass cheeks as he pounded me. I looked up at him as he fucked me. His face was twisted in pleasure, his hair damp with sweat, perspiration running down the sides of his face and dripping onto my stomach. He panted as he went balls deep inside me and then back out again. I guided his thrusts with my hands on his ass, encouraging him. I wanted him inside me, all of him, every last drop of his creamy load.

"I want all of it," I told him, gazing into his eyes. "Give it to me."

Stefan knew exactly what I meant as he picked up his pace, furiously slamming into me, his big balls smacking against me.

"Fuck," he croaked, several thrusts later. "I'm coming."

He gave one last thrust and then I felt his huge cock expanding and contracting inside me as squirt after squirt of his hot seed filled me. When he was done, he pulled out of me with a sigh.

As I sat up, I felt a dull ache up my side and knew I would be sore for days after the brutal pounding Stefan had given me, but it was well worth it.

A sheen of sweat covered Stefan's powerful chest as he breathed in and out, recovering from his exertion.

"That was naughty," I said, glancing down at the sticky mess sliding down my leg. I don't know why, but I suddenly had one of my urges, and I scooped up a fingerful of it, sticking it in my mouth and sucking it totally clean. Sure, normally, I'd realize just how gross I was being, but dammit, it was Stefan's, and I was pregnant!

Stefan grinned, both at my comment and my lewd display. "Yeah, it was. Come on, let's get you cleaned up and home. And don't worry about the frat. I'll make sure none of them ever disrespects you again."

Chapter 15
Bella

I avoided Jace for the next week, despite his numerous attempts to contact me. My parading with Jace had done little good to stave off the rumors surrounding the night of the Sacrifice anyway. People still continued to talk shit and make up stories.

Plus, I was done with all the harassment and misogynistic attitudes of the males of Alpha Gamma. If someone wanted me to hang out with them, I demanded respect. I should have never subjected myself to it in the first place.

Whatever. Fuck them all.

They had no idea what Stefan was to me.

In fact, our bond could only grow stronger.

* * *

I was eating at NSU'S food court with Sara between one of my classes, enjoying a beautiful, bright, and sunny day when trouble came knocking.

To go along with the beautiful day, I had on a pretty white and yellow sunflower dress and matching yellow earrings. To top it off, my makeup was cute, my hair was freshly flat-ironed and styled, and I felt good, confident.

Sitting across from me at a two-seat table, Sara, God bless her soul, was dressed in an unflattering black number that made her look like the Queen of Darkness sitting in the light, but I wasn't friends with her because of her fashion sense.

We both were currently enjoying a juicy cheeseburger with fries and a soft drink. Normally, I avoided fast food, but I think I was starting cravings early. I was absolutely filled with dread that this fast-food eating would soon become a normal occurrence and I would be shopping in the plus-sized aisles of Walmart.

Since finding out I was pregnant, I'd been devouring any and all the information I could find online and at the local library. It sucked that I couldn't talk to anyone about it. It sucked even more that I couldn't talk to my mom about it.

But how could I have gone about asking her? "Oh, hey, Mom. I'm pregnant with Stefan's baby and I need a little more info about all the ups and downs. Can you fill me in?"

I could only imagine the ensuing thud when my mother fainted and hit the floor.

"It looks like you have a lot on your mind," Sara remarked, breaking me out of my reverie.

A soft breeze ran through the area, ruffling my hair as I took a big bite out of the juicy burger. I let out a moan of satiation as the flavors of meat, cheese, lettuce, onion, mayo, and tomato merged inside my mouth.

"I'm just happy to be eating," I replied after I had chewed down the bite.

"You know, I've never seen you eat so much," Sara said, looking at me with concern while she fingered the straw of her drink. "You sure that all this stress isn't setting you on the path to binge-eating?"

Sara's concern for me amazed me. We hadn't really known each other when I came to NSU. Our friendship had been one of convenience, really, yet she had taken up for me after the night of the Sacrifice as if she'd been a childhood best friend.

"You know, you might be right," I said. While I'm sure the stress was causing me to crave food a little, the theory did not totally convince me. In my mind, it was more likely pregnancy cravings. But of course, Sara didn't need to know that. "Kappa had a lot of nerve for making me pretend to go out with that asshole, Jace."

Sara took a sip of her drink. "Oh, yeah. Whatever happened with that? You were complaining about him every day and then suddenly, you stopped."

"I stopped pretending to be his girl," I replied, fingering my burger. "I couldn't take it anymore. I figured that the investigation was almost through, and I didn't think it was going to influence the final decision one way or the other, so I told Jace to fuck off."

Sara reached across the table and gave me a high-five. "Right on, sister!"

We both shared a good laugh and then Sara asked, "What about Stefan? What has he had to say about all of this?"

I froze. After our steamy sex session in the janitor closet, Stefan and I had agreed to cool our relationship again until we were away from here.

"He just wants me to be happy," I replied quietly, taking a sip of my drink.

Sara was staring at me. "That's cool, but uh . . . hey, I've been thinking. Do you think you could get Stefan to go out with me?"

I nearly spit my drink into her face.

"Are you okay?" Sara asked when I began hacking

and coughing. "I'm just saying, your stepbrother's really hot, and if he's single . . ."

I held up a finger. "Hold that thought," I gasped. "I've got to go to the restroom."

I got up and left the table. To be honest, I was partly evading Sara's question, but I really did have to pee.

The nearest bathroom was closed, so I had to go to another one, down a corridor behind the food court.

The area was deserted and no one was in the bathroom. After relieving my bladder from what seemed like a gallon of fluid, I washed my hands, checked my makeup in the mirror, and then walked back outside.

I only got two steps before I heard a deep voice growl, "Why have you been hiding from me, Bella?"

I turned around to see Jace Randall staring at me, standing near the women's bathroom door. He had dark circles under his eyes and looked like he hadn't slept for days. Dressed in a dark hoodie and sweats, he looked like he was dressed for a foggy day and a jog, not a bright, sunny one.

My body went cold all over as I realized Jace must have been stalking me.

"I tried to be nice and give you a chance," Jace continued, not giving me a chance to respond. "But you didn't want me. All because you're in love with your stepbrother."

I glanced around. No one was nearby. "I'm not in love with my stepbrother," I refuted.

Jace sneered. "Save it. We know that you are. I can see it in your eyes whenever his name is mentioned." Slowly, Jace began to advance on me and I began to tremble. I debated on running away, but I knew Jace was going to catch me.

I'm sure someone is around here somewhere, I thought. *I mean, it's not THAT far from the food court, for crying out loud. He can't be trying to harm me in such a public place.*

I tried to calm my nerves, thinking that Jace was only here to rant and rave his displeasure at my rejection. I'd let him say his piece and then go on about my way.

"First your brother comes here and takes over the top Alpha spot, and even when he screws you, his own stepsister, he becomes even more popular." Jace scowled at me as he advanced. "How is that even possible? Can you tell me that, Bella?"

My mouth was dry and I had no reply. Nothing I could say would make him stop hating Stefan, so why bother?

"And can you also tell me why you rejected me over him?"

"I didn't reject you because of him," I said tersely. "I rejected you because you are an asshole and I'm not attracted to you."

Jace stopped directly in front of me, his eyes burning. "I'm afraid that's not the correct answer, Bella."

Looking into his eyes, I was hit with the sudden realization that Jace had come after me with an agenda, and if I didn't act, I'd be in serious trouble.

Not giving him a chance to show me what it was that he was going to do, I surprised him by clawing him across the face with my long fingernails, drawing blood and some of his skin.

Jace let out a surprised cry of pain and grabbed at his face. "Ow, you bitch! The fuck you do that for?"

Not wasting any time, I ran away, my heart pounding in my chest, hoping to reach the food court before Jace gave chase.

I counted several seconds before I heard his footsteps pounding behind me. He was closing in on me fast.

"Help!" I yelled desperately, but I was too far away from the food court for anyone to hear me and no one was nearby to help. There was too much noise in the food court for anyone to hear either.

Jace was so close now that I could hear him breathing as he quickly closed the distance.

"Shit," I gasped, feeling as if my lungs were about to burst. I was running as fast as I could, but I was wearing sandals and Jace was a powerful athlete. There was no way I was getting away.

I cried out as he grabbed me from behind, his arms encircling my waist.

"Where do you think you're going, bitch?" He growled into my ear, his breath hot on my neck. "You're going to fucking pay for scratching me."

I struggled against him briefly and then opened my mouth to scream, but he quickly clamped his hand over my mouth.

"Shut the fuck up," he snarled, bearing down hard on my jaw, preventing me from parting my lips to bite him. "No one is going to help you."

He began dragging me away from the food court and away from salvation.

"This is all your fault," Jace hissed angrily as he

pulled me away in the opposite direction. I couldn't believe there was no one walking nearby to witness him, but that's my luck for you. "For thinking you were too good to sleep with me. You walk around in those sexy clothes, flaunting your tight body and being a major cock tease, and then act surprised when a guy wants to fuck you. But not just any guy. No, you have the most popular guy in the school thirsty for it. And what do you do? You turn me down. No girl has ever turned me down. Ever. I mean, any girl who turns me down must have some serious issues. And then I realized that you do have serious issues. You slept with your brother, for Christ's sake. What girl in her right mind does that?"

I struggled against Jace's grip and tried to swear at him, but all that came out was a garbled mess. He was one to talk. Jace was obviously obsessed with getting revenge on Stefan and having sex with me.

"And sometimes, sick people need medicine," Jace said into my ear, his words sending a chill down my spine. "And I have just the medicine you need." He pressed his body into me as he made me walk forward, and I could feel his hard cock rubbing up against my ass.

I began to tremble within his grasp as I realized what he was going to do to me.

"Yeah," he whispered in my ear, aware of my fear and probably getting even more of a kick out of it. "I'm going to show you just exactly what you're missing."

I tried to look around for help, someone, anyone, but Jace kept my head in one position as we continued to move forward. Still, I couldn't see anyone in the vicinity.

Surely, someone had to see what was going on.

Feelings of despair overwhelmed me as the desire to scream, yell, bite, and kick faded away. Even if I could somehow manage to fight back, Jace was too strong. He had absolute control in this situation, and he was going to have his way with me whether I liked it or not.

We were just about to round a corner and probably disappear from any last chance of help when a deep, familiar voice said, "Let her go."

My heart sang with joy and relief.

Jace whirled around clumsily with me in his arms. "Fuck off, Livingston."

"I warned you not to lay a finger on Bella," he said darkly, "and I told you what would happen if you did." His eyes strayed to me briefly before going back to Jace. For a moment, I wondered how he had miraculously appeared right at that moment, but then I realized that even though we were supposed to keep our distance, Stefan had been watching me from afar this whole time to make sure I was safe.

I loved Stefan even more in that moment.

"I'm warning you one last time," Stefan said in an even tone, ignoring Jace's bait. "Let her go."

Stefan's eyes strayed back to me again and then back to Jace. Slowly, it dawned on me that he was sending me a subtle message. If he rushed Jace, who knew what he would do to me before Stefan reached him? He needed my help.

Jace shook his head. "Not going to happen. You've been a thorn in my side ever since you transferred to NSU."

Stefan's eyes flickered one last time to mine, and I almost felt a shared connection between the both of us. I knew what he wanted me to do.

Stefan's voice cracked like a whip. "Now, Bella!"

Jace had gotten distracted by Stefan's appearance and had relaxed his grip on my jaw, just enough to allow me to open my mouth.

I bit into his palm as hard as I could, breaking skin, the taste of blood and sweat flooding into my mouth. Jace let out a pained cry and let go of me, and I rushed away just as Stefan rushed forward.

I spat Jace's blood from my mouth just as Stefan collided into Jace's body with a loud grunt. The two went down on the ground, rolling over each other, each one grappling for domination.

Injured, Jace was at the disadvantage, only managing to score a couple of blows to Stefan's back, which did little to stop him. After a brief struggle, Stefan overpowered Jace and straddled his midsection.

Then, he began sending powerful punches into Jace's face. "I told you not to lay a fucking hand on her!" Stefan roared, landing punch after punch.

Nearby, people were coming out of the woodwork, gathering to see the fight. I stared at them in disbelief. Where were these people when Jace was dragging me away?

I turned my attention back to the fight. As much as I felt Jace deserved the beatdown he was getting, I knew I had to stop Stefan before Jace was severely injured, or worse, dead.

I rushed forward and grabbed Stefan's arms before he could deliver another punch. "Stefan, stop!" I cried. "You're going to kill him."

Stefan turned on me, his face twisted in fury. I

took several involuntary steps back, my blood chilled. Stefan looked truly frightening. He had a small cut on his lip and his nose was bleeding from the scuffle, but it was his eyes that horrified me.

They were filled with pure, unbridled hatred and rage.

"Please," I pleaded. "Look at him. I think he's learned his lesson now."

Jace lay there, moaning and groaning, his eyes rolling around in his head, eyes almost swollen shut. I should have felt a small sense of satisfaction at his current condition, but all I felt was sick to my stomach.

"We have to leave," I told Stefan, who looked like he wanted to finish the job. I glanced at all the people who were showing up. "Now, before more people show up."

This had been the very thing I feared since the beginning—Stefan's anger being unleashed on someone and causing trouble. Given the circumstances, I suppose he had no other choice, but this probably would have never happened had I not been forced into pretending to be Jace's girlfriend in the first place.

Stefan turned around and stared at Jace. For a moment, I feared he was going to fly back into a rage and finish the job, but then he climbed to his feet and stepped over Jace's prone form.

By this time, a small crowd had gathered, and people were whispering amongst each other. Several of Stefan's frat brothers and Jace's buddies came running up.

"Stefan, man, what the fuck?" one of them demanded as the others quickly knelt on the ground and began trying to revive Jace.

Stefan ignored him and reached out his hand to me. "Come on, Bella, let's go."

With one last look at Jace's battered face, I took Stefan's hand and let him lead me away.

"Where are we going?" I asked Stefan as we made our way across the campus.

I had no idea what in the world was going to happen now. Stefan had beat the shit out of Jace. Who knows what lies Jace would make up? All any of the bystanders saw was Stefan beating his ass.

The thought frightened me more than just a little.

But the answer Stefan gave me was one that I had least expected.

He looked over at me and replied, "Home."

Chapter 16
Bella

"You think they bought it?" I asked as I watched Stefan dump his duffle bag on his bedroom floor.

We were back at home and I was helping Stefan unpack his things. When we got back home from NSU, both of our parents had been relieved and perplexed to see us back mid-semester.

Of course, they had immediately inundated us with questions about why we hadn't answered their phone calls for weeks and bitched about how worried sick they were.

Any longer, my mom said, and she was going to have called the sheriff to come look for us. It was only the carefully designed messages that Stefan left on his father's voicemail that had stayed her hand.

Stefan, being the devious devil that he is, made up a story that there had been several assaults on NSU campus and that he wanted to bring me back home because he feared for my safety.

He made up some story about me receiving threats from several athletes for speaking out against a sexual assault that had taken place on campus. These athletes, he explained to my parents, would probably not be punished because of their valuable status to the school and would likely be able to carry out their threats against me and be able to get away with it free and clear.

Stefan had even admitted that he got into a fight with a fellow frat brother on my behalf, which resulted in more threats against me.

Rather than risk more fights, Stefan had brought me back home.

Both of our parents, who I thought would be pissed as hell that we were wasting a semester of their hard-earned money and that Stefan had gotten in trouble once again, praised Stefan for doing the right thing and were happy we were both safe.

Luckily for us, the story of our having sex hadn't reached our parents' ears, and they'd only heard small rumors about a scandal on our campus involving a popular fraternity. Still, there was the problem of what Stefan had done to Jace. From what I understood, Todd made up a story about what happened to Jace so that the school wouldn't investigate the fraternity further. So, Stefan made good use of the ignorance of our parents to weave a tale that was so good that I almost believed it over the events that really happened. Some of it had truth to it, anyway. I was threatened, and Jace did attempt to assault me.

Stefan grinned at me. "Hook, line, and sinker." He walked over and gathered me up into his arms, delivering a solid kiss to my lips.

I burned with desire, a feeling of happiness in my heart. Now that we were home, I could have Stefan all to myself. The thought of having sex with him right under our parents' noses filled me with breathless excitement and dread at the same time.

Our kisses quickly became more passionate, and Stefan pushed me back onto the bed. He gently lowered himself on top of me, smothering my neck with kisses. "You know, Evelyn and Dad are supposed to be going on vacation here soon, after his big project with the Governor," Stefan murmured, his deep voice filled with unbridled lust. "We'll have the whole house to ourselves."

"What's that supposed to mean?" I purred softly, knowing the answer. Stefan's strong hands on my body and his lips pressed against my skin felt incredible.

He grinned and kissed me hard on the lips. "Making up for lost time and mistakes. Starting with lots and lots of time in bed together."

I smiled and replied dreamily, "I think I can come to love that."

I pulled him down into another deep kiss, and we rolled around on his bed until I felt a sharp pinch and cried out.

Stefan pulled back immediately, his forehead creased with concern. "What's wrong, Bella? Did I hurt you?"

"I don't think so," I replied, rubbing at my hip. "Something just dug into my side."

"Hmm." Stefan pulled back off the bed and onto his feet. "Move," he ordered.

Dutifully, I rolled off the bed, revealing a medium-sized orange package with Stefan's name on it and no return address where I had been lying.

"The hell is that?" I wondered.

Stefan stared at the item with suspicion. "I have

no clue."

"I think it must have been on the bed before we even walked in," I suggested.

"Must have," Stefan muttered absently, his eyes on the package. After a moment, he picked it up and examined it.

He shook the package close to his ear, but it didn't make much of a sound. Gritting his teeth, veins bulged on Stefan's biceps as he tore open the top part of the package. He peeked inside before pulling out a folded piece of paper. When he unfolded it and read it, his face went white.

My pulse began to race, my heart pounding so hard that I thought even Stefan could hear it. "What is it?" I asked breathlessly. "What does it say?"

Stefan's voice sounded strained. "It says *For brother and sister.*"

"Throw it away!" I hissed immediately. "Now!"

Stefan folded up the piece of paper and stuffed it in his pocket, shaking his head. "I can't do that, Bella." He glanced at the package apprehensively. Whatever the package contained, it wasn't anything big. "Someone wants to give us a message."

"All the more reason to chuck it out the window. Please," I begged. "Get rid of it."

Stefan stared at me. "Do you really want to do that? Obviously, it's someone who knows who we are and where we live." Stefan shook his head. "As much as I want to please you, we have to see what it is."

I crossed my arms, glaring at him. "Fine, whatever. Just do it."

I held my breath as Stefan reached inside the

package and pulled out a small, black, square-shaped item.

"What the hell is that?" I asked in confusion. Then I recognized it a moment later.

It was a flash-drive memory stick.

Whatever was on the drive, I knew it couldn't be good.

After a moment, he walked over and grabbed his laptop off his desk and brought it over to the bed, powering it on.

I waited anxiously for it to boot up, holding my breath.

When the screen booted up to the OS window, Stefan stuck the flash drive in the USB slot.

I thought I would explode as I waited for it to load.

When the folder and thumbnail file finally popped up on the screen, my heart jumped. I peered at it closely. It was a video file. A crushing dread descended upon my body and I began to get dizzy.

Stefan turned to me, fear in his eyes, his hands trembling. "Are you ready?"

Of course I wasn't ready. But Stefan had to go open the bag of worms, and now I had to look.

I nodded, feeling like I was going to faint.

Tapping the laptop's trackpad, he double-clicked the file.

A dark room appeared on the screen. It looked somewhat familiar to me. A few seconds later, two individuals walked into the room, one led by the other, and my heart dropped in my chest as I watched in horror as the couple, who were dressed in costumes, proceeded to have hot, steamy sex. Even as I was horrified, I couldn't help it, knowing who it was. It got me aroused, seeing how just passionate, how nasty and hot we'd been. No wonder Stefan made the connection that we both wanted it.

Still, someone had recorded us. The fact smacked me in the face when the video got to the point that I took off his mask, and then a little bubble popped up with our names and our student ID photos superimposed on them. Stefan looked at me then, his eyes filled with horror.

Stunned, I could only return his look as I realized the ramifications of watching our own sex tape.

* * *

"Who could have done this?" I asked breathlessly from my perch on Stefan's bed, my pulse racing in my ears. Part of it was my horror, but another part of it was that I wanted that night again, to do it over and over and over.

Stefan slowly closed down the laptop screen, his chiseled features white as a sheet, his large hands visibly shaking. He was caught up in the horror of the implications, of the threat we'd just gotten. Besides when I told him about the baby, I'd never seen him so afraid. Being the strong alpha male that Stefan was, that alone made me even more frightened about our current predicament.

"It was Jace." Stefan's deep voice came out in a feral growl that I felt within the pit of my stomach. "It had to be."

I stared at the laptop and then the small flash drive that contained the damning video of Stefan and me having sex, wishing I could drop it into a pit of molten lava. "But why? And how? The Sacrifice was before the investigation and your fight with him. What would be his reason . . ." My words trailed off as I remembered Jace's words.

We'd been out on one of our 'dates,' and I'd asked him just why he was so hard up for trying to fuck me and to embarrass my brother. Jace had already had two beers, and apparently, he was loosened up enough that he told me the truth rather than some of the typical bullshit he'd fed me the rest of the time.

I've been here a whole fucking year, working my way up the social ladder, becoming one of the most popular athletes on NSU's campus. Meanwhile, your stupid brother just transfers here mid-semester, gets into Alpha without even trying, and is now considered the top dog by the fraternity. How fucked up is that?"

"He hated me the moment I joined Alpha Gamma, that's why," Stefan replied, confirming what I already knew. "I'm better looking, stronger, and I was just as popular. And you know what?"

"What?"

"I don't think this is the first time that this sort of thing has happened. The recording part, that is." At my raised eyebrow, Stefan continued. "I wouldn't put it past them. I mean, after all, they record all of their hazing."

"They do?" I asked with some surprise, though I should have known better. It's stupid, but a lot of college kids these days aren't too bright.

Stefan stopped pacing to nod. "Yeah. I've seen a couple of them. Some real fucked up shit, let me tell you. But when the investigation storm hit, they had someone smuggle them out of the Alpha dorm and hide them."

I remembered what some of the girls had to do to join Kappa, and seeing how the guys were probably ten times worse, I was suddenly filled with curiosity. "Did you have to get hazed to join Alpha?"

Stefan's handsome features twisted into an appalled expression that I would have thought adorable if not for our circumstances. "Fuck, no! What kind of dude do you take me for, Bella? Do you honestly think I'd let someone stick a rod up my ass? Or let someone force me to snort some guy's ball sack?"

I couldn't help but laugh at Stefan's tone. On the other hand, the idea of some guy being humbled by Stefan did have a bit of a kinky appeal all of a sudden. "No. You're not the kind to be sniffing."

"It's not funny." Stefan rolled his shoulders and neck as if working out a kink. "As soon as the fellas heard that I transferred to NSU and was looking for a frat to join, they let me join on my own terms."

Stefan's expression turned thoughtful. "But still, whoever sent this must want something from us. Why else would they want us to watch . . ." his voice trailed off as his eyes fell upon the package that the USB device had arrived in.

Slowly, he picked it up and looked inside before turning it upside down. Sure enough, a folded-up note fell out into his palm. Stefan glanced at me once before opening and reading it.

My heart jumped in my chest at the frozen expression on Stefan's face. "What does it say?" I inquired breathlessly, fearing the answer.

Without answering, Stefan handed it to me, my

heart feeling as if it was going to pound out of my chest as I read the words scrawled in large print.

TELL THE TRUTH OR ELSE.

The taste of sawdust filled my mouth as the note fell from my hands to the bedroom floor.

"Oh, God," I whispered, my limbs shaking violently, my heart racing faster than a track horse. The room started spinning around me and I felt like I couldn't breathe. My vision narrowed until it was one black dot, and all sound began to fade away.

"Don't start panicking, Bella," I dimly heard Stefan say in the background. To my faded hearing, he sounded extra muffled. "Everything is going to be okay. We'll get through this as usual . . . Bella?"

I fell back on Stefan's bed, my eyes rolling into the back of my head. I honestly don't know how long I was passed out—probably only a few seconds—but I awoke to the gentle touch of Stefan's hands on my forehead.

"Bella," he breathed in relief when he saw my eyes flutter open. "You kind of scared me there."

"I don't know what just happened," I said weakly. "The room started closing in on me and I felt like I couldn't breathe."

Stefan delivered a soft kiss to my lips and cupped my cheeks in his hands, stroking them gently. "It's okay. You were probably just having a minor panic attack."

I stared up into Stefan's eyes. They were so beautiful, but what really touched me was the love and concern for me reflected in them.

"You think so?" I asked.

"Yeah." Stefan brought his lips down on mine again, more firmly than the last. "But I know something that will relieve some of that stress and make it a little better."

"What's that?" I asked, excited by the huskiness in his tone.

Stefan's eyes flashed. He began kissing me on my neck, each kiss burning more than the last, and then worked his way down my stomach. He lifted my blouse, exposing my belly that was still flat and not yet showing the life that was growing inside it.

When he was done ravaging my midsection, he deftly undid my jeans and slid them halfway down my thighs. By this time, my panties were soaking wet and my limbs were shuddering with anticipation.

And Stefan was never one to disappoint. He pulled my panties to the right side of my thigh, exposing my swollen clit and wet lips. With a sound of hunger, he placed his mouth around my mound, sucking and slurping up my juices with powerful suction.

My lips parted and I let out a half-moan, half-cry of pleasure at the incredible sensation. "Shit!" I cried out, my thighs quavering around Stefan's neck. "That feels so good."

Stefan paused for a moment to grin up at me, his lips wet. "Good."

He returned to kneading my clit with his teeth, this time with even more force. I dug my nails into the bedding to deal with the incredible sensations washing through my body and clenched my teeth, fighting to stay quiet. My parents were still in the house, and though our house was quite large, I was sure they'd hear me if I kept this up.

After a moment, Stefan stuck two fingers inside,

sliding them in and out as he slithered his tongue over my clit, sending shockwaves of pleasure rolling through my body.

Fighting to keep all sound in, I reached down and grabbed Stefan's hair while he went to town, running my fingers through the soft silkiness and making it a tousled mess.

Stefan stared up at me as he kept his mouth glued to my pussy, his powerful fingers ramming in and out of me. Gazing into his eyes, I was struck by the intensity and the incredible sensations that were sweeping through my body. It became too much to hold in.

The room began to swim in my vision, my body temperature rising. I could feel the tidal wave building deep in the depths of my stomach, demanding release.

I parted my lips to cry as I felt it coming, ready to explode like a supernova, when the door swung open and a familiar voice demanded,

"What on earth are you two doing in here?"

Chapter 17
Stefan

In an instant, I saw shock register on Bella's face as the door to my bedroom swung open and panic gripped me. Moving incredibly fast, I pulled back from between Bella's thighs and shoved her away from me, quickly jumping up from the bed and out in front to obstruct the view, hoping Bella would pull her pants on in time.

Garbed in a red evening gown made of silk, her hair done up into a French bun, Evelyn, my stepmother, strode purposefully into my bedroom, looking ready for battle.

She came to a halt in the middle of the room, and I briefly wondered if she had seen me between her daughter's legs.

If she had, we were up shit creek. There was no way I was going to explain that shit away.

I could already see the look of outrage on her face.

Evelyn placed her hands on her hips and stared at me suspiciously. "What were you two doing?" she demanded.

Don't crack, don't crack, I chanted to keep calm. What made matters worse was that I had a boner as large as the Empire State Building. Good thing my cock was pointed downward in my jeans so it wasn't sticking out in a way that was obvious.

I casually took my forearm and wiped Bella's sweet juices from my lips. "Nothing," I replied, thinking fast. I nodded to a half-empty coke can that was conveniently sitting on the nightstand next to my bed. "I was just sharing a drink with Bella, talking about what we planned on doing now that we're back at home." I cringed inwardly, hoping she'd accept my flimsy excuse, keeping my exterior calm and collected.

Evelyn peered around me to get a better look. Behind me, I heard the bed creak and I hoped that Bella had gotten her pants on in time. "You sure about that? You two scrambled away from each other faster than two squirrels chasing after a nut as I walked in."

I let out an inward sigh of relief and relaxed. She hadn't seen what we were doing after all, and I chuckled nervously to myself.

Before I could reply, Bella was at my side with a scowl on her face, her arms crossed around her chest. She had apparently managed to get her jeans back on in time, though her clothing looked rumpled.

"Jesus, Mom," Bella hissed with venom. "Do you know how to fucking knock?"

I could tell that Bella was using faux anger to deflect some of Evelyn's curiosity, but I didn't think it was necessary. It was obvious Evelyn hadn't seen me whipping Bella's pussy with my tongue, so there was no need for the extra theatrics.

Evelyn appeared taken aback for a moment by Bella's rage. "I didn't think I had to, seeing as this is my house and that you two just got back home. I was just coming up here to tell Stefan something, and I didn't realize you were both in here," she replied when she had regained her composure. "And I most certainly don't appreciate how you're talking to me. You may be grown now, but you're still my little girl. I know Stefan says you were having trouble at school, but that doesn't mean you can come home and take it all out on me."

"Well, learn some basic manners and I won't have to," Bella snapped.

I nudged Bella with my elbow, hoping she'd take the hint. She was taking the fake anger thing a bit too far.

Evelyn stared at her scowling daughter, looking like she was about to explode. I knew I should head things off before things got out of hand, so I moved forward, put my hand on her elbow, and then led her out into the hallway.

"Evelyn," I said, lowering my voice so Bella wouldn't hear once we were a few steps away from my bedroom. "Please don't take anything Bella says to heart. She really is going through a rough time after what happened at school. I'm sure she doesn't mean to act this way."

Evelyn glanced at the doorway to my room, looking like she wanted to march in there and grab Bella by the hair and demand an apology. "Why do I think that you are making up excuses for Bella again, hmm? You don't think I remember how she acted before you guys left off to college? You saw it yourself."

"But this is much worse than that," I pointed out, not in a million years willing to say that I knew exactly why Bella had been acting that way, or that I'd been treating her like shit intentionally because of our mutual desire and inability to do something about it. Instead, I fell back on our cover story, which wasn't really all that much of a cover. "Bella was harassed by a pack of assholes the entire time she was at NSU. She's traumatized and is having trouble dealing with it."

Evelyn gave me a hard look and I tried to quell the surge of anxiety that rose inside.

I'd been hoping that my parents wouldn't question my story about what had happened back at NSU. While they both seemed to eat it up, I knew that it would only be a matter of time before more questions arose.

One thing that we had going for us was the fact that they had no idea of how Bella and I felt for one another. I mean, to them, there had never been any signs of inappropriate attraction. I was too busy trying to bang any girl with two legs, and Bella was too busy being a cold-hearted bitch to me.

So, I was pretty sure that even if the rumors of Bella and me having sex ever made it back to their ears, they'd just dismiss the notion.

After a moment, Evelyn glanced at my doorway and then bit her lower lip thoughtfully, the anger dissipating from her face. "Was it really that bad?"

"It was," I replied.

"My God." Evelyn lowered her voice to a whisper. "Do you think your father and I should file a complaint against the school?"

"No," I said quickly.

Evelyn raised an eyebrow. "Why not? If those boys you were talking about caused Bella this much distress, they deserve to be punished."

I shook my head. "That's not going to happen. Those guys are like the most popular dudes in the school and they have rich parents. You'd just be wasting your time filing against them."

Evelyn scowled. "Your father has money too. He can make things happen."

"I know, but it's probably better if we just let it all be in the past. You know the Governor won't want to risk a scandal at a state school, and Bella wasn't hurt. It sucks, but it'll be fine." God, I can bullshit when I need to.

Evelyn, for the first time, looked hurt. "But I'm her mother, Stefan. I should be the one she comes to first with these types of things."

"I know." I said, placing a reassuring hand on Evelyn's shoulder. "But don't worry. I'm sure Bella will come to you with everything that she's going through when she's ready. In the meantime, I'll continue giving her the support she needs. Trust me, I won't let any harm come to her. In fact, I kicked the living shit out of one of the dudes who was harassing her."

Evelyn's face lit up like a light bulb. "Did you? We aren't going to be hearing threats of a lawsuit like before, are we?"

"No, it wasn't that bad. But he got the message."

"All right, Stefan, I hope that's the case. I really do appreciate your being there for Bella," Evelyn said as she pulled me in for a warm embrace.

"It's no big deal," I told Evelyn as we pulled apart. I beamed at her to make her feel even more at ease. It was hard not to gag on my next words. "As her stepbrother, it's my duty to be there for her."

"And that's all I can ask of you." Evelyn turned to leave. "I'm going to go talk to your father about Bella. Maybe he'll know what to do."

Shit.

The fraudulent smile on my face was frozen. "You do that."

When Evelyn was gone, I returned to my bedroom to find Bella sitting on the bed, staring at the flash drive resting in her palm.

She looked up at me as I closed the door behind me and locked it. "How'd you get rid of her?"

"I just told her that you were going through some things and that I was providing the shoulder you needed to cry on, and that you'd come to her with your problems in due time." I approached the bed, my eyes on Bella. "It's not too far from the truth when you think about it."

Bella stared at me. "And what did she say?"

I paused in the middle of the floor. "She mentioned talking to my father, but I'm not sure what else. Look, Bella. We've got to be strong. We can't crack under pressure. Besides, Evelyn just asked me that as a question. I told her that you were fine, so I doubt she'll make anything of it." When Bella refused to look my way, I sat down next to her, took two fingers, and lifted her chin toward me. "Can you be strong for me? For us?"

Bella stared at me a long time, her lips quivering, tears in her eyes. Finally, she sniffed. "I'll try."

I kissed her softly on the cheek, still mindful of the taste of her juices on my lips. "Good."

Bella held out the flash drive to me. "But what are we going to do about this? And what about the threat? Who knows what they have planned for us—"

"Shh." I took the drive from her hands and set it to the side.

"One problem at a time." I moved my hand down to Bella's thigh and gave it a light squeeze. "Did you come before your mom came barreling her way in here?"

Surprise flashed in Bella's eyes. I knew what was she thinking—how could I be thinking about her sexual needs after what had just happened? "No," she replied softly.

Grinning wolfishly, I pushed her back onto the bed and began tugging at her jeans. "Then let's handle that first before worrying about anything else."

I slid Bella's jeans off her long legs, the smell hitting me like a drug right in the nose. Bella could see it too, and she smiled, getting into it. We scooted down to the edge of my bed, taking the time to arrange ourselves so that if someone did decide to barge in again, I could drop behind my bed and even roll under it while Bella had her back turned to the door.

"I love you," I whispered, looking up into her eyes as I brought my head forward and kissed her still moist lips. Bella moaned softly, running her right hand through my hair as the first shocks went through her and I buried myself in her wet folds.

Bella was delicious, moist and tender, and as I licked and nibbled on her pussy, I lost myself in pleasuring her.

"Oh my God, Stefan," she whispered as I found her clit and nibbled it. Her thighs quivered as she wrapped her legs around my head, and she leaned back, unable to control herself any longer. "That's it, eat my pussy."

Her nasty talk made me grin and lick harder and faster, wanting to wash away all her worries, all the stress from her body. Somewhere inside this luscious frame, my child was growing, and I loved it. I loved her, and I wanted to show her just how much.

Bella's clit swelled and her heels dug into my back as she pulled me in. She was trembling on the edge and wouldn't be able to take much more. I sucked on her button, and she exploded, biting her forearm to keep her screams inside as her thighs clamped around my head and cut off my air for what felt like eternity while she came on my tongue and lips.

When it passed, Bella lay back, her eyes dazed as I got up, wiping more of her delicious juices off my lips and licking my fingers clean. "Feel better?"

"You do that to me every morning, and I think I'll never be stressed for the rest of my life," Bella whispered, wiping her forehead. Her eyes drifted downward, where my cock had shifted in my jeans, no longer running down the leg but totally making a tentpole. "You look like you need some help now too."

"No time," I whisper, glancing at the clock. "You know they'll be calling for dinner soon."

Bella sighed and reached over, cupping my cock and making me moan. "Then as soon as I can, I'm giving you dessert. Or maybe I'm getting dessert, a thick load of Stefan's cream in my mouth."

I grin, knowing that whether she'd been one before or not, my stepsister was an amazing cock sucker. That she was eager for me too was just the cherry on top. "We'll see. For now, though . . . I love you."

"I love you too."

Chapter 18
Bella

"I'm going to need you to come work for me tomorrow, Stefan," Terry said over breakfast the next day.

We were all sitting at the kitchen table, having cheese-covered eggs, buttered toast with jam, sausage, and bacon. I was particularly hungry, digging into my eggs. I'd slept well, even if Stefan and I hadn't had the chance to let me return his oral favor. I'd been hoping to get the chance today, so Terry's words didn't make the morning begin well.

"What?" asked Stefan, a look of surprise coming over his face. He looked sexy as usual, dressed in a wife beater and pajama sweats, his hair tousled from just waking up.

He had the biggest plate at the table, piled high with sausage and eggs. Stefan liked to eat meats since he followed a low-carb diet.

I could have just stared at him all day if not for the fact that it would rouse suspicions with my parents.

Terry paused in his sip of his steaming morning coffee. My stepfather was dressed up in a nice business suit, ready to go to work for the day. Despite that, he had bags under his eyes and looked like he hadn't gotten a good night's rest. Apparently, running a construction business was a stressful job. "You didn't think I'd let you come back home and just do nothing, did you?"

Stefan looked appalled. "Of course not, but—"

"I spent a lot of money on your and Bella's tuition. While I understand how things can happen unexpectedly and cause a change in plans, I'd fully expect you to have a damn good reason for quitting mid-semester and coming home. And thus far, the reason you both have given me isn't good enough."

"But I had plans. I was going to get a job so I could move out and get my own place," Stefan protested.

"And I had plans on you and Bella finishing your degrees and not wasting my damn money too!" Terry snapped. "And how do you expect to get a job that's worth a damn with just a high school education, huh?"

Stefan's features became tight with anger, and I took a small break from stuffing my face, fearing that there was about to be a big blow-up. "I have every intention of going back to school."

"You do?" Terry asked, looking unconvinced. "When?"

Stefan glanced at me and fell silent.

Terry continued on. "We're finishing up the theater. My entire company is riding on this, and I sure can use an extra hand."

"I don't want to work construction," Stefan said flatly.

"Why not? You're physically fit and in tiptop shape. It'll be no problem for you."

"It's not what I want to do, Dad," Stefan said firmly. "It's not my style. Construction is a poor man's job."

Terry paused, and a glare so vile twisted his face that I actually felt goosebumps rise on my skin. "I don't give a shit what you want to do. The moment you left that university, you gave up that right. You're going to fucking work for me as long as I need you or until you take your ass back to school."

"Fuck you!" Stefan rose from his seat so fast that he knocked over his chair and it clattered against the kitchen floor.

"Stefan!" my mother cracked. This whole time, she had been sitting there quietly, watching the exchange—a miracle for her, let me tell you—but now, she had an expression of alarm on her face.

Looking like she'd had a better night's sleep than Terry, Mom looked well put-together as usual, her hair done up in a sophisticated bun, her makeup immaculate. She was wearing a nice business suit, but I had no idea why. Actually, I did have an idea why. My mom was a housewife who didn't work, but for some reason, she liked to pretend she did.

Stefan froze, trembling with anger. I fear that if Mother hadn't said anything, Stefan and his father would have come to blows.

"Stefan," I chimed in softly. "Please sit down."

My words seemed to have an incredibly calming effect on him. He swallowed audibly and then picked up his chair off the floor and sat back down.

"Fine, Dad," Stefan said quietly, his demeanor subdued. "I'll come in to work with you today."

Both of my parents tossed curious glances my way, amazed at how easily I had calmed the situation.

"Glad you saw it my way, Son," Terry said with a nervous chuckle.

After that, we all ate without saying a word until my mother broke the silence.

"I scheduled an appointment with a psychiatrist for you, Bella."

I froze in the process of stuffing my face with a mouthful of eggs. "What?" I asked.

"You have an appointment this Friday with Dr. Kern."

"But I don't want to see a psychiatrist!" I cringed at how shrill I sounded.

My mother took a sip of her orange juice and then wiped her mouth with her napkin and set it down to study me. "Stefan told me that you had a very hard time while at school. I'm just trying to help."

"But I don't need a . . ." I paused mid-sentence when I felt a sharp nudge against my leg underneath the table. I glanced around the table. Stefan had his head lowered, but I knew it was him.

I swallowed angrily. I didn't know why he would want me to go along with my mom's desire to send me to a psychiatrist. The only thing that I could figure out was that he didn't want me to arouse suspicion.

"Is there going to be a problem, Bella?" Mom asked me. She was leaning forward in her chair, gazing at me with an I'm-ready-for-your-bullshit look.

She was clearly expecting me to have an outburst, and I had been seconds away from proving her right. As I thought about it, I realized that arguing with my mom in my current condition would only cause more stress and make my situation worse.

Since my mom had impressed upon me that stress had caused her to have a miscarriage when she was younger, I was absolutely terrified.

I needed to minimize stress at all costs.

"No, Mom," I replied finally, my eyes going back to the eggs impaled by my fork. Food was just about the only thing that gave me comfort these days. "I'll go."

* * *

"Dad is totally busting my balls," Stefan said as he brushed past me to grab a box of tools off a shelf. We were in Terry's shed that sat at the very end of our back yard, able to get a private word in together for the first time all day.

After breakfast, Terry had told Stefan to go get himself re-acquainted with a set of tools because it would help him ease into the tasks he would have Stefan doing at the construction site. He'd stop by after lunch to take Stefan to the site.

Back when we were younger, the shed used to be one of Stefan's favorite places, and he would take delight in building stuff with his dad. But much to Terry's disappointment, it was a pastime Stefan soon abandoned when he came of age and got into sports.

Up until that point, Stefan had assured Terry that he would go into the construction business when he got older, but he changed his mind not long after.

"There's no glory in it," Stefan would say back then, infuriating my stepfather. "I'm going to be something much greater."

Stefan, it seemed, had a huge ego even then.

"You'll be fine," I said, leaning against a metal shelf filled with equipment, tools, and screws. "At least, for now."

Stefan set the box of tools down on a table in the middle of the room and glanced at me. Dressed in a tank top, his powerful biceps were on display. I had to admit, he looked right at home amongst all the manly tools. "Are you just saying that because you want to side with Dad? Because I remember how you used to side with him back in the day when he complained about me not following in his footsteps."

"I'm saying that because you would probably excel at anything Terry tasks you with."

Stefan opened the toolbox and grinned at me. "You have a honey tongue, you know that?"

I laughed lightly. "When it comes to you, yeah, I do."

"That's why I love you."

A feeling of warmth spread through my chest at his words.

"I always feel so good when you say that," I said softly.

Stefan pulled a large hammer out of the box and examined it.

"Do you, now? Well, you'd better get used to it—you're going to be hearing it for a long time."

Even though his words sounded kind of corny, they filled me with hope for our future. Stefan's attitude, at least so far, had been one of protective assurance, and it made me feel safe that I could trust him not to abandon me when things got rough.

Setting down the hammer, Stefan walked over to one of the shelves filled with dented metal shavings and brought a large sheet back to the table. "But you know what? After thinking about it, maybe this is what I need for right now. It will get my mind off all the problems that are going on with us and provide me with an outlet to relieve some stress." Stefan gripped the hammer tightly and brought it down on the metal, filling the shed with a loud clang.

I jumped at the sound. "I think it will be good too. But it can't last for long."

Stefan studied the dent he had made in the metal and then looked over at me. "I'm aware of that. We have, what? Two, maybe three months before you start showing enough for it to be a problem?"

I almost burst out laughing. With the way I'd been eating, I wouldn't be surprised if I started showing as early as next week. "Maybe a little less than that." By now, my pants were already starting to feel a little too snug around my hips, ass, and thighs. It would only be a matter of time before I had to go up a size. Having always been a size two my whole life, the thought horrified me.

Stefan's expression grew thoughtful. "I'll just have to think of something before then. In the meantime, we'll keep an eye out on how you're growing. If it starts looking like it'll be a problem, we'll just have to try to conceal it with bigger clothing. You know those baby doll dresses that flare out that you used to like to wear?"

"And when that stops working, then what?" I asked.

"Then we leave." Twisting his face into a grimace, Stefan brought the hammer down against the metal again, harder than before.

I stood there quietly for the next few minutes, watching him pound away at the metal like a smith at his forge, admiring his powerful arms at work.

"Why'd you nudge me when Mom said she's taking me to see Dr. Kern? I don't really want to go to that stupid psychiatrist," I said when Stefan had taken a break from the pounding. The sheet of metal now looked banged up, and I really didn't know what Stefan planned with it. Maybe he was just taking out his frustrations.

Stefan looked over at me, wiping the sweat from his brow. "I wouldn't worry about that. You see how Evelyn is acting. It's better that you just go along with it. It can't be that bad. Just answer the man's questions and call it a day. I'm going to be one taking you to your appointment, so we'll come up with some crap to say."

"You are?" I asked with some surprise. "Not Mom?"

Stefan nodded. "Yeah. I already cleared it with Dad. He says there's not much work to be done on Friday, so he's fine with me taking you to your appointment. I had to do a little convincing with Evelyn though. She wanted to be the one to take you."

Stefan's willingness to be there for me whenever I needed him touched me.

"Thank you," I said simply. "But . . . there's still the matter of what happened back at school. How long do you think it will be before they hear about it?" Both Stefan and I were shocked to find out that no news station or paper had run the story about the scandal shaking NSU yet. It only showed how badly the school wanted to keep Alpha Gamma's and Kappa Beta's customs under wraps. Coincidentally, it was a boon for Stefan and me.

Stefan shifted, staring at the dented-up metal. "Well, we have one good thing going for us."

"What's that?"

"I overheard Evelyn talking with Dad, and she

was bitching about how the school wouldn't tell her any details about our situation because of the pending investigation."

"But what happens when it ends?"

"I'm not sure, but even if they told them everything, do you honestly think that either of them would believe that we're fucking?"

I thought about it for a moment. I didn't see either of them, even Mom, of all people, believing such a tale unless she was provided with undeniable proof.

"No," I said finally. "I don't think so."

Stefan nodded. "Exactly. They'll believe anything I tell them when it comes to that. We both just need to keep an eye out on all mail that comes through and listen for any calls from the school."

I nodded. "But if they see that tape . . . all bets are off."

Stefan readied the hammer and then brought it down with impressive force, causing sparks to fly off the metal. "Then we have to make sure that they never see it."

Chapter 19
Bella

"This is so cute!" I squealed with delight, fingering a tiny pink jumpsuit.

It was Friday after my appointment at the psychiatric building, and Stefan had brought me to a baby clothing store across town to do a little bit of stress relief. I had some reservations about going inside, seeing as how I was nowhere close to due, but once I was in, I fell in love and quickly forgot about my horrible experience.

The psychiatrist had sucked. With all sorts of intrusive questions, stuff that made no damn sense as to why I might actually be there, and just wasting my time, I'd been eager to leave. It didn't help that I had to lie my ass off the whole time, feeling that he could see it plain as day, so Stefan's little surprise was appreciated.

There were all sorts of vibrant colors all over the place, adorable stuffed animals, toys, cribs, and of course, adorable baby clothes. Looking at it all filled my heart with a strange kind of bliss.

"Why are we even over here in the girls' section?" Stefan grumbled. He was standing behind me with his arms crossed. While he appeared irritated, I knew it was all an act. I'd seen him making googly eyes at a little bib that said *Daddy's Princess* on it, even if he pretended otherwise. "We're having a boy."

Raising an eyebrow, I paused, turning around to face him with the little jumpsuit pressed against my chest. "And how would you know?"

Stefan flexed his powerful biceps. "Because I know." He lowered his voice to a furtive whisper. "I just have a feeling."

I chuckled at his antics. "Well, I still want a girl," I said. "I know Mom would want a darling little granddaughter too."

As soon as the words left my mouth, I froze. My mom would have absolutely loved having a grandchild . . . but that would be after I had gone to school, graduated, and landed a good job.

I just wasn't sure how she'd react to Stefan being the father. I could only imagine the look on her face when she finally found out. Terry would probably try to strangle Stefan to death with his bare hands.

"Do you two need any help?" a light voice asked.

I turned to see a young pregnant woman, probably in her late twenties, standing there and smiling at us.

"Um, we're just looking," I replied, flustered.

Am I going to look like that? I worried.

The woman had to be at least seven months into her pregnancy with a belly the size of a giant pumpkin. If I got that big, I worried what Stefan would think of me. And at the rate I was currently eating, I could easily see how I could wind up there.

The woman looked at me closely. "How far along are you?"

I glanced down at my belly. Was I showing already? Nope, still flat, but my thighs looked a bit bigger.

For a moment, I debated on lying, but then I

thought, what the hell? I was in a store for pregnant women. No one would know that I was here.

"Almost two months," I replied.

The woman smiled. "You have quite a way to go then." She looked over at Stefan, and her expression changed. I could tell she was admiring him. "And is this your husband?"

Stefan and I glanced at each other. "Not yet," I said before Stefan could reply. "This is my boyfriend." For some reason, it felt incredibly good to say, freeing. We'd lied to the whole world for too long, and being able to say it just once, even if it was to this stranger, was just what I needed.

"Darn," the woman said. "I was hoping he was your brother or something. My boyfriend left me when I told him I was pregnant and I've been looking for a real man."

"Well, I'm sorry to hear that," I said, not knowing anything better to say. Seriously, this was getting damn weird. Was she working at the store or looking for another man?

"It's okay," the woman said, resting a hand on her belly. She sighed dreamily at Stefan. "You both look pretty young. How old are you?"

"We just graduated college," Stefan replied smoothly. He chucked a thumb at me. "Good DNA, that's all. She has a degree in biology and I'm an assistant coach."

"Oh. Well, that's nice." She smiled again at us, mainly at Stefan, as another costumer walked into the store. "Well I wish you both good luck."

She waddled off to greet the new costumer and I

turned to Stefan. "Kind of desperate, wasn't she?"

Stefan grinned. "When you need it, you need it."

I scowled. "What's that supposed to mean?"

"It means we're having a boy."

I slapped him on the arm. "Are not!"

We continued looking around the store for several minutes until I had my fill.

"Can I buy this?" I asked Stefan as we were about to walk out of the store. I was still holding the baby girl jumpsuit and had forgotten about it.

Stefan peered at me skeptically. "You sure you want to do that without really knowing the sex? And what if Evelyn were to find it?"

"I'll hide it where she'll never find it. I just want to have it to look at whenever I'm sad."

Stefan made a face, like he knew I was being nuts. "Fine. If that's what will make you happy, go ahead. You just have to promise that Mom will never see it."

I grinned, happy to have gotten my way with him. "I swear."

We walked up to the counter and prepared to pay for the little outfit. I was overcome with giddy excitement. This would be our first official purchase as parents and I couldn't be happier.

When the cashier asked for payment, I suddenly turned and took off toward a section of the store.

"Bella, where are you going?" Stefan called.

"I'll be right back," I sent over my shoulder.

I ran and grabbed the item and rushed back to the counter, breathless.

"Here," I said, setting the baby blue outfit on the counter next to the pink one. I smiled up at Stefan and winked. "Just in case."

Chapter 20
Bella

I spent the next few weeks doing chores and running odd errands for my mom. Since I wasn't going to school, she said, I needed to make myself useful in the meantime.

She felt so strongly about this that she fired the housemaid so that I'd have to do more work. Now, under normal circumstances, this would've made me go flip mode on my mom because I felt she was being absolutely hateful.

But, given the circumstances, I didn't want to argue. I didn't want any more stress put on my body than I was already dealing with.

So I became Mom's personal slave, doing any and everything she told me to. I was to clean both floors of the house, wash the dishes, do everyone's laundry, take Terry's suits and her dresses to the cleaners, go pick up take-out, and anything else that struck her fancy.

I supposed this was her way of punishing me for daring to quit college in the middle of the semester, but if she really knew what was going on with me, maybe she wouldn't have been so quick to make me her slave.

Or, maybe she'd just kill me?

I sure didn't know. Just how bad was Mom's temper?

On top of working me like a dog, Mom would pester me with incessant questions. I'm sure she was only trying to figure out what happened back at college, but some of her questions were downright bizarre.

I had no idea where these questions were coming from. Maybe the shrink had talked with her or something, but I was relieved that she wasn't hounding me about NSU.

The other problem I had was eating. My appetite had seemed to more than double since being back home. I wanted to eat anything and everything. To make matters worse, I developed odd cravings for things like oysters and scallops when I had never been a big fish eater.

But I knew such things were perfectly normal. In my free time, which was very little, I read up on pregnancies and the changes a woman's body will go through during it. A changing appetite was one thing that popped up again and again, but it only made me more nervous. I knew that if I kept eating like I was, I might wind up as big as a barn.

I hardly got to see Stefan during these times since he was always at work with his dad. But when I did get to see him, oh my.

He would often come home from work covered in sweat, dust, and dirt, dressed in jeans and a torn-up, dirty shirt that would expose his flesh here and there. But every time I saw him, I swear my ovaries started mass-producing hormones that screamed at me to tell Stefan to take me right then and there on the living room floor. It wasn't that out of bounds, though. Stefan just looked like a walking ad for cologne, something unapologetically manly like Brut or Old Spice, something for a real man. And Stefan looked like the walking embodiment of a real man.

Surprisingly enough, Stefan seemed to love his job and I was happy for him. But I couldn't help but worry about what was going to happen to us. We had an unknown blackmailer waiting for us to make a move and a baby complicating matters.

Due to the volatile situation we were in, it was only a matter of time before we would be forced to leave the house and find shelter elsewhere. That, or tell the truth.

* * *

It was on a Friday afternoon that I found myself doing laundry for the family. Stefan and Terry were at work, and Mom was somewhere in the house pretending to be doing something important.

I had been on my feet pretty much all day and was ready to sit down, but I knew that I wouldn't catch a break long before Mother had some other chore for me to do.

I was loading in a bunch of white clothing in the washer when I came upon a pair of Stefan's underwear.

I peeked at them, wondering if they had been worn because they looked clean. Then I was hit by an errant thought. My hormones were raging, and I couldn't help but imagine him standing before me in nothing but his boxers.

I imagined getting down on my knees and slipping his huge cock out of the slit and sliding it into my mouth. Maybe it was the hormones or maybe it was just that it was Stefan, but sucking his cock until he blew a load in my mouth was constantly on my mind. I must have been standing there appearing to be in ecstasy.

"Hey, I forgot to tell you to make sure you don't

put bleach in—what in the world are you doing?" There was my mom, standing there in the doorway, staring at me like I was nuts.

I jumped like a rabbit and tossed Stefan's boxers into the washer. "Uh, nothing," I replied quickly, my mind racing, "I was just checking if those were dirty or not."

My mom made a face. "You sure about that? You were practically inhaling those things." My mom shook her head. "Anyway, don't forget that I need your help cooking dinner. This is a big day for Terry, so I want to have a nice dinner ready for when he comes home."

"Okay, Mom," I said dutifully, closing the lid on the washer. "I'm on it."

My mom beamed at my obedience. "You know what, Bella? I don't know what happened to you at that school, but I really like how you're acting now. Like a changed young woman."

"Thank you," I said with a sweet smile. "I just think I needed a little change of perspective, that's all."

Mom just ate it up. "I think so too. Now, all we have to do is find you another school to go to."

I sighed when my mom left. I didn't say anything to her because I didn't want to argue, but there was no way I could go back to school. I mean, I eventually wanted to, but with the pregnancy, I wouldn't be able to go next semester.

* * *

Stefan and Terry returned home hours later when Mom and I were putting the finishing touches on the pot roast in the oven. The smell of meat filled the house as I added buttered rolls onto the top rack of the oven.

Terry was the first one in, dressed in his usual business attire, his face lit with excitement. "Evelyn!" he shouted. "We finished the theater, and it's magnificent."

My mom, who had been drying her hands at the sink, let out a squeal of delight and ran out of the kitchen into Terry's arms. "Congratulations!"

The two embraced each other and kissed multiple times before my mother pulled away. "Now you won't mind continuing to pay for Bella's education."

Terry glanced my way, his smile dimming slightly. "I suppose not. As long as she's going to stick with it."

Stefan walked in behind my parents and my jaw almost dropped to the floor. He was covered from head to toe in dirt and sweat, but that didn't matter to me. Forget looking like a model, he looked like a god in his torn jeans and tank top with his massive biceps on display.

Feelings of strong desire ran through me and I needed to hold on to the kitchen counter for support.

"Sweet Jesus, Stefan," my mom complained as she surveyed the sexy mess that was Stefan. "Do you just roll in the dirt for fun at the construction site or something?"

"Cut him some slack, Evelyn," Terry grumbled. "The boy is one of the hardest workers there. In fact, he might be one of the reasons for our success."

Evelyn stared, a smile spreading across her face. "I suppose so."

I breathed in deeply, trying to cool my heated blood. I don't know what was going on, but my hormones were raging out of control. I just wanted to rush forward and jump into Stefan's arms, making him take me on the kitchen's island for all to see.

"Dad's right, Mom," Stefan added, grinning to show he meant no offense. "I do work hard." He turned to Terry. "Hey, Dad, why don't you take Mom out to dinner to share your success? Since Bella and I have been back, I haven't seen you two spend much time together."

Terry's face lit up and he snapped his fingers. "You know what? That's a good idea, Stefan. How about it, Evelyn? I know it's piss poor since Stefan had to bring it up, but I've been neglecting you. How about we go out to eat at your favorite restaurant?"

My mom glanced back over at the stove. "But what about the roast in the oven? Bella and I spent a good deal of time preparing it."

Terry shrugged. "Let Bella and Stefan have it."

Stefan rubbed his stomach. "Don't worry, I can polish it off. I'm absolutely ravenous."

"See?" Terry asked. "Problem all taken care of."

Evelyn smiled. "I'll try to get ready as fast as I can."

Terry grinned back. "You do that. I'm going to wash up too and change suits."

They walked off together upstairs, leaving me alone with Stefan. When Stefan turned his gaze on me, I felt like I was melting.

"How was your day?" he asked in his deep baritone. He walked over and set his hat down on the kitchen's bar.

"Okay," I said, my eyes glued to his glistening biceps. "Mom worked me like a slave as usual."

"She needs to lighten up," Stefan said with

irritation. "She has no idea what you're going through."

"It's okay. It gives me something to do while you're gone, but I don't know how much longer I'll be able to do it before . . ."

Stefan nodded quietly. We both knew what that meant.

"Let me make your plate," I said, tearing my gaze away from his sexy body. "I know you have to be ready to chow down."

"I'm about to pass out."

I went about fixing Stefan a plate, piling it high with meat and potatoes. Once again, I felt good doing something so simple for him. I finally figured it out. All the hours of doing housework—this is what I want. I want to be his. To serve him.

When I set Stefan's plate down, he tore into it like a starving dog. I got a kick and a little something else out of watching his powerful jaws at work while he chewed. While I watched, I stuffed my face with the buttered rolls I'd put in the oven right before Stefan and Terry walked in. They were absolutely delicious.

Stefan groaned in contentment when he was done with his food. He practically licked his plate clean. "That was really good. If you keep that up, I might hire you to cook for me one day."

"Shut it, silly," I said. "I had help from Mom."

"That's why I said, if you keep it up."

"So, what are you going to do now?" I asked. I hoped Stefan sensed the hidden meaning.

But it looked like he was blissfully unaware of the opportunity our parents leaving us in the house alone might give. I got it—he was tired—but I almost had *Fuck me, Stefan* written on my forehead in red marker.

Stefan got up from his seat, oblivious. "I'm going to take a hot shower and then jump in the pool for a swim."

I waited for him to ask me to join him—anything—but he didn't, and he walked off upstairs to his room without inviting me and I was left with a feeling of disappointment.

My mom was down the stairs twenty minutes later, dressed in a sparkling silver evening gown.

"Mom," I breathed. "You look absolutely beautiful."

"Why, thank you, Bella," my mom beamed. "It feels nice to hear that at my age."

Terry was down next, and he didn't look much different than before, dressed in one of his usual business suits. "All ready?" he asked Evelyn.

My mom smiled up at him. "All ready," she repeated.

They both left the house and I was left with a strange feeling of loneliness. After I had put up all the food, I walked up to my room.

I was about to take a shower when I remembered Stefan. I walked over to my window and looked out. Stefan just so happened to be crossing the lawn to the pool at that moment. He was dressed in swimming trunks, with no shirt on, carrying a towel. Even from this vantage point, I could see his well-defined abs.

Stefan's words came back to haunt me. *We need to play this smart.*

But why play anything when there was no one around? After a moment, I made up my mind. I walked over to my closet and dug out one of my sexiest bathing suits.

Sometimes, a girl just has to say what she wants. And I wanted him, I thought as I changed quickly, making sure my butt was just properly outlined in the high-cut leg holes. Ignore that, Stefan.

Night air caressed my skin, causing goosebumps along my flesh as I strolled outside into the backyard.

The cool earth enveloped my bare feet as I made my way over to the swimming pool, garbed in a red silk bathrobe that covered my bathing suit.

I stood at the edge when I reached the pool, watching Stefan swim laps back and forth, his powerful arms sending up large splashes of water along the sides.

He seemed oblivious to my presence, so I was content to stand there, taking joy in watching his powerful body at work.

Stefan finally seemed to notice me, halfway through a lap, and he literally flipped his body over in the water to get a better look at me.

"Bella," he said with some surprise as he waded in the water, his blonde hair plastered to his skull. I liked the look on him. He looked incredibly sexy when he was wet. And I could tell with one glance that I had his attention. "I'm glad you decided to join me."

"Of course I was going to come join you," I replied. "I couldn't let you swim out here all by yourself." I nodded at the water. "Is it cold?"

Stefan grinned at me playfully, wiping water out of his eyes. "It's just right. Come on and jump right in."

I dipped my toe into the water and jerked it back instantly. "Liar," I accused him.

Stefan chuckled, delighted he had tricked me. "Come on, it's not that cold."

I scowled, placing my hands on my hips. "It's fucking freezing."

Stefan threw back his head and laughed, sinking into the water by several inches. "I love it when you talk dirty. But seriously, it's not that cold." Stefan swam his way to where I was standing and grabbed ahold of the edge. He looked up at me, his eyes flashing with dangerous excitement, his deep voice husky. "Especially when you have me to warm you up."

A warm flush came to my cheeks as excitement coursed through my body. "Well, when you put it that way . . ."

With sensual flair, I took off my bathrobe and tossed it to the side, revealing my red one-piece swimsuit.

Stefan's eyes went wide with surprise. "Holy shit," he sputtered.

"What?" I asked, immediately self-conscious.

"You've put on some weight."

I frowned, almost wishing I'd kept on my robe. Was I really already becoming a whale?

Stefan noticed my displeasure and shook his head vigorously. "No, it's amazing. You've filled out in all the right places." He bit his lower lip as he ogled my curves and continued to shake his head in amazement, boosting my self-confidence.

"I hope you will still feel the same way when I get even bigger," I said. While I was pleased Stefan wasn't bothered by the little weight I'd put on, I knew more was to come as my pregnancy advanced.

I'd be a fool to think that looks weren't important to Stefan. He was a young, All-American, red-blooded male who was incredibly handsome and could have any girl he wanted.

But if I didn't want to worry myself to death about the issue, I'd have to take his word for it.

Stefan stared at me as if he was appalled by my lack of faith in him. "I'm going to want you even more."

"Well, since that's settled . . ." I dipped my toe in the water and kicked, splashing Stefan in the face.

"I'm going to get you for that!" Stefan yelled with surprise, wiping at his eyes.

"You have to catch me first," I said.

Stefan was quick to oblige, rocketing out of the pool so fast I hardly had time to react. Shrieking, I took off for the house. I only got to the edge of the lawn before Stefan's powerful arms wrapped around me, pulling me close.

"Where do you think you're going?" he whispered in my ear, his breath hot on my neck. I squealed with surprise as he hefted me up into his arms and brought me back to the edge of the pool.

"Stefan, no!" I cried, recognizing his intent, squirming against his solid grasp.

"All is fair in love and war," he grunted. And in one smooth motion of muscle and grace, he scooped me up and literally threw me into the water.

I gasped with shock as the cold water hit me and I heard a muffled sound of a large splash behind me.

Blinded, I began to swim away from him, but I was no match for the seasoned athlete, and he quickly caught up to me with several powerful strokes and pulled me into his arms.

My body thrummed with electricity at being so close to his. His abs pressed against my stomach, and down below, I could feel his cock pressing against my thigh, already starting to get hard.

I wanted nothing more than to please him, but we were outside, and who knew who could see us or when our parents would be back?

"Got you again," Stefan panted, staring me in the eyes and making my heart flutter.

I swear, my stepbrother was too gorgeous to be real with his amazing chiseled cheekbones. It didn't help matters that his big cock was rubbing against my thigh, making my hormones rage out of control.

"What you just did wasn't fair," I said breathlessly, trying not to think about the throbbing log against my thigh.

"Neither was kicking water in my face."

I wrapped my arms around his neck, pulling him closer. Stefan's eyes flashed, and he pressed his lips into mine. I surrendered to him, allowing him to hold my body up in the water. His tongue swirled around in my mouth, mixing the taste of our saliva and chlorine.

His bulge was still increasing in size as we pressed against each other. Steam rose around us, and I wondered if it was from our combined body temperature. Stefan's hard body felt warmer than an oven, and his passionate kiss was blasting heat through my stomach like a furnace.

Stefan suddenly broke away from our kiss, filling me with longing and disappointment. "They could be back home any minute. We don't want to get too frisky."

While I was disappointed that we didn't have sex right then and there, I knew Stefan was right. With everything that had already happened, it wouldn't do for us to get caught bumping uglies in the pool.

On top of that, I was impressed that Stefan could resist a quick fuck with how hard his cock was. It only made my respect for him grow stronger.

With some reluctance, I paddled away from Stefan. I was immediately struck by how cold I was once I was away from him, and my teeth began to chatter.

"You know what, Stefan?" I asked, flipping over in the water to face him.

"What?"

I splashed him in the eyes. "You're a total buzz kill!"

Stefan let out a surprised gasp and grabbed at his eyes. "I'm so going to get you for that!"

I laughed uproariously and began to swim away. In seconds, Stefan was chasing me around the pool and we began splashing each other repeatedly, engaging in a vicious water fight.

Feelings of nostalgia rolled through me as we played, reminding me of old times when we were younger. For once, I found myself forgetting about everything, my pregnancy and the threatening note, lost in the bliss of the moment.

"Enough!" I cried when Stefan had overwhelmed me with a burst of water splashes that blinded me and made it difficult for me to breathe. "You win!"

"That was fun," I murmured to him after I caught my breath. "Reminded me of old times, when we were kids."

Stefan grinned at me. "Yeah, it kind of did, didn't it?"

I still couldn't get over how hot Stefan's body felt, and once again, steam surrounded us. Warmth spread up from my nether regions all the way to my chest, and I felt a burn behind my ears as I stared into my stepbrother's eyes.

My hormones raging through my blood, I couldn't think straight with Stefan's cock pressed against me. I couldn't fathom how he could be next to me with such a boner and resist fucking me.

But more than anything, I wanted him. I wanted to taste him.

Suddenly, I felt bold. Powerful. Stefan was going to give me what I wanted. I pulled Stefan close and began guiding us toward the end of the pool toward the steps.

Stefan didn't take my meaning at first. "What do you think you're doing?" He grinned at me as I paddled us into shallow water. "Who said you could take control of this ship?"

Not saying a word, I led him to the steps of the pool and pushed him down on the higher step. Then I knelt in front of him on the lowest step and began pulling at his swimming trunks.

Stefan glanced all around, finally grasping my meaning. "What are you doing, Bella?" His voice had a slight note of panic in it. "Some of our neighbors can see into our backyard and might see us."

"Fuck them," I growled, managing to get his shorts down several inches. The tip of his cock appeared, big and bulbous, and my mouth was instantly filled with saliva.

"Bella, I really don't think you shouldn't be doing this..." Stefan fell silent as I jerked down his shorts and his huge cock popped out and smacked him against his abs.

Hungrily, I grabbed it, feeling how hard and throbbing he was, and stuffed him into my mouth.

I started slurping his cock greedily, trying to take every bit of his thick shaft, my mind going back to the day that I lost the dildo-sucking contest to Veronica.

"Bella..." Stefan groaned.

I ignored him and slurped his huge head with relish, swirling my tongue along the sensitive parts, and I gripped his shaft with my left hand while bringing my right around to cup his balls.

Massaging them gently, I bobbed my head up and down, stroking in tandem.

Stefan let out a deep groan. "Fuck, that feels good."

I went further down his shaft, taking as much of him as I could without gagging.

I marveled at the feel of his cock throbbing in my mouth, each pulse a powerful jolt against my tongue. How I wanted to taste his juices.

I massaged his balls more vigorously while going up and down on him like a madwoman, my saliva mixing with chlorinated water on his dick.

"I'm gonna come soon," Stefan groaned.

Good, I thought, as I almost made it all the way down to the base of his shaft. *That's what I want, to taste your sweet, thick cream.*

Before that could happen, Stefan suddenly tapped

me on the shoulder urgently.

"Bella," he half-groaned, half-whispered. "The lights are on back at the house. Our parents are home."

I ignored him and continued to stroke and suck stubbornly, wanting him to nut in my mouth.

"Bella!" Stefan choked. "Stop it."

For all his objecting, Stefan had yet to pull me off his dick.

In the distance, I heard a door opening and my mother calling Stefan's name. This would have been the time I pulled away and pretended nothing was going on. But I couldn't. I desperately wanted Stefan's seed and I wasn't going to stop until I got it.

Stefan tapped me several more times on the shoulder and I could hear my mother approaching. Knowing I had only seconds left, I squeezed Stefan's balls and slurped his head as hard as I could.

I was rewarded with a gasp and his hot, creamy liquid flooding my mouth. His milk was sweet and tangy. I took as much of it as I could before Stefan began to pull up his shorts.

Pushing away, I drifted beneath the waves of the pool and swam toward the deep end.

It wasn't a moment too soon either, because my mom reached Stefan a second later. Down on the deep end, I wondered how long I could hold my breath before I had to surface and if my mom could see me.

I could hear Stefan and my mom talking, but sound was too muffled to understand what they were saying. When it felt like my lungs were about to burst, I swam to the surface, hoping I'd have an explanation ready. I broke the water, gasping in air.

When I recovered, I swam over to the edge and grabbed a hold. I was surprised when strong hands reached down and pulled me out of the pool.

"Don't you ever do that again," Stefan scolded me, but at the same time, I could see that he loved it, too.

I wiped water out of my eyes and shivered from the cold breeze against my skin. "Did she see me?" I asked.

Stefan shook his head and nodded to where my mother was just now stepping back into the house through the back door. "No, and we were damn lucky too. Thank God all she came out here to ask me is if I wanted some of the food they brought back from dinner."

I grinned. "It was worth it."

Stefan's expression grew more serious. "I don't know what's gotten into you, Bella, but this isn't a game."

I gawked at Stefan, my teeth chattering. "Well, you almost did the same thing when we were in your bedroom and Mom walked in on us."

And I only wanted to repay the favor, I thought.

"It wasn't the same. The door was closed and I wasn't expecting her to just barge in. We're outside, right? Anybody could've seen us."

"Okay," I said acidly. So that's how he wanted to play it. Damn him. "I get it."

Then he walked off back to the house, leaving me alone to shiver in the dark.

Chapter 21
Stefan

Construction work. It's pretty much all I knew day and night. But now that the theater was done, work had slacked off a little.

The spare time was both refreshing and frustrating. Working on the site, I'd found that I liked what I was doing. If anything, being able to take out all my stress on metal and wood helped, and I came home every night feeling like I'd at least gotten a good workout in. Trust me, lugging fifty-pound bags of concrete around works even a good athlete.

So I liked having some more rest. But I missed being able to let off my energy, and I sort of missed the guys. I'd been accepted on the job site quicker than I thought I'd be, mainly because I busted my ass. Some of them gave me some shit about being the 'boss's kid,' but that only lasted about a day or two before there was respect in their voice.

If there was anything strange about working, it was Dad. He was constantly texting someone on his phone, it seemed, and whenever I'd come into his makeshift office, he'd slam the lid on his laptop closed. His face was always pink and flushed and he'd have this guilty look on his face.

Oh, shit. Dad's getting into porn.

I got it, I guess. Evelyn was still pretty well put together for a woman her age, but I'd heard that a lot of men still had urges beyond what their wives would be cool with. Still, whacking it in your office? Not cool, Dad, not cool at all.

Still, I didn't know what sort of arrangements he and Evelyn had on that side of their lives, and I didn't want to know. I was just glad I didn't have to look forward to walking in on Dad with his cock in hand and *Dirty Anal Debutantes* on his laptop or something.

Speaking of jacking off, I spent a lot of my new spare time doing just that and thinking about Bella. Because I had warned her that we had to be careful while in the house with our parents, I wanted to set an example for abstinence. Jacking off while imagining her lips around my dick allowed me to do that, kind of. And Bella knew about it. She'd approached me with a raised eyebrow and a wastebasket full of gummy tissues one day. "For me?"

"Because of you," I whispered low enough so that nobody could hear. "Sorry."

"Don't be," she whispered back, blushing. "I'm doing the same."

Trust me, it was better for us both for us to relieve tension that way instead of fucking every chance we got. It was far less risky and it allowed me to control my raging hormones so that I could think clearly. And Bella was cool with it too.

Even still, it was difficult. All I could ever think about was how she sucked me off in the pool. Whenever I thought about it, I got an instant hard-on.

One day, I would pay Bella back for all the torment she had put me through with her naughty antics.

* * *

I was helping Dad move a new chair into his office one evening when another warning arrived. Evelyn was gone from the house and Bella was off doing some chore her mom had for her.

My dad hadn't stopped pampering Evelyn with the dinner the night the theater was completed. He had continued to splurge on Evelyn, giving her vouchers to massage parlors and beauty spas.

Evelyn, it seemed, was enjoying every minute of it.

I grunted as we set down the new leather chair exactly where my father wanted it.

"Thanks, Stefan," my dad huffed, wiping sweat from his forehead. "Don't know how I'd have done it without you."

"Pay the movers," I supplied jokingly.

My dad chuckled. "Yep, you're right. Good thing you came back from school, huh?"

If my dad only knew the real reason.

"I guess."

"You don't sound too enthused." My dad walked over to his desk and sat down. Then he glanced around as if looking for something. "Hey Stefan, why don't you go check and see if the mail came today? Usually, one of you three has a stack on my desk right about now."

A shock went through me. I had forgotten all about checking the mail before work today.

"Sure thing, Dad," I said quickly. I walked out of his office and made my way through the house. Once outside, I broke into a sprint to the mailbox. I snatched it open and breathed a sigh of relief.

The mail was still inside.

I took it out and then froze when I saw it—a package just like the one that had contained the sex tape. I wanted to throw it away, but I knew I had to see what was in it.

My heart pumping, I stuck the other stack of mail in the crook of my arm and ripped open the package. The only thing that was inside was a folded piece of paper.

The message read:

TIME IS RUNNING OUT FOR YOU BOTH.

Rage ran through me as I stared at the words. It pissed me off because I felt so helpless about the situation. The entire time, I said I would protect Bella, but how could I protect her against a faceless enemy?

On top of that, what the blackmailer wanted us to do was a paradox. If Bella and I told everyone the truth, it was almost like everyone seeing our sex video anyway.

So what was the point?

After staring at the letter long enough, I folded it up and stuffed it into my pocket. I walked back in the house and delivered my father's stack of mail onto his desk.

"Are you all right, Son?" my dad asked, gazing at me with concern. "You look a little pale."

"I think I'm a little tired," I replied. "Been up all night."

"Get some rest, Son. You've worked hard enough and deserve it. Matter of fact, I'll let you take the entire next week off."

"Thanks, Dad," I said. "I owe you one."

I left his office and headed up to my room. My immediate impulse was to tell Bella about the new note, but I figured she didn't need any more stress.

No, if I wanted the threats and letters to stop, I had to do something. I had to go to the source.

I quickly changed into dark sweats and a dark hoodie and then left the house.

Firing up my car, I pulled out of the driveway and made my way to NSU.

It was time to pay someone a little visit.

* * *

Under a full moon and a clear, starry sky, I waited behind a bush, biding my time. Back when I was in Alpha, I had jogged with Jace on several occasions late at night, so I was well aware of his routine.

I knew that he jogged by the same sorority house every weeknight around the same time. He had a couple of girls who sometimes invited him in for a workout that had nothing to do with jogging. With him distracted by potential pussy, this was a perfect time to confront him about the threatening notes and the sex tape.

Sure enough, Jace came jogging by the bush I was waiting behind, his feet lightly hitting the pavement. I waited, and as soon as he got near, I jumped out in front of him. "Surprise, motherfucker."

Upon seeing me, Jace ran onto the opposite lawn, but he tripped several steps in. By the time I got to him, he was already on his feet, but it didn't matter. I collided into him with a grunt, knocking him onto the lawn.

We rolled around in the grass, grunting and growling at each other. Jace managed to get several glancing blows to my right cheek and break free.

I shrugged off the blows and caught him before he could run off, knocking him face-first into the grass. I jumped on his back and grabbed ahold of his right hand, twisting it behind his back and eliciting a sharp cry of pain.

"Get the fuck off me," Jace growled, struggling against my grip as I used my weight to hold him in place.

"No," I snapped back.

Jace tried to maneuver his body out from under mine, but I twisted his arm again, causing him to howl out in pain.

"The fuck do you want, man?" he cried.

"I want to know why you sick fucks recorded the Sacrifice between me and Bella."

Jace stopped struggling, trying to turn his face to look up at me. "Huh? What the hell are you talking about?"

I debated on whether I should release Jace. I didn't want to continue struggling with him and possibly wind up in a fight on the campus lawn.

Besides, I needed to see Jace's face when I accused him of trying to blackmail Bella and me.

I braced myself for an attack and released my hold on Jace. Jace immediately jumped to his feet and glared at me with hatred.

I returned his scowl, ready to duke it out if I had to. My face was pulsating where he had struck me, and I was itching to return the favor, knowing that I'd probably have several bruises by the next morning.

"The video you sent me," I replied. "What are you going to do with it if we don't do what you want?"

Jace's features twisted into a confused glower. "The fuck are you talking about, Livingston? What video?"

I studied Jace for a moment, noticing his expression and body language. As far as I could tell, he appeared to be telling the truth, though I knew better than to trust him.

Taking a deep breath, I quickly told him about the video and the subsequent note.

Jace was shaking his head as I finished my tale. "I don't know if Alpha Gamma records Sacrifices, but I can assure you I had nothing to do with any video, nor did I know anything about it." He laughed. "But when I think about it, I wish I had done it. Then I could totally humiliate you and your brother-loving sister."

I clenched my teeth and resisted the urge to pound Jace's face into the ground. It wouldn't be helpful right now.

Jace continued. "Still, you're a dick for assuming it was me. I'd much rather duke it out in a fair fight than humiliate you. These pussy ambushes you keep doing are getting old. First, getting your sister to bite my hand, and now, stalking me at night during a jog. What's next?"

I ignored his attempt to piss me off and make me lose control. "I know that they record the hazing ceremonies. You showed me a few of those tapes yourself. You know where they moved those videos?"

"No, I don't. Todd would know about it more than me, though. But, even if I did know, what makes you think I'd tell you anything after how you betrayed our fraternity?"

I snorted. "I didn't betray shit."

"Yeah, you did. It's because of you that we and Kappa are under investigation."

"You mean because you couldn't treat Bella like she was deserving of respect? I mean, you're lucky to be alive after what you tried to do to her."

"Oh, yeah? And what did I 'try' to do to her?"

"Don't try to play stupid. You know damn well on the day we left that you were trying to take her back to your place so that you could have your way with her."

Just thinking about it made my blood boil, and it was very difficult not to rush Jace and kick his ass again. I knew if I didn't leave his presence soon, that's exactly what would happen.

"Is that what you really think? I just wanted to talk to her and tell her I was sorry about my behavior."

What a crock of shit. "Sure. Keep telling yourself that."

I turned to leave, knowing I'd get nothing else out of Jace besides the urge to beat the fuck out of him. Despite my animosity toward him, I actually believed that he was telling the truth.

But if it wasn't Jace, then who was it?

As far as I knew, I had been beloved on campus, even more so after the Sacrifice. Bella, on the other hand, had been hated by a lot of females. The list of possible suspects could be larger than I originally thought.

The very thought made my blood run cold, and I wondered if I would be better off telling Bella that I had handled the problem and we no longer had anything to worry about.

Just as I was about to disappear around the corner, Jace called out to me. "Livingston!"

I was tempted to ignore him, but something in his

voice made me turn around. "Yeah?"

"If I were you, I'd take a look at Kappa. This isn't the first time some hot freshman's been run off campus by some of those Kappa bitches. Just sayin'."

I nodded and turned, breaking into a jog myself. Maybe Jace was right or maybe he was full of shit, but I thought he was right.

Guys like the Alphas, when they've got beef, come for you to beat your ass. And after the ass-kickings are finished, they tend to let it go unless there's another reason not to.

It's girls who tend to go for this behind the back, mental torture shit.

Chapter 22
Bella

My cravings had spun out of control. I was either always eating something or always thinking about eating something.

It was the very thing I feared when I found out that I was pregnant—gaining weight. Even Stefan had already made a comment on my weight when I disrobed for him out at the pool. While he still seemed attracted to me, what was he going to think when I went up another ten pounds? What about when I went up twenty?

These thoughts continuously hounded me, and I feared that Stefan would eventually grow disgusted by the new me. Coupled with the fact that our parents might know the truth by that time if we didn't find a way to conceal it from them, I was downright terrified.

Still, even those thoughts couldn't keep me from eating or wanting to eat. I was just too damn hungry. It made me suspect the little one growing inside me was a boy and wanted to grow up to be a powerful athlete like his father.

Due to my constant cravings, I found myself raiding the fridge for something to eat at one A.M. when I heard the front door open and shut.

I quickly closed the fridge and spun around as footsteps approached the kitchen doorway.

It was Stefan, dressed in black sweats and a black hoodie, and he was staring at me.

"Stefan?" I asked with surprise. "What are you doing out so late?" The last I knew, Stefan had gone to bed hours ago. Immediately, I was hit with suspicions of him going out to clubs to pick up girls . . . until I saw his face.

A purple bruise shadowed his right jaw and his face looked swollen.

"And what the hell happened to you?" I gasped with horror.

Stefan's eyes flashed down to my flimsy gown and to the curves it barely concealed before going back to my face. "I just got back from NSU."

I made a face. "NSU? What in the world for?"

"To see Jace."

I grew silent for a moment, immediately knowing what that meant. "Jace did that to you?" I ventured.

Stefan nodded. "It wasn't much of fight though. He caught me by surprise with a few lucky punches, but I got in a few as well."

I turned and began searching through the cabinets. "Let me see if I can find something to put on your bruises."

Stefan approached me from behind and pulled my hands away from the cabinet, turning me around to face him.

"I'll be fine," he told me, his voice deep and commanding. "Nobody can hurt me when I'm trying to help you."

My pulse began to race and I felt heat from being close to him. I swear that every time he was near, the temperature in the room went up by several degrees.

I stared at his bruises, wishing I could heal them

with a simple touch. "But your face—"

"I'm fine," Stefan reiterated firmly. "But I have to tell you something."

Judging by the tone of his voice, I knew it was bad. I tensed up, preparing for the worse.

"Jace didn't send the video."

I gaped, stunned. "If he didn't, then who did?" I finally managed.

"I don't know."

"Are you sure it wasn't him? Jace hates your guts so I wouldn't put it past him to lie."

"I'm sure. He's a douchebag for sure, but he didn't do it, and he doesn't think anyone at Alpha did either. He claims that they have never recorded our Sacrifice that he knows of."

"What could that mean?"

Stefan's gaze made me go cold all over. "That it's probably someone from Kappa Beta."

My mouth opened but no sound came out. How was it possible? I could have totally seen one of the guys from Alpha staging the recording seeing as how it was inside their frat house and it was totally a guy thing to do, but one of the Kappa girls? It seemed highly unlikely.

"I can't believe it," I whispered. "I mean, how would they pull it off?"

Stefan grabbed ahold of my arms and my body temperature went up by several notches. "I don't know, probably snuck in for the price of a blowjob, but it's true. And it makes sense if you think about it, actually. If it were Alpha Gamma that had recorded it, it would have been all over the campus by now. Like Jace said, he'd have started shit with me straight up, and in that, I do believe him. No, this little mind game, stab you in the back bullshit that's being played on us has female written all over it. I bet you it's one of those sick bitches at Kappa who hates your guts."

I couldn't take anymore—the pregnancy, the investigation, the blackmail, my mother's suspicion—it was all just too much. Maybe we should just tell the truth and be done with all this craziness. The thought had crossed my mind more than once, but I always chickened out when I thought about my mother's reaction.

As the thoughts filled my mind, my vision began to fade and I felt myself falling forward, but strong, loving arms caught me.

Chapter 23
Stefan

I held Bella in my arms, carrying her upstairs. The wooden steps were quite sturdy, built in the last twenty years, but they still managed to let out a creak every other step.

Cringing, I repositioned Bella in my arms and tried to balance my steps, praying that neither of our parents would be awoken by the noises.

As I made my way up, I glanced down at Bella. With her long hair flowing out like a banner, delicate features, and sensual lips, she looked like Sleeping Beauty. I wanted to kiss her right there on the steps. But, at the same time, I couldn't help but feel a twinge of guilt at her current condition. I knew that it was my ranting that had stressed her out, that had probably caused her collapse.

Being as quiet as possible, I finished making my way up the stairs and brought Bella to her room. Good thing for me, the floorboards didn't creak when I passed our parents' room to get to Bella's. It was bad enough that Evelyn was already suspicious of what Bella and I were up to.

Inside her room, I gently nudged the door shut with my foot and then carried my burden over to the bed. There, I softly laid her down. I stood back up and stared down at her.

Lying in the bed, she looked even more like Sleeping Beauty now. A lock of her hair had fallen across her face. I reached down and pushed it away, still in awe of how beautiful she was to me.

What amazed me even more was that I was still in awe of her beauty. Usually, a girl's looks lasted as long as our last fuck. Not for Bella—every glance at her face was a privilege for me, and it never got old.

I reached down and gently pressed my fingertips against her lips. Soft velvet caressed my fingers.

I need to leave, I told myself as burning need clutched my stomach.

But I couldn't leave. Despite everything I had told Bella about being careful while we were in our parents' house, I wanted to be there, in the bed with her.

Driven by impulse, I bent down and firmly pressed my lips against hers, enjoying their softness.

Bella's eyes fluttered open and I reluctantly broke our kiss. "Stefan?" she asked weakly.

"Yes?"

"I'm sorry. I just felt like a wall was closing in on me and—"

I pressed a finger to her lips. "Don't worry. I want you to stop worrying so much. No matter what happens, I'm not going to let anything happen to you. We're in this shit together, you got me?"

Bella nodded slowly.

Now was the perfect time to bid Bella goodnight and head back to my room. But seeing her lying there, looking all vulnerable, made me want her so badly that I couldn't help myself.

I bent down and locked lips with her again, this time more forcefully. Her soft lips were a delight to experience, and I think I tasted a cherry lip gloss, something I hadn't tasted when I first kissed her.

Still, it wasn't bad, and it actually enhanced the experience. I parted my lips and demanded entry to Bella's mouth with my tongue. She let me in eagerly, and our tongues mated, melding together. I ran my hands up and down her curvaceous body, feeling her heated flesh.

After a moment, Bella broke away, sparking disappointment.

"Should we be doing this, Stefan?" Bella asked breathlessly. She stared up at me with question, her eyes burning with lust. "I mean, remember what you said at the pool—"

I locked lips with her again, cutting her off, and lay down on top of her, driven by passion. Bella relaxed underneath my weight, surrendering to my advance. After several juicy tongue twists, I broke away and began covering her neck with passionate kisses. Bella ran her fingers through my hair, moaning softly in my ear.

I gripped her nightgown in my hands and pulled it above her chest. I pulled back from her neck to hungrily eye her breasts and stiff nipples. They seemed larger and fuller than I last remembered. Pregnancy was doing wonderful things to Bella's already amazing body.

I lowered my head to them and began sucking on her hard nipples, kneading them gently with my teeth. This elicited a moan from Bella, and I felt her buck slightly beneath me. Emboldened, I swirled my tongue around her nipples, flapping my tongue rapidly back and forth.

Once I had my fill, I drifted down her stomach, kissing her soft skin until I reached her panties. Eagerly, I pulled them down her thighs until I had them off and then tossed them onto the floor.

I pulled Bella to me by her waist, making her spread her legs out in front of me, and then went in. I licked her clit back and forth with my tongue, savoring the sweetness.

Using my fingers, I spread the flaps of her lips wide while I sucked and slurped on her clit.

Bella reached down and grabbed me by the hair, moaning softly. "Don't stop."

My confidence soared and I continued, enjoying the tastes of her sweet juices. I stuck two fingers inside, marveling at how warm and wet it felt, and began sliding them in and out sensuously.

Down below, I could feel my cock expanding inside my sweats, demanding release. With my other hand, I reached down and fondled my cock, feeling pre-cum stain my sweats. I wanted badly to take it out and fuck her.

"I'm close to coming," Bella moaned.

I banged her harder and faster in response, bearing down on her clit with all the force my tongue could muster.

And that was all it took.

Letting out a soft cry, Bella convulsed underneath me as she came. The whole time, I kept my mouth clamped down on her clit, sucking in all the sweet nectar she had to offer.

When it was over, I stepped off the bed and stood up. I took off my hoodie and shirt and dropped my sweats, my cock springing out, bouncing up and down.

Fresh from the throes of her orgasm, Bella eyed my dick with need. She wanted it. She wanted it bad. And boy, was I going to give it to her.

Bella sat up in the bed, moving forward as if she wanted to service me, her hand going for my rod. I swiped her hand away and shook my head.

She was going to get it in the way I wanted her to.

I roughly pushed her back onto the bed and climbed my naked body atop hers. Then I entered her with a grunt, causing her to gasp, letting her pussy adjust to my large size. Her insides felt like warm pudding wrapped around my dick. It was a comforting sensation that made me feel like her pussy was where I belonged. I was home.

Slowly, I began to gently thrust inside her. Even though I wanted to fuck her like a wild beast, I had to be mindful of our parents.

I ran my hands up her stomach as I humped and grabbed ahold of her breasts. At the same time, Bella's hands drifted down my back and grabbed ahold of my ass, squeezing and digging her nails into it.

I started to go deeper and deeper inside her, and the deeper I went, the closer to Heaven I got.

My stomach seemed to twist into a tight little ball as a fiery tempest grew inside my balls. Bella seemed to sense this, and she bore down on my dick, pulling me closer to Nirvana.

"God, I'm coming," I croaked.

With one deep, final thrust, a powerful release washed over me and I let out a strained gasp as my seed squirted out into her warm insides.

I collapsed in the bed beside her a moment later, feeling totally spent, covered in a sheen of sweat from my efforts.

Bella looked at me as I caught my breath, the sparkle in her eyes telling me that she had enjoyed every moment of it.

"That was beautiful," she said softly.

I grinned and kissed her on the forehead. "I'm glad you liked it."

I kissed her again and then rolled out of the bed.

Using towels from the adjacent bathroom, Bella cleaned up the immediate mess we had made and then went in the bathroom while I replaced the bed sheets.

"What are we going to do about this?" Bella asked when she returned. She was sitting on her bed, garbed in a different nightgown, her face creased with worry. "If it's as you suspect and it's someone from Kappa, there's no telling what they'll put us through before this is over." Bella then began to run through the list of possible suspects, mainly Kappa's president and her sidekick. "They threatened me, you know."

Neither of us had the courage tell our parents about our relationship as the author of the tape wanted us to.

So the only thing I had to do was make sure I screened every piece of mail that came through the house before Bella and I left off to our own place. Then, we could tell them and not care how they reacted.

"I don't know," I finally replied. "But we'll think of something."

Chapter 24
Bella

"The governor is throwing a party this weekend to open the new theater, and he's going to be giving me an award for it," Terry announced at the dinner table one evening over a plate of steak, rice, and potatoes.

I was seated on one side of the table with Mother, and Stefan was on the other side with his father. He hadn't given much eye contact throughout our meal, and I was a bit disappointed. A part of me, the naughty part, wanted to stick my foot across the way and massage him with it. I could only imagine the look on Stefan's face if I did.

My mom let out a startled gasp. "Why, that's wonderful, Terry!"

"Congratulations, Dad," Stefan chipped in, grinning and clasping hands with his father in a bro-like manner.

"Congratulations, Terry!" I added.

Terry beamed at all the praise we piled on him for the next five minutes before dropping another bombshell.

"And you all are expected to attend."

Stefan and I let out a groan simultaneously, but my mom clapped in an excited fashion.

"There is no negation here," Terry warned the both of us, seeing our sour expressions. "You both have to go."

"But I don't even have anything to wear," I

blurted. I regretted the words as soon as they left my mouth.

"You know what that means, don't you?" asked my mom.

I knew if I didn't answer, she would say what she wanted anyway. "What?"

My mom beamed. "It's time to go shopping."

* * *

"My gosh, Bella, are you gaining weight?" my mom asked as she struggled to zip up my size-two ball gown, a beautiful white, frilly number that reminded me of a wedding dress.

Of course I was gaining weight, but I didn't want to tell my mother that.

I sucked in my breath, trying to become as small as possible. I wanted to fit in the dress as much as she wanted me to. Not being able to fit in it absolutely terrified me, and it meant I was saying goodbye to one of the things that had been permanent in my life.

My precious size two.

"Finally," my mom huffed as she managed to pull the zipper all the way up my back thanks to my efforts. "I hope that holds."

I held in my breath as long as I could.

"I can't breathe," I gasped, letting go of the air. The dress made several popping sounds, and the zipper unzipped itself halfway down my back.

"Lay off the donuts, why don't you?" Mom half-joked.

I can't, I thought. *The baby is hungry.*

I decided to remain mum on the issue. I couldn't argue that I wasn't pigging out every five seconds. I thought about blowing up at her about shaming me but decided not too. It'd come off as too fake. Mom was getting wise to my fake rants and my real ones.

"All right, let's get you out of that thing and let's try some other ones that are, um, maybe two sizes bigger."

Two sizes? I about fainted.

I must have tried on several different gowns, a couple of size threes and a couple of fours. Unfortunately, I felt the most comfortable in a four.

When I finally found the one I wanted, I quickly forgot about the disappointment of going up two dress sizes.

"This is the one!" I proclaimed.

"That looks great on you!" my mom exclaimed at the dress I decided on.

It was a dashing red lace number that showed off my new curves in such a flattering manner that even a blind man would be impressed. The bottom part of the dress flowed behind me in a train. I would have to be careful with it at the party, but I suspected there would be other women there with similar dresses.

I twisted my body around, checking out my back side.

Eat your heart out, Stefan, I thought, shocked at the new fullness of my ass.

Baby got back.

"Thanks, Mom," I replied.

Mother wrapped her arm around my waist and beamed into the dressing room mirror. "I'm sure you're going to turn heads." Ruffling my hair, she kissed me on the cheek.

The only head I want to turn is Stefan's, I thought in protest, but I knew better than to say so.

"Now," my mom said with a grin, stuffing all the dresses I had tried on into my hands to put back on the hangers. "My turn."

* * *

I was filled with giddy excitement when we arrived back at home in my mother's black Mercedes Benz. I had a new dress that I was sure would knock Stefan off his feet, and I actually looked damned good in it despite gaining weight. I had been dreading going to the party before, but now I actually had something to look forward to.

"Bella, can you get the mail?" my mom asked when we were halfway to the front door.

Shit.

I was so excited about everything that was going on, I had forgotten to check it earlier in the day. But, judging by the stack of the mail stuffed in the box, so had everyone else.

As I glanced over the bundle, I was glad when nothing was out of the ordinary.

Lucky. Damn lucky.

Chapter 25
Bella

The governor's party was a ritzy affair. Prominent people, young and old, from all over town were in attendance. Dad had rented a limo for our arrival—a long, white, pristine one that had a bar inside and plush, cream-colored seating.

I absolutely enjoyed the ride and was kind of disappointed when it was over.

When we stepped out, serving men quickly rushed up to usher us into the estate. As we were led in, I marveled at the estate's grounds. Lush, green, freshly-cut grass surrounded the walkways. Marble fountains and statues were erected at each intersection, inspiring points and stares.

I always thought we had been pretty well off, but the governor's mansion was on another level.

Inside, the opulence continued, with vast, vaulted ceilings, white marble floors and walls decorated with Victorian finery. The furniture was also either white or cream-colored with gold trimmings.

"Holy shit," I overheard Stefan muttering to Terry, "this dude is loaded."

Terry chuckled and muttered something in response, but I didn't quite hear what he said.

We were led into a packed ballroom filled with elegantly dressed people. Tables lined with real gold plates and silverware were situated around the room.

All around us, there were packs of people talking

to one another. Quite a few male eyes turned on me when I stepped into the room, but I was surprised I had quite a lot of competition in the young female demographic.

There were plenty of girls who had absolutely gorgeous dresses, their hair and makeup immaculate. I tried not to look at them. There was no need to compare.

And there was one person in the giant ballroom who wasn't checking out the competition either, and that was Stefan. He'd had his eyes on me since we left the house. He hadn't said much to me on our way here, not to arouse suspicion for our parents, but I could tell that he really liked the way I looked in my dress.

A couple, an older man and woman, walked up to our little group and began speaking with Terry. That's when Stefan took his opportunity to approach me.

"You look absolutely gorgeous in red," Stefan told me under the murmur of the crowd, stepping up close so that I could hear him. "Absolutely stunning."

A flush ran through my chest and up through my cheeks. I was glad he appreciated the work I'd gone through to look good for him.

Before the party, Mother and I had gone to the beauty parlor and had gotten our hair, nails, and makeup done.

"You look good too," I replied. And I meant it.

Stefan was dressed in a black and white tux, a bowtie at his neck. With his hair slicked and parted to the side, he looked unbelievably GQ, as if he'd just stepped out of a high-powered photo shoot.

I had already caught more than a few girls stealing glances at him, and it made me feel more than a little protective—and slightly jealous.

But I couldn't let him see it, not when I had promised that I would be strong for us.

I mean, how could I break down when Stefan was being so cool about everything?

Despite the worry over our heads, Stefan looked like he was on top of the world.

"I want to sweep you off your feet and carry you up to the balustrade overlooking the ballroom," Stefan said. "So I can show off my future bride to everyone."

The words 'future bride' brought up strong emotions inside me and I nearly started crying in front of everyone. But with great control, I kept my face from cracking and simply said, "I would love that."

That was another bad thing about my pregnancy. My emotions were starting to go up and down like a rollercoaster.

The governor interrupted our little conversation when he walked up with a young, handsome blond man with vivacious green eyes and dressed in a tux similar to Stefan's at his side.

The governor was a big man with broad shoulders, greying hair at the temples, and a bald pate on the top of his head. He looked rather imposing, but I guess if you're the governor, you have to be.

"You have some beautiful children, Terry," the governor remarked after shaking hands with Terry and my mother, mainly looking at me.

My mom beamed. "Thank you, Gary," she replied, even though the governor hadn't been talking to her. "She got her looks from me."

I can't believe she said that, I thought, holding

back a roll of my eyes. *Seriously, Mom, we get it. You're hot for a woman your age. Certified MILF. Don't go fishing for compliments.*

"Governor, meet Bella and Stefan," Terry announced. "Bella and Stefan, this is Governor Gary Rich."

"Pleased to meet you, sir," I said diplomatically, taking the man's hand. He gripped it firmly and shook it and then shook Stefan's.

"It's a pleasure." Gary turned to the young man beside him, who was smiling at me. "This is my son, Cory. He's a lawyer for one of the top firms in the city."

Cory stepped forward and grabbed my hand, bringing it to his lips for a kiss. "Nice to meet you." His eyes flashed as he looked at me.

"Nice to meet you too," I replied, blushing. I didn't mean anything by it—it's just a natural reaction.

Beside me, I felt Stefan stiffen, but he remained silent.

When Cory moved on to shake Stefan's hand, he hesitated a second before taking it. "It's a pleasure," said Cory.

"Likewise." Stefan's voice was strained. I was worried the two of them, obvious alpha males, would go at it, but then an aide came over and Cory had to leave, defusing the situation.

Terry and the Governor continued chatting for a few minutes before the Governor pleaded that he needed to greet more guests and walked off.

As soon as the man was out of earshot, Terry turned on Stefan. "What was all that about?" he demanded.

Stefan glanced at me. "I didn't like the governor's son."

"Why not?"

Stefan shrugged his shoulders. "I don't know. There are just some people you don't like on sight. He's one, that's all."

We spent the next thirty minutes walking around and talking to snobby rich people. Stefan hardly spoke whenever introduced and kept his eyes either on me or roving around the ballroom.

I soon grew tired of shaking people's hands and of people walking on the train of my dress. I nearly tripped because of it. Luckily, Stefan caught me in his arms.

When it was time for the food to be brought out, I sighed with relief. I'd had it with the fake smiles and the fake greetings. Somewhere along the way, I started suffering from cramps and it had become difficult for me to stand, and my smiles started to look like I was constipated because I was in so much discomfort.

Our family was seated at a small table near the right center of the room, near the stage that had been set up for a presentation.

"This is just mind-blowing," my mother muttered, eyeing the expensive silverware.

"Tell me about it," I replied, situating myself in the seat in such a way where my sides hurt less.

The wine and drinks came out first, followed by the food. My mom raised an eyebrow when she saw me have the waiter load my plate with clams, oysters, and scallops, but I didn't care. I was hungry.

While everyone ate, several people got on stage to speak about boring crap. But my attention was turned to the stage when someone announced the governor.

"Ladies and gentlemen, your host for the evening—your beloved Governor, Gary Rich!"

The room erupted in applause, but I was too busy eating to clap.

The governor walked up on stage and stood there before the podium, basking in all the adulation for a full minute before motioning everyone to quiet down.

"Thank you everyone," Gary said into the mic. "I thank you all for coming." Then he launched into a speech about how glad he was to serve the people of our state as our governor. I zoned him out and continued to eat my meal until he started talking about Terry.

"I've known Terry for a very long time, back when we went to high school together, and he is nothing but the consummate professional. When I first envisioned a new theater for our capital city, Terry was the first man who came to mind who I thought could make it happen. So, without further ado, I proudly present to you, The Gary Rich Theater!" The room burst into applause as the screen behind Gary dimmed. "My son, Cory, will do the honors of showing you all the video of our spectacular new center." Gary gestured to Cory, who was standing somewhere off-stage, out of view. "Cory."

There was movement around the side of the stage, and everyone waited for something to come on the screen. Time ticked by and people began muttering to each other.

Gary leaned away from the mic to speak to his son, but his voice was still picked up. "What's taking so long?" he whispered loudly.

I heard the muffled sound of Cory's voice, but

couldn't understand what he was saying, and it looked like Gary grew agitated by whatever his response was.

"Got it!" Cory called out quickly after several moments. He ran up on stage and casually wrapped his arm around his father's shoulders. "See, Dad? I'm useful for something after all."

The whole room burst out into light laughter but quickly quieted down as video came on the screen.

I was in the middle of eating an oyster, not paying attention or looking at the screen, when I heard someone say, "What the hell is that?"

I looked up and my heart nearly stopped. Beside me, Stefan stiffened.

Oh, no. God, no.

The familiar scene of me being led by hand into a room by a half-naked gladiator was on the screen.

"What is this?" Gary demanded of his son, away from the mic again but still being heard.

Cory stared at the screen, looking perplexed. His response was faint, but I still managed to hear it. "I don't know, Dad. This is not the footage I put into the player."

"Take care of this."

"Yes, sir."

As the scene on the screen became more risqué, people around the room began muttering among themselves and looked uncomfortable.

Suddenly, a scream pierced the air.

A second later, I knew why. On the screen, there was Stefan, still masked, going down on me.

"Eat that pussy!" My pleasured moan rolled out over the entire room.

"My God." I saw an older man cover his young

daughter's eyes with his hand.

"Cory!" The governor roared, no longer caring about decorum. "Get that God damn video off the screen now!"

Cory's voice was filled with panic as he frantically pressed buttons on the player. 'I'm trying, Dad, I'm trying."

"Turn the fucking thing off!" The governor yelled again, his face red with rage.

A sudden, high-pitched laugh suddenly drew my gaze away from the damning video and shock rolled through me. There, sitting several tables away, was Veronica George, dressed in finery, smiling at me with devious pleasure.

You bitch, I thought. *Stefan was right, it was a Kappa. It was you this whole time.*

"Surprise, surprise, Bella," Veronica called sweetly.

Stefan turned and looked at me as my mother turned and stared at us both in horror. "Well," he said in solemn tones that said he already accepted his impending doom, "This is not going to end well."

Chapter 26
Stefan

Our sex tape was still playing out on the large-screen TV before the shocked audience. In it, Bella and I still wore our masks as I fucked her like a wild beast, my ass flexing with each powerful thrust, but it was fast approaching the moment where Bella recognized me and tore my mask off.

To me, it didn't matter if my face was revealed in the video. Our parents had probably already recognized us from the moment we appeared on-screen, elaborate costumes or not.

I was just waiting for their shock to wear off and for the shit to hit the fan.

Thankfully, the screen abruptly went blank, silencing Bella's moans and my feral grunts just as I was about to blow my load, and just before Bella tore off my mask, revealing my identity. For the party guests, I felt some small consolation that the mysterious couple on screen having sex would remain a mystery . . . at least for now.

"I got it off!" Cory, the governor's son, shouted with triumph from where he had been furiously hammering on a laptop that had been feeding our sex tape to the large screen before just yanking out the cord connecting it to the video system. Cory studied the laptop like it was defective, flipping it over on its side before setting it back down on a small stand. "I don't know why the hell it wouldn't shut off before. It was like the whole system froze when I tried to close the video."

"Finally!" Gary, the governor, snapped. He stomped across the stage and over to his son. "You would have thought you were a damn imbecile with computers with how long it took you." The governor tried to be quiet with his next words, but his furious whisper was still clearly audible over the outraged chatter in the room. "What the hell was that all about, Cory? Was that one of your damned pornos?"

The young man looked appalled. "No! Of course not, Father. I would never keep a file like that on my work laptop. You know me better than that."

The governor looked unconvinced and gave him a stare.

Cory scowled. "I swear. Someone must have tampered with my laptop while we were going around greeting everyone." Cory pointed sharply at the CD that he pulled from the laptop. "See here, the CD is named *Gary Rich Theater Presentation.*"

"Wait," Cory added. "This isn't my handwriting. Someone must've replaced it somehow. Someone got on my laptop and put this CD in instead—I just assumed it was the same CD. I'm so sorry, Father."

The next few words of their conversation were lost in the loud chatter of the outraged guests, but I could tell by the look on both of their faces that they were discussing what to do about the culprit.

After a moment, the governor turned and walked back onto the stage.

"Ladies and gentlemen," the governor spoke into the microphone in an apologetic tone, "I am very sorry about what you just saw. I can assure you that this wasn't intentional in any way. My son, Cory, is a young man of integrity and would never conspire to pull off something so offensive—even in jest. It is our belief that someone with an agenda has tried to sabotage this party and tarnish my reputation. I'm sure you are all aware that as governor, I have no shortage of political enemies who wish me out of office. Rest assured, we'll find whoever did this. They're not going to be laughing when we find out who's responsible. In the meantime, I implore you all to remain seated so my son can locate the real video file and we can continue on with our evening."

But the outraged crowd wasn't buying the governor's explanation and people began filing out of the ballroom in droves.

"Sick bastard!" a woman yelled as she swept from the room with her husband and two children in tow.

"I'll never vote for him again," someone else added.

The governor raised his hands imploringly. "People, please calm down and remain seated. This is all one big misunderstanding." But his pleading went unanswered as people continued to file out of the room.

Beside me, Bella tensed as she prepared for the explosion that was about to be unleashed on our heads by our parents. Underneath the table, her hand grabbed a portion of my right thigh and squeezed, her nails almost piercing the expensive material of my pants and digging into my flesh.

I gritted my teeth and ignored the sharp pain her nails caused. If digging her claws into my flesh helped her retain her calm before the storm, then so be it. I was going to be her rock through whatever bullshit that was about to go down.

Evelyn still seemed to be numb from shock, her eyes darting to the blank screen behind the stage and then back to us. My father looked disgusted, his face filled with disbelief as he watched people flee the ballroom.

I braced myself for the barrage that was coming at any moment, summoning the energy I was going to need to defend our relationship.

Before anyone could say anything, a peal of high-pitched laughter assaulted my ears.

It was Veronica George, strutting her way to our table, dressed in an evening gown that showed off her big fake tits and hugged her thin body in all the right places.

"Hi, Bella," Veronica purred in a cheery tone that made me want to jump up and throttle her. "Hey, Stefan! That was such a great show, wasn't it?"

Bella dug in harder and I winced. Bella had sharp nails. I was sure she'd made a hole in my pants by now.

Veronica grinned at Bella. "Didn't think your past would catch up to you, did ya?"

I swallowed back the rage that rose from the pits from my stomach. The only thing that saved Veronica from needing a plastic surgeon was the fact that I'd been raised to never put my hands on a female.

But I was tempted.

God, I was tempted.

I sucked in my breath to send a scathing reply her way. I wasn't going to hold anything back now since I had absolutely nothing to lose, but then Veronica turned her gaze on my father.

"Hello, Terry," she said in a low, sultry voice, placing her hands on our table and bending forward so that her cleavage was on maximum display. "You haven't been texting me as much lately. Why's that?" Tossing a triumphant glance at Evelyn, Veronica strutted away from the table, leaving hysterical laughter in her wake.

Much to my surprise, Evelyn snapped her gaze around on my father like a hawk. My dad looked like he'd just seen a ghost, his face pale, his hands trembling.

"What the hell was she talking about?" Evelyn demanded.

Bella and I traded surprised glances. We'd been expecting Evelyn to erupt on us, demanding to know why we were on that video having sex while dressed in costumes.

My father remained silent for many moments as everyone in the ballroom continued to file out before finally letting out an explosive breath. "I have a confession to make."

Chapter 27
Bella

I couldn't believe it. The whole party had seen Stefan and me having sex on tape, including our parents. Yet, for some miraculous reason, neither of our parents had recognized that it was us on the screen. Yes, we had on costumes and masks, but they still should have been able to identify their own children.

The only logical explanation I could come up with was that, given the situation, the last thing they would've expected was a sex tape involving their children to be shown in front of everyone.

In other words, it simply hadn't registered to them that those two young people on the screen fucking each other's brains out were me and Stefan.

Whatever the case, I wasn't going to waste time pondering the issue.

We had been granted a temporary reprieve, and I intended to make the most of it. It was funny, actually, that I had Veronica to thank for saving my ass.

Had she not come along when she did, providing the perfect distraction with her comment to Terry, I'm sure my mother's shocked mind would have eventually put two and two together.

But it was only a matter of time before she did.

And it wouldn't be long.

* * *

"Now, would you like to explain what the hell that girl was talking about?" demanded my mom when we were all back home from the governor's party, spread across the living room.

My mom stood in the middle of the floor, her arms crossed across her chest, while Terry sat on the couch, his head in between his hands.

She looked like some enraged ice queen in her magnificent ball gown as she scowled expectantly at Terry.

Stefan and I were seated opposite of Terry on the other couch in the living room, Stefan on one end and me on the other.

Stefan still looked like he had stepped straight out of a GQ magazine, with his overcoat resting on the arm of the couch and his dress shirt open at the collar, giving a peek at his sexy chest underneath.

His eyes on his father, he sat with his legs spread wide like he owned the place. Even with everything going on, it was hard not to stare at him. He practically oozed confidence in the face of our shaky predicament, which turned me on even more.

In fact, he'd handled the whole situation at the party way better than I did. While I'd been about to pass out, Stefan seemed like he'd been ready to fight.

Fortunately, it hadn't come to that . . . yet.

Terry brought his head up out of his hands and glanced at the glass of red wine sitting on the coffee table in front of him.

As soon as we'd gotten back home, Terry offered to pour all of us a glass to help prepare us for whatever secret he was about to reveal. Obviously, my mother had immediately declined, and though I could have used a sip to calm my nerves, there was no way I was drinking alcohol while I was pregnant. Stefan had surprised me when he had accepted. He was one who usually shunned alcohol, claiming that it made him unfocused, and as an athlete, he always wanted to perform with a clear mind.

But now he was on his second glass.

Terry picked up the glass in front of him and took a sip. "Please don't go crazy when I tell you this, Evelyn," he said quietly, setting the glass back down on the table.

"I'll make no promises," my mom replied stiffly.

Terry sighed and glanced over at us. "I've been unhappy in our marriage for a while now. I'm sure I'm not alone."

Shocked silence descended over the room like a dark blanket, and Stefan and I exchanged worried glances.

"But that gives me no excuse for what I've done," Terry said quickly when my mother's features twisted with outrage. Terry proceeded to tell us all about his online fling with *Sororitybabe95*, A.K.A Veronica George, going into very explicit detail. How it had started with just a random invite to his social media, and how it had progressed from there, trading pictures, texting, sexting . . . and while Mom didn't quite get it, I did. Veronica had somehow planned all of this. I don't know when she started it. It must have been before the Sacrifice, for some reason, but the more I heard, the more I felt like I'd been a fly in her trap for months.

I listened to Terry's account, feeling an array of emotions—disbelief, shock, horror, and then, finally, outrage. Sure, I was mad at Terry, but I was even more pissed at Veronica. How could she do something like that? What had I done that was so awful to made her want to seduce my stepfather and cause trouble in our family?

As far as I knew, sleeping with my stepbrother wasn't against the law. And by accident, I might add. What gave that slutty tramp the right to judge me?

And if she called this revenge because of the sorority facing a shut-down, then she was wrong about that, too. Alpha and Kappa had been engaging in questionable practices since their inception. So, even without what happened during my Sacrifice, it would've only been a matter of time before their unscrupulous actions caught up with them.

Fuck her, I thought angrily. *Fuck her and all those crazy Kappa bitches.*

My mom's next words pulled me out of my reverie with a jolt.

"I want a divorce."

Terry jumped to his feet, his arms outstretched as he moved toward my mother. "Now, now, come on, Evelyn, I want to work on things. There is still counseling and—"

"Don't fucking touch me!" Mom screamed, swiping Terry's hands away. "Don't you ever fucking touch me!"

Sobbing, my mom pulled up the edges of her gown, hiking them above her ankles, and fled the living room. I moved to go after her, but Stefan made an imperceptible gesture and I sat back down on the couch.

This is between Dad and Evelyn, his eyes seemed to say to me.

Terry turned to look at us. "I've really screwed things up, haven't I?"

"Just go talk to her, Dad," Stefan bade. "I'm sure she'll listen when she calms down."

Terry cringed and glanced down the hallway. "Wish me luck, guys." Shaking his head, he left the room.

"Whatever you do, don't faint on me," Stefan was quick to say to me when Terry was gone. He picked up his glass and downed the wine in one gulp. "I've had enough shocks for one night."

"We came so very close to being found out," I said, ignoring his attempt to make light of the situation. "I thought for sure that Mom was about to jump our shit."

Stefan nodded. "I did too."

I stared at the space between us. I badly wanted to move across the couch and into his arms, but I knew I couldn't. We'd already taken too many liberties, and we were now sitting on a ticking time bomb.

It was just the matter of when before it exploded.

"We're still screwed, though, as soon as the Governor or his son looks at the end of that video."

"You mean the video on this CD?" Stefan held out a broken CD entitled *Gary Rich Theater Presentation*. "Nope, I handled that during all the commotion when everyone started leaving."

"Oh, I never even saw you do that! But why do you think they didn't recognize us? I mean, even with our costumes on, they could hear our voices. How would my mom not have recognized me?"

"Well, that's an easy one. We only recognized ourselves because we knew already. The video was pretty dark, and think about it from their perspective. They would've never in a million years thought it was us unless they actually saw our faces. Hell, even then, they probably wouldn't believe it. I'm sure everyone there just assumed it was an attempt to embarrass the Governor."

"I guess," I admitted. I had already reasoned as much myself. The fact that Stefan had come to the same conclusion made me feel a little bit more secure about the situation.

"Exactly. They had no clue what the fuck that was. I'm just glad Cory finally shut it off in time, or we'd be singing a different tune right about now. Lastly, Veronica came along and unknowingly covered our tracks with that comment toward Dad. Evelyn is going to be focused on that for now, buying us a little more time."

"I still can't believe what happened," I said with a gentle shake of my head. "Veronica really was determined, tracking Terry down online like that. But I just don't understand how Terry could let himself get caught up in her web."

Of course you know how, I told myself. *He's a man, and all men have two heads, and sometimes, the smaller head wins.*

Stefan clenched his jaw. "Even though Veronica baited him, I'm going to find it hard to forgive him for what he did. Hell, I'd seen him in the office. I thought he'd been watching a few pornos or something, not online cheating. He could have easily turned her down after he found out what she was about."

"But is it really that easy though?" I asked. "Come on, you're a guy. My mom is getting up there in years and doesn't have the body of a young twenty-year-old. I mean, it's not bad, but it's not Veronica's. What man, young or old, wouldn't find it hard to resist someone with a body like Veronica's?"

I had to admit, I was asking this question for my own benefit. I wanted to see Stefan's reaction because, despite all that he'd said to me about my ever-changing appearance, I couldn't help but feel a little self-conscious about gaining weight.

Stefan stared at me. "Yeah, it is that easy. I'm a man of my word. If I commit to something, I'm in until it's over. That's it. I thought Dad was the same type of man, as he raised me to be that way, but I guess I was wrong."

"I don't know. My heart bleeds for Mom, but at the same time, I feel bad for Terry. It was kind of our fault."

Stefan glowered. "Dad's actions put him in the position he is in now. He doesn't deserve your sympathy . . . or mine, for that matter."

I grew silent in the face of Stefan's anger. I was shocked, actually. He seemed to be more upset about what Terry did than I was.

"In fact, I'm going to need you to stay completely out of this."

"Why?"

"Judging by how serious Evelyn sounded, things are about to get really, really ugly. I'm sorry, Bella, but I know Evelyn almost as well as you do. She won't hesitate to use you as a pawn should this come down to a divorce."

"But Mom is going to need me—" I began.

"Have you forgotten our little secret? This whole mess has put tremendous stress on the both of us. Now add the stress of a divorce to that, and what do you think that will do to your body and the—" Stefan's voice trailed off.

I couldn't deny the truth in Stefan's words. I was already under tremendous stress given everything that happened, and a contentious divorce just might put me over the edge.

To punctuate Stefan's words, the sound of muffled screaming wafted down the stairs to our ears, followed by some rumbling.

Mom must be kicking Terry's ass, I thought in despair. *Look at all the strife that bitch Veronica has caused in our family.*

Stefan made a face and looked up at the ceiling. "You hear that? No telling how long that's going to go on."

The screaming intensified, and I wondered if the neighbors down at the end of the block could hear my mother's screeching.

"Then what are we going to do?" I asked fearfully.

Stefan grabbed the wine bottle sitting on the coffee table and poured what was left of it into his glass. Then, to my surprise, he turned back the entire glass in one gulp before replying to me.

"I have to get you out of here."

Chapter 28
Stefan

Shortly after I had assured Bella that I had plans to get us out of the house, my dad had come back downstairs. He looked defeated and as if he'd rolled in the hay a couple of times while receiving several mean punches to the eye.

He'd looked at us once, not saying a word, and then headed to his office. As much as I wanted to stay out of the whole affair, I felt like now was the time to confront him.

I was angry about what happened. As a man of supposed integrity, it pissed me off that he'd let a slutbag like Veronica George take advantage of him.

I knew the temptation, God I knew, but that didn't make it right. A strong man was never cowed by temptation. He was always in control of the situation, no matter what.

And as a man of my word, I'd take control of the chaos and protect Bella at all costs.

I stomped into my dad's office and slammed the door behind me. "That was pathetic! How could you hurt Evelyn like that?"

My dad, who was sitting at his desk, looked up from his laptop at me with surprise. I expected him to explode on me in a rage—wanted him to, even—but he just sighed. "I couldn't help myself, Son."

I shook my head with disgust.

My dad sat back in his chair and studied me

coolly. "Tell me, what would you have done? You, the ultimate jock, who has probably slept with more girls than you can even count."

"What does the number of girls that I've slept with have to do with anything?"

"Don't pretend to act like a goody-two shoes, Stefan. You know exactly what I'm talking about."

"No, Dad, I don't."

"Stefan, we're men," Dad said as if that explained everything. "Young, pretty women are our weakness."

"No, Dad, that is your weakness," I argued. "And you should've never let that weakness get the best of you. Fuck, I thought you were jacking off to porn, not Skyping with another woman!"

Dad stared at me, and I saw anger and shame in his eyes. I felt a surge of satisfaction. Finally, the emotion I'd been hoping for. "Is that what you've come into my office for?" he demanded angrily. "To badger me about my mistake when I already feel like shit? Trust me, Evelyn has already let me hear it. I don't need it from you too."

I shook my head. "No. I came to tell you that I'm moving out."

Surprise registered on Dad's face. "What? What for? Are you planning to go back to school?"

"Not right now," I replied.

"Then why are you moving out?"

"To give you guys space. We're just going to complicate everything even more."

Dad sat back in his chair. "Why in the world would you want to leave at a time like this? I'm going to need all the help I can get to keep Evelyn from divorcing me and taking me for all that I'm worth."

"Dad, she's just pissed. She'll get over it. It was just some online thing, for crying out loud. And I'm taking Bella with me," I added boldly, not giving him a chance to respond.

"What? Why?"

"She's been through a lot in the past few months. She doesn't need to be here while you two work this out."

"I really don't understand much of any of this, Stefan. Why would Bella want to move some place with you? Doesn't she have plans to go back to school? And how the hell are you going to support yourself?"

These were all valid questions, but of course, I couldn't answer them.

"You said I'm one of your hardest workers," I explained. "I hope to still work for you to support myself."

I hated my job working for my father, but it would do until I found something else that could support Bella and me. Although Bella wasn't too far along yet, I didn't want her to have to get a temporary job too. Besides, I wanted to be in control and provide for us both. It made me feel . . . powerful.

My dad let out a derisive snort. "Why the hell should I help you when you're being so difficult?"

"Because you know what you did wasn't my fault. You need to clean this up yourself. You taught me that a man cleans up his own shit."

Dad gaped at me. "Son, my company is at stake here. If Evelyn divorces me, I stand to lose everything. *Everything*. That means no construction company, no job, no paycheck, nothing! How the hell would I be able to pay you a salary? Huh?"

My dad shook his head. "No, what you're going to do is stay here and do everything in your power to convince Evelyn that divorcing me is a bad idea. With your and Bella's help, Evelyn should see reason."

I glowered at my dad. This was exactly what I hadn't wanted from the beginning—being used as pawns by our parents.

"We are a family unit, Stefan," my dad continued. "I'm sorry, but I need some support. If you and Bella don't help me on this, don't expect financial help from me in getting your own place. If you do that, you're on your own."

Silence filled the space between us and I studied my father. I could help him, of course, but I didn't want to. Yes, Veronica had been the woman, and she wouldn't have approached Dad if it weren't for me and Bella. But did it matter? He still had a choice. He could have just ignored her. Either way, he'd just given me an ultimatum, and my pride demanded that I rebel just out of spite.

"Like I said, we're moving out," I growled.

Without another word, I turned and walked out of his office, slamming the door behind me.

Chapter 29
Bella

"How's the baby coming along, Bella?" Mother asked.

My mother smiled as she looked at me and I smiled back. The joy reflected in her eyes made my heart sing with elation, filling me with happiness.

We were sitting around a table out on the deck in the backyard with a group of women, all family members and close friends, enjoying a cup of cold, fresh lemonade. It was a warm, sunny day, with clear blue skies and soft breezes that felt soothing against my skin. The perfect day.

I rubbed my swollen belly. I was wearing a bright, yellow sundress that matched the beautiful summer day. "My little one is coming along just fine." I glanced down at my stomach, smiling sunrises as I felt the baby kicking inside me. "Any day now."

"Do you think it will be like it's father?" one of the women asked, a sour-looking old woman who was dressed in a gaudy dress, topped by a stylish hat with a feather sticking out of it.

I held in a frown. The way the woman had said 'it's' rubbed me the wrong way, but I brushed the feeling away. Perhaps she hadn't meant any offense by it. "I think that it's a he, and yes, I think he will be just like Stefan."

The woman smiled at me, but it only made me feel more uneasy. "That is wonderful, Bella. But I have *one question."*

The nausea I felt inside intensified. "Yes?"

The woman's face became a mask of black anger. "What kind of slut fucks her stepbrother and then ends up pregnant with his bastard?"

* * *

"Bella, calm down! You're going to wake up your mother!"

I gasped as I came awake in my darkened bedroom, my forehead and entire body covered by sweat. A dark silhouette stood over my bed. Crying out in fear, I lashed out. The shadow was quick, though, and caught my hand.

"Bella, it's me," said a familiar voice. "Stefan."

"No," I moaned softly, struggling to break free of the powerful grip. "You lie."

I felt strong arms wrap around me, restraining me from fighting back. "Calm down, Bella. It's me, Stefan."

Feeling his warm flesh pressed against mine brought me back to the present. "Stefan," I sobbed with relief into his shoulder. "I had the most terrible dream."

Stefan pulled back and studied my face in the dark. To my surprise, he still had on his expensive clothing from the party, but now the front of his dress shirt was unbuttoned even further, teasing that beautiful chest and washboard abs of his. "Would you like to talk about it?"

I wiped away the tears flowing down my cheeks as images of being taunted and shunned slowly faded into the darkness. "No," I said finally. "I'm just glad it's over."

Stefan stared carefully at me for a moment before

saying, "Okay. But once you feel better, I want to know what it was all about."

"All right." I peered closely at him, trying to keep my eyes on his face and not his chest. "Why are you in here this late? Was I that loud?" The last time I saw Stefan was just before Terry had come back downstairs from arguing with my mom, looking absolutely defeated. Stefan said he was going to speak with his dad for a moment before going to bed. He refused to tell me what he was going to talk about, but I could only assume it had something to do with the plan he had for the both of us.

"It's not that late. But yeah, you were really starting to wail as I came in."

"What did you say?" I asked immediately, thirsty for details. "To your dad, I mean."

"Well, first, I told him that he should be ashamed for having an online relationship with some chick half his age, and then . . . I told him we're going to move out together."

Stefan went on to tell me about how Terry wanted us both to stay and help him convince my mom not to leave him.

I gaped in disbelief when Stefan was done with his story. "What? Why in the world would you tell him that? We're only going to draw more attention to ourselves."

"Well, we're going to have to come clean eventually. At this point, I'm just concerned with getting you out of any stressful situations."

I shook my head. "I still don't understand. Why don't we just help him? We know exactly why Veronica stalked Terry and did what she did. Knowing that, I have no problem with trying to convince Mom that a divorce would be a bad idea, especially when that's exactly what Veronica would want."

I just couldn't understand why Stefan was being so hard on Terry about the whole situation. Even knowing Veronica orchestrated the whole thing, and given the fact that Veronica was a young, hot babe—God, I hated to admit it—why couldn't he give his dad a break?

Stefan sure is riding on the moral high horse, I thought, *while I'm sitting here with his baby growing inside me.*

"Growing up, Dad always told me to take responsibility for my actions. And you know what? I listened. That's why I'm trying to get us out of this mess. I've created a problem, and I intend to deal with it. Whether Veronica planned it or not, Dad created his problem, and I'm sure he'll get himself out of it."

The way Stefan said *problem* when he was referring to our situation struck a chord inside me. Is that what he thought of me and the baby? As a problem?

Was that all I was to him, some problem to deal with?

Stefan must have seen my worried expression. "Bella, what's wrong?"

"Should have never done it," I whispered, black depression washing over me.

"Should have never done what?"

"Any of this," I replied. "That stupid contest, the Sacrifice. Look at everything that's happened. We're hiding a secret from our parents and Mom is threatening to divorce Terry. Jesus, Stefan, Terry is going to hate my guts when he finds out the truth behind all of this."

"Don't say that," Stefan pleaded. "Haven't I told you before to stop being so hard on yourself? No matter what reason Veronica came after Dad, whether we caused it or not, his actions are his own. It could just have easily been some other girl. He has no one to blame but himself, you hear me? Himself."

But I still couldn't get over the feeling that we were responsible. "Fuck her," I hissed angrily. "And fuck this whole, fucked-up situation!"

Stefan placed a hand on my arm. "Stop it, Bella. You're losing control."

I brushed Stefan's hand away. "No! I'm tired of all of this shit!"

Stefan remained calm in the face of my fury. "Bella, you're getting too loud. You're going to wake Evelyn."

"I don't care! I doubt she's asleep anyway," I snapped.

Stefan gripped me by both arms firmly and stared me straight in the eye. "But I do. Get a hold of yourself and stop this nonsense now."

After defiantly staring him in the eye for a moment, I looked away with a sigh. He'd won. "I'm sorry," I said softly. "I'm just so stressed about this whole situation and I'm feeling overwhelmed by it all."

"I know. That's why I'm trying to get you out of here."

"I just wish there were some other way . . ." my words trailed off as my eyes drifted down to the opening of Stefan's shirt, where his powerful chest was on display.

I ran my fingers down the opening of his dress shirt, enjoying the feel of his flesh against my fingertips. Hungry, I continued all the way down until I hit the waistband of his dress pants.

Stefan looked at me with confusion. "Bella? What are you doing?"

My nightmare had shaken me to the core. All of my fears were haunting me, and the lies we were telling our parents were starting to get to me. I needed to feel something, anything.

Stefan placed his hand over mine, halting me at his zipper. "Bella, we can't do this now."

Unheeding, I shoved his hand away and began unbuttoning his pants anyway. It took me nearly thirty seconds to unzip them—I swear the expensive material had a safety lock on it—and then I managed to pull his pants and underwear down slightly.

I was disappointed to see that he wasn't rock-hard and ready when his cock came out, but my breath caught in my throat anyway.

Even flaccid, it was a wonder to behold, with the perfect-shaped mushroom head that looked juicy and oh, so succulent.

I grabbed ahold of it, relishing how it felt in my hands. It was warm. Hot. A jolt ran up my fingers as his cock twitched and blood began pumping through it.

A desperate note had entered Stefan's voice. "Bella..."

I ignored him, daring him to stop me. For some reason, I felt powerful holding his dick in my hands, feeling the blood plump through it.

Some say a man's dick was an extension of his ego, and for Stefan and his nearly 8-inch cock, it had to be a major source of his confidence. It thrilled me to be holding his symbol of pride in my hands, having him completely at my mercy.

Swiftly, it grew inside my grip until his luscious head was fat and swollen.

I squeezed the shaft of his cock and waited expectantly. Sure enough, a large drop of precum came out of the eye, and I rubbed it all over his head and down his shaft, lubricating him.

"Bella . . ." Stefan was moaning now. I knew I had him.

Disregarding his feeble protests, I began jerking him off, stroking from the top of his head down to the bottom of his shaft. While I stroked him, images from my dream assailed me. Gripped by fear, this only made me stroke him harder.

"Fuck," Stefan cursed as I paused stroking to squeeze his cock to get more precum to come out. He'd gone slightly dry.

This time, I was rewarded with even more fluid, and I relished spreading his juices all over his fat dick. I added a little saliva and resumed jerking him off, pumping his big cock as fast as I could.

The sound of fleshy friction filled the room as I jacked him furiously. I gripped his head as tightly as I could every time I stroked to the top, adding a slight twist to it and making sure to stimulate the most sensitive part of his head.

"Fuck, if you keep doing that, I'm gonna come," Stefan moaned. He lifted his ass off the bed, arching his back a little. Satisfaction rolled through me as I noted the expression on his face, his features twisted in effort as if he was trying to lift a mountain, sweat rolling down his jaw.

This only made me feel more powerful. I was in control of this strong male specimen who had been a thorn in my side for years because of my attraction to him.

I pumped as furiously as I could, angrily jerking his huge dick up and down. "Come for me," I commanded him, looking straight up at him. "Give it to me," I repeated.

"Ah, fuck!" Stefan gasped, his face twisted as if he was in agony, his forehead covered in sweat.

Powerful jolts went through my hands as his dick contracted rapidly, sending squirts of hot liquid all over the place. Stefan must've had a build-up, because it went everywhere—on the bed, my gown, and his dress pants.

I felt hot liquid roll down my wrist as his cock continued erupting like a volcano. I held on and squeezed, getting every last drop until his dick stopped contracting.

Stefan let out a huge sigh and lowered his ass back onto the bed when it was over.

"Fuck, are you happy now?" he demanded as I let go of his dick. He seemed to know that my actions were some sort of power play meant to exert some control over him, but at the same time, it seemed he didn't want to press the issue, as if he was scared of what my reaction might be.

He got up from the bed and grabbed tissue from the box of Kleenex sitting on my nightstand and began wiping at his dick and then furiously at his pants. "I hope this washes out. These pants cost 300 bucks." When he was done, he pulled his pants back up, zipping them closed. Even in the dark, I could see the stains all over them.

"I'm sorry. I'll wash them out for you," I apologized, though I wasn't really sorry. For some reason, I was in no hurry to wipe his mess from my hands and arm. I wanted to feel a part of him on me.

Stefan sighed and dropped the tissues in the wastebasket next to the night stand. I would have to empty that before the next morning. I wouldn't want Mom to come nosing in and wonder why come-encrusted tissue was sitting in my trash bin. "I'm sure it will. But I'm going to need all the nice clothes that I've got since I'll probably have to start looking for a job."

I stared at him. "So we're really moving out?"

Stefan nodded and grabbed more tissue. Then he walked over to my bed and began wiping at the mess he'd made on my bedspread. It being dark, I knew he would miss a few spots. But it was okay. I would get them later. "Yes. We're not staying here."

"Why don't we just stay and help Terry?"

Stefan stopped wiping and turned to look at me. "Look at it this way—even if Evelyn does decide to stay with Dad, what do you think is going to happen when you start to show? I just don't see them happily cheering you on, Bella. And that's assuming they don't know that the baby is mine." He shook his head. "No way. If you think it's bad here now, I would hate to see what it would be like then."

As much as I hated to admit it, Stefan was right.

We couldn't stay here. I had about another month before I would really start to show. Of course, I could just wear big clothing, but even that would only last so long.

"We have to think about the baby first right now. Besides, they'll have plenty of time to sort it out without us around. We'll just get in the way." His voice had a note of stone in it.

"My mom is a very proud woman," I said flatly. "Even though it was only some online thing, from what your dad said, I don't see her forgiving him easily. I can't just tell her to forgive him without giving her a good reason. She'll just think I'm being sympathetic to him and taking his side."

"Just let them deal with it. Maybe we can try to smooth things over later if things aren't looking good. But look at the bright side—we'll have all the time in the world alone."

While being alone with him sounded amazing, I also wanted to do everything I could to keep our parents together. I didn't want their split to be any fault of mine, but I was just going to go along with Stefan. "All right. I just won't say anything then."

"Good." He finished wiping away at the wet spots and then got up and threw the tissues in the waste basket. "Do you want me to . . .?" He nodded at me, and I instantly understood what he meant. "You'll have to be very quiet, though. No screaming when I get into it." He grinned mischievously.

I should have been jumping at the offer, but Stefan hadn't exactly asked for me to get him off, so why should I expect anything in return? On top of that, I hadn't really been in the mood before I did it, and I definitely wasn't in the mood now after discussing our parents.

Besides, it seemed more like he just felt obligated, and not because he really wanted to. And I didn't want him to do it if he felt that way.

I shook my head and surprise showed in his eyes.

"You sure?"

He scratched at the back of his neck when I didn't reply and said, "We'll go look at some apartments tomorrow."

I shifted in the bed, careful to keep my semen-covered hand away from my sheets. "How are we going to afford moving out, Stefan? You said Terry wasn't going to let you work for him if you leave."

"I have money saved up, just enough for us to get a place and to give me time to look for a job."

"Stefan . . . I'm scared."

He gave me a Stefan grin, but while it helped, it didn't take away all my worry. "Have a little confidence in me, okay? I told you. I'm going take care of you no matter what, okay?"

"Okay," I said finally.

He walked over to the bed and planted a soft kiss on my lips and then nodded at my arm. "Now go clean up and get some sleep. We have a long week ahead of us." He playfully ruffled my hair and then walked out of the room, quietly closing the door behind him.

Chapter 30
Bella

"Mom?" I asked delicately.

My mother half-turned from where she was sitting at the vanity as I closed her bedroom door behind me. I sucked in a breath as I surveyed her appearance. Dressed in one of her favorite gowns that looked mightily rumpled, with no makeup on, she looked awful, and had obviously been sulking before I'd walked into the room. Her eyes were red and puffy looking.

I'd decided to pay her a visit after avoiding her most of the week. Between the constant arguments with Terry, and me and Stefan scouting around for an apartment to move into, I hadn't found the time to speak with her for more than a few minutes.

But since Stefan abruptly left today to go looking at apartments without me, I decided I would break down and have a little talk with Mother, though I wasn't sure what I was going to say.

On one hand, I wanted to tell her that divorcing

Terry would be a big mistake, and on the other, I wanted to tell her the truth and just end all this madness.

Stefan warned me repeatedly not to get involved in our parents' relationship woes, but I found myself unable to resist trying. I felt that I owed her at least that much.

I just didn't know if I was going to be able to get her listen to me, or only succeed in pissing her off.

"Yes, Bella?" my mother's voice was scratchy.

"What's going on?" I asked.

She peered at me while wiping at her cheek with the back of her hand, causing the right strap of her gown to fall off her shoulder. "What do you mean?"

"Are you going to leave Terry?"

My mom stared at me for a long moment and then tugged the strap of her gown back onto her shoulder. "I don't know yet."

"Maybe after you calm down, you guys should just attend marriage counseling like Terry said. It might do some good."

Mother scowled at me. "Well, that's nice of you to suggest such a thing, as if it's just so easy to do when you weren't the one hurt by what he did, Bella," she said acidly.

Oh boy, I thought. *She's got the acid tongue out. Careful, Bella.*

"I'm sure that it meant nothing to him. Besides, it was only an online thing. It wasn't really cheating . . . was it?"

I knew I was really pressing the issue, but I had to get my mother to see a little reason. I didn't know exactly how far Terry had gone with Veronica, but it couldn't have been that far.

"It isn't? It's a different form, but it's still cheating, and that's taking his word for it that it never progressed further. I'm having a hard time believing that. And God knows what your stepfather did every time he saw all that stuff." She stared at me, rage burning in her eyes. "Did you see the girl?"

Of course I had seen the bitch. She was one of the reasons Stefan and I were in so much of a mess.

"My God, Bella," my mother continued. "She is so young, she's your age, for crying out loud." There was a bitterness in my mother's words that left a sour taste in my mouth.

"Yeah, I saw her," I said in a casual way that would not reveal that I knew Veronica. "She looked like a slut with no class. She's nothing compared to you." I walked over beside my mom and gently stroked her hair, trying to console her as she'd done for me so many times before.

My mom looked up at me, and I saw a flash of gratitude in her eyes. "Thank you, Bella, for coming to talk to me."

After a few moments of silence, I spoke up and said, "I think you should remind him of what he's missing. I know what he did has hurt you and made you angry, but you shouldn't let all those years of happiness go to waste."

A scowl twisted my mother's features. "Whose side are you on, anyway? Mine or Terry's?"

"Yours, Mom. You know that. I just want to see you happy again."

I sucked in a deep breath. I knew she wasn't going

to like what I had to say next. "I also wanted to say that Stefan and I will be moving out."

My mom reared back with surprise. "What? Moving out? Are you two going back to school?" she asked, sounding hopeful.

"No, we're moving into an apartment."

If Mom looked surprised before, she was absolutely floored now. "What?" she exclaimed.

My hands began to feel clammy as my pulse began to race. "Didn't Terry tell you? Stefan talked with him the other day about moving out."

My mother scowled darkly. "Please, I haven't listened to a word that man has said since he revealed what a rat bastard he is." She shook her head. "Just make me understand here. Why the hell are you and Stefan moving into your own place together? You should be concerned about going back to school."

I licked my lips. I didn't have adequate answers to her question. I could only avoid them. "You and Terry need your space."

"If I divorced your stepfather, this house will most likely be mine. I've already spoken with my divorce lawyer. Terry will want to retain his business, and I don't care about taking that from him, but the house and a generous percentage of other assets would be mine. Terry would no longer be here. You don't need to go anywhere, Bella."

And where would Stefan be? I wanted to ask. For some reason, I knew that Stefan would no longer be allowed here if she went through with it, at least not until she had time to get over her anger.

"And with the money from the settlement, I can

send you to whatever school you want."

I froze, my mouth going dry. "I can't go to another school, Mom."

She stared at me. "Why the hell not?"

I couldn't answer. How could I? The truth would end me . . . and maybe even end her. So I kept my lips closed.

"Don't you have goals?" my mom demanded when I didn't answer. "Dreams? Aspirations? Just because a bunch of boys gave you a hard time at college, doesn't mean you have to give up on life."

"I know, Mom."

"So help me understand what is going on, Bella. Since you've been back, you and Stefan seemed to be stuck together like glue. Had he not gotten the job working for Terry, I don't know what we would've done to separate you two."

"Let's not talk about this right now, Mom. I don't want to argue with you." I'd come to offer her support. Now I wish I'd never stepped in her room. Stefan was right—I was only asking for more trouble.

My mom glared at me. "Why does it seem like everyone in this damn house is hiding secrets from me, huh?"

"I'm going to go, Mom," I said softly. "I have some packing to do."

"Bella, I'm not done talking with you, young woman!"

"Bella!"

Hardening my heart, I walked out of the bedroom.

Chapter 31
Bella

"Open your eyes," Stefan said, removing his hands from in front of my shades.

"Oh my God, it's beautiful!" I exclaimed to Stefan, stepping through the doorway.

Tears filled my eyes at the sight before me.

It was a beautiful one-bedroom, one-bath studio with cream-colored walls and matching carpet, and a small kitchen and stove. It wouldn't have taken much to make me happy, but it really was a nice place.

The fresh smell of paint filled my nostrils as I looked over at Stefan. "I love it!"

Stefan stuck his hands into his pockets and grinned as he surveyed the room with me. He looked quite handsome, as usual, dressed in blue jeans and a freshly ironed, white South State University t-shirt. He had an SSU hat on, turned backward. "I knew you would. The first and last was cheap enough on this place that I have just enough for us to survive until I find a job."

I ran into his arms. "I'm so happy!" I crowed. For a moment, I almost forgot about all the issues facing us, basking in joy at having our first place together.

Stefan squeezed me lightly, peering down at me. "Didn't I tell you I would come through for us?"

"Yes, you sure did."

He kissed me hard on the lips, leaving me breathless. "And I'm going to continue to do so, no matter what happens. Don't ever doubt me."

"I won't," I said, flashing him a hopeful smile.

* * *

"I got a job!" announced Stefan. He was in our small living room, sitting on the cream-colored couch, one we had purchased with a newly opened credit account at a nearby furniture store, his laptop perched on the coffee table in front of him.

"That's wonderful, Stefan!" I called over the sizzle of bacon. I was in the kitchen, cooking Stefan a breakfast consisting of sausage, bacon, and eggs. It was a morning routine I'd taken up as soon as we had moved in, and I found that it filled me with a sense of domesticated joy.

It had been nearly two weeks since we moved in, and I couldn't have been happier. That wasn't to say the transition had been all roses, but it was truly a joy being able to wake up next to him. The best, though, was that we made love every night without worry of anyone walking in on us.

Back when we moved in, Stefan rented a moving truck and hired someone to help him move some of our furniture from back home into our new place. When I tried to come along, he told me to stay at the apartment because he expected trouble from our parents. Instead, he told me to give him a list of things that I wanted from the house and he'd get it.

Sure enough, when he got there, Terry had been waiting for him. The two had an exchange of words, but apparently, it hadn't gotten too bad. Even still, since then, we'd tried to keep our distance from our parents as best we could.

The only thing that bothered me was deserting my mom when she was having marital problems. But I would no doubt start to show soon, and even if I didn't, she may pick up on it some other way.

"What kind of job is it?" I asked as I turned the burner off and piled the bacon and sausage along with the eggs onto a plate.

"Modeling," Stefan replied.

My heart fell in my throat as I poured a glass of orange juice. "Modeling?"

"Yeah. I'll be modeling for a company that sells their apparel from fashion magazines and catalogues."

"What kind of modeling?"

Stefan cleared his throat. "Clothing and underwear."

I guess I should feel proud that he was mine, but I couldn't help but feel a little jealousy too. If Stefan was going to be taking sexy pictures for some magazine, there was no telling how many girls would end up ogling his body.

"How in the world did you manage to get a modeling job? Don't you have to have an agent for that?" As far as I knew, Stefan hadn't said anything about modeling since we'd been at our new apartment. The jobs he'd applied for so far had all been typical nine-to-five jobs that only required a high school diploma.

"I saw an ad online looking for professional models. The requirements were that you have to be good-looking and be physically fit. I said fuck it and sent in a few pictures and said I was representing myself. That was yesterday, and there is already a response today."

"They must have really liked you," I remarked.

I brought Stefan's breakfast along with his glass of orange juice over to the coffee table and set it before him. He closed his laptop and set it aside on the couch and then patted the seat next to him.

I flopped down next to him, trying not to let my disappointment show.

"You're not pleased, I take it?" Stefan asked as he grabbed his fork and began digging into the pile of eggs.

I pushed an errant strand of hair out of my eyes. I swear, since my pregnancy, my hair volume had increased so much that it drove me absolutely wild. "Well, it's not that. I always thought you could be a model. I just don't know how I feel about you modeling in your underwear."

"I figured you would feel that way," Stefan said, grabbing his glass of orange juice and taking a gulp. "But you shouldn't worry. It's a totally professional environment from everything I've seen, and the pay is pretty good. I looked it up online, and even for an amateur model like me, I could fetch a hundred dollars an hour. I'd only need to get a few sessions to pay for most of our expenses."

I smiled. "Well, that does sound wonderful."

Stefan bit into a piece of bacon and then flashed me his killer grin. "I've gotta put these good looks to use for something."

I grew silent, unable to offer much of a response. After a moment, Stefan seemed to notice that I didn't have a plate of food.

"You're not going to eat?"

I was feeling a little sick, and just the thought of eating made me feel queasy.

"I'm not hungry," I replied.

Chapter 32
Stefan

Lights flashed rapidly in my eyes, nearly blinding me as I stood before a large green screen in torn blue-jeans and no shirt on, striking a masculine pose.

"You're doing beautiful, Stefan," my photographer, named Jenny, a young woman with chipmunk cheeks and short brown hair, purred as she peered through the lens of her camera. "Absolutely beautiful." There was a flurry of activity behind her as people scurried about, shouting commands. I was one of several models doing a photo shoot at the same time, and multiple green screens were set up as models were brought in and out for various shoots.

She was one of the first women I'd met when I entered the studio, and I found her to be slightly bossy almost immediately, but I attributed it to the demands of the profession.

After all, photographers were used to issuing orders to get the models to pose in the way that they wanted.

Jenny peered over her camera and motioned at me. "Can you pull down your pants a little and show a little of your underwear?"

I shifted on my feet and did as she asked.

She beamed at me, her eyes seeming to feast on my body. "Good." More flashes went off.

What am I doing here? I asked myself.

It seemed so surreal. Although I knew I was good-looking, I'd never thought I'd end up modeling because I had dropped out of college to support my pregnant stepsister. But the pay was good, and considering how hard it was to get a good job with only a high school diploma, I wasn't going to complain.

"Very good, Stefan." Jenny straightened and motioned at one of her staff members, who went scurrying off to one of the other green screens. "I'm going to bring Cara, a swimwear model, over to take a few pictures with you, okay?"

"Of course," I said, trying to seem casual by flashing an easygoing smile.

A second later, Jenny's assistant returned with a tall, curvaceous, dark-haired beauty dressed in a barely-there bikini in tow. I quickly averted my eyes as she made her way toward me.

"Cara, this is Stefan, a new model who is having

his first shoot," she introduced us. "Stefan, this is Cara."

The beautiful model held out a hand to me and flashed a pretty smile as she appraised my muscular torso. She seemed attracted to me, and her eyes seemed to be silently saying, *I don't know you, but let's go fuck after this.* "Nice to meet you, Stefan." She had a foreign accent—some type of European. I wasn't sure.

"Hey," I said shortly, gripping her hand briefly and letting go.

Jenny gestured at me. "Cara, can you move beside Stefan and do your thing? Give me cool confidence, like you own Stefan."

I swallowed as Cara moved beside me and did as Jenny commanded. The beginning of anxiety began to grip my stomach. While I was used to keeping my cool in tense situations, I hadn't been expecting to take pictures with a beautiful foreign model.

It's totally natural to feel attraction for a beautiful girl, I told myself to assuage my growing anxiety. Still, considering the rant I'd given my dad jut a few weeks before, I still didn't feel right.

Jenny took a few pictures and gestured again. "Now, can you rest your head against his shoulder?" Cara did as she asked. Jenny began to peer into her camera but stopped short. "Move in a little closer. Good."

Jenny took a few more shots, all while having us change to various poses together, some involving Cara placing her hands on my abs and grabbing my ass. Each one made me start feeling more uncomfortable than the last, and it was becoming difficult to maintain the poses. "Good, the both of you. Now, Cara, can you place your hands on Stefan's crotch?"

Cara let out a little giggle and placed her hand on my junk, and I immediately tensed up.

If Bella knew this was happening, she'd be pissed, I thought. *And what if this winds up in a magazine and she somehow happens upon this picture?*

"Stefan, can you cup Cara's left breast with your right hand?"

Sweating, I began to reach for Cara's breast before pulling away.

Jenny pulled back from her camera, noting my apprehension. "Is there a problem?"

"I don't mean any offense," I said to Cara before turning to Jenny, "but this isn't what I expected. I didn't sign up for this."

Jenny frowned. "It was in your contract that you signed."

When I didn't offer a rebuttal, she gestured at Cara. "It's not a big deal. It's just a picture. Now, will you please perform the pose?"

Cara placed a reassuring arm on my shoulder, rubbing it gently. "It's okay, handsome boy," she purred in her heavy accent. "I'll guide you." Smiling, she took my hand and placed it on her breast.

Desire roiled through me and I quickly snatched my hand away. Cara looked like she'd been struck by my rejection, but I didn't care.

"I can't do this."

Several of the studio hands stopped what they were doing to stare at me, and Jenny scowled.

"Either do as you're told and take the photo with Cara, or leave."

Without saying a word, I walked over and gathered up my clothes that I'd taken off for the shoot and walked out.

* * *

"What happened?" Bella asked as I walked back into our apartment during mid-afternoon. "Did everything go well?"

She was perched on the couch, dressed in tiny shorts and a cut-off top, browsing my laptop. Each day, it seemed Bella put on a few more pounds. I didn't mind it, though. I actually liked seeing Bella, who'd been thin all her life, with a little more meat on her bones.

I walked over and sat down next to her, tossing my extra clothes along the arm of the couch. "I walked out of the photo shoot."

Surprise etched across Bella's features as she placed the laptop on the coffee table and repositioned herself to face me. "What? Why?"

My eyes were drawn to Bella's top. She wasn't wearing a bra, and her hard nipples pressed against the flimsy material.

My first instinct was to make up some BS, but then I thought better of it. I quickly told Bella what happened, leaving out only the 'fuck me' eyes the model gave me. I did the right thing. No need to go bragging about it.

"I left because I didn't want you to get pissed if you ever happened upon those photos. I want to do right by you."

Bella bit her lip, but I saw appreciation flash in her eyes. "You didn't have to do that just for me, Stefan. I would've been annoyed, but I would have understood."

Sure you would have, I thought. *But you deserve better than having to.*

"It's okay. I'll just find another gig."

Hopefully.

It sucked because the pay would've been good for us, but Bella seemed to already be suffering from self-esteem issues, and I didn't want to further exacerbate the problem.

"Well, maybe I can try to help by getting a job," Bella suggested.

I shook my head. I'd rather go down to the plasma center and get money out of my damn veins than have Bella go through that stress. "No, I already told you that I'll take care of everything."

"But—" Bella began to protest as my cell ringtone went off.

I raised a finger to silence her as I dug it out of my back pocket and checked it. I half-expected to see a call from Dad or Evelyn, or even the modeling company, but the words on the screen shocked me.

Call from James Carter.

What's he calling for? I wondered. The last time I had talked to my old coach at South State, he'd been pissed at me for causing so much trouble by beating up my teammate. He got even more pissed when I was subsequently forced from the school because of my actions, leaving the lacrosse team without their All-Star player.

"Coach Carter?" I answered.

"Stefan, my boy!" Carter greeted enthusiastically. "How good to hear your voice again. How have you been doing?"

I glanced at Bella, who was staring at me with an inquisitive expression. "I'm doing well."

"Good, good. How's things going at North State?"

I paused. "Uh . . . I'm no longer enrolled there, actually."

"Well that's just wonderful news!"

What the hell?

I reared back and looked at the cell with surprise, as if I was looking him in the face, before bringing it back to my ear.

"Listen, Stefan. I talked to Jared Stroing's parents and cleared everything up. They are fine with you returning to South State as long as you and Jared promise to get along. I have secured a sports scholarship for you so you can attend the next semester free of charge. All you have to do is show back up."

I sat there in dumbstruck silence, unable to believe what I was hearing.

"This is a wonderful opportunity for you, Stefan. I'm talking about something that could lead to a professional career." Coach Carter continued. "You were one of the best athletes I have ever seen, and I never stopped believing in you."

I swallowed deeply. Coach Carter had just re-ignited my dream of being an All-Star athlete. Besides Bella, it had always been one of the driving forces in my life. Heck, since I'd been back at home, I found that I missed playing sports immensely.

"Um, that's wonderful, Coach Carter," I said dumbly.

"Wonderful?" Carter asked incredulously. "It's fucking fantastic!" He chuckled. "So what do you say, huh? Come back and lead these kids to greatness."

I wanted so badly to accept Coach Carter's offer, but I had a baby on the way and Bella to think about. There was no way I could return to school and sports and take care of Bella at the same time, at least not right now.

"Uh, I'm going to have to get back to you on that, Coach," I said.

There was a short pause over the line. "All right, Stefan." He sounded slightly disappointed. "But I want to remind you that an offer like this isn't going to last long. I'll be expecting an answer back from you soon."

"Who was that?" Bella asked as soon as I was off the phone.

The expression on her face caused a heavy feeling in my chest and I fucking hated it. "It was my old coach back at South State, Coach Carter."

"What did he want?"

I let out a sigh, knowing I should probably keep my mouth shut on the offer, but I knew that Bella wouldn't stop until she knew what was said. "He was offering me a scholarship to return to South State to resume my position as captain of the lacrosse team."

I saw the fear flash in Bella's eyes immediately. "Oh that's great, Stefan," she said without any emotion. She eyed me closely. "What are you going to tell him?"

I laughed nervously. "Is that a joke or what? Of course I'm going to tell him no."

Silence filled the room as Bella studied me.

Her scrutiny made me feel uncomfortable, and I kept talking to fill the void. "I have you and the baby to worry about. I can't accept the offer, not right now."

"You should do it," Bella said suddenly.

I stared at her. 'Huh?"

She looked away from me. "You should do it," she said, her voice sounding weak. "Don't worry about me and the baby. I'll find a way on my own."

"What are you talking about, Bella? I can't just leave you alone to fend for yourself."

Bella turned back to me and I could see tears streaming down her cheeks. "But this is your life-long dream we're talking about here."

"My life-long dream was to be with you."

I thought my words would bring her solace, but Bella turned back away. I reached out to grab her, but she pushed my hands aside and wiped at her tears.

"I ruined you," she said quietly.

I felt like I'd just been punched in my stomach. "What?"

"I ruined your life when I got pregnant. This was my nightmare, Stefan. In my dream, you were there right at the end, and you said that I ruined you and your future. It broke my heart. Now, it's all coming true."

"Bella, I had no idea. You didn't ruin anything. We both wanted this, remember?"

Bella shook her head, refusing to look at me. "We don't know what we really wanted. We weren't even thinking. That's why I'm pregnant in the first place."

I grabbed ahold of Bella, overpowering her resistance, and turned her to face me. "Listen. I need you. We need each other. I could never leave you. Never." I kissed her hard on the lips, pressing her into me. When I broke it off, she was breathless and I saw a spark in her eye.

I let go of her and stood up from the couch, feeling my pulse begin to race. I had to do something to release the pent-up frustration and make us both forget about our current situation.

"I know just what you need."

I walked over to the stereo I had brought from home and turned it on. Loud music filled our apartment.

I walked back over, pulling off my shirt as I went, and pulled Bella on her feet. Then I pulled her into my arms and began devouring her neck.

Chapter 33
Bella

"Don't you think our new neighbors are going to complain about the loud music?" I asked breathlessly as Stefan smothered my neck with passionate kisses.

Stefan pulled back and grinned at me. "I'd rather them complain about loud music than the sounds of us making love."

He resumed kissing me all over my neck, hot, burning kisses that made my flesh sizzle with electricity. Breathless, I gave in to his assault.

He seemed to be trying to assure me through his passion that he would never leave me. I wanted to believe him. I wanted to believe that he was going to love me and our baby forever.

I gave in, and I wrapped my arms around his neck as he ran a hand up the side of my body to my breast and squeezed my nipple through the flimsy fabric of my cut-off top so hard that I gasped.

Then his tongue was entering my mouth as he fondled me, and he swirled it around mine like a twisting nether, devouring all I had to give.

The next thing I knew, he was ripping my shirt off, exposing my breasts and erect nipples. Down below, I could feel his bulge pressing up against my stomach, and desire burned through my abdomen.

Hungrily, I unbuttoned his jeans and pulled them down his chiseled ass cheeks until they rested around his thighs. His hard dick was suddenly pressed against my stomach, and I could feel it pulsating against my skin.

Grunting, Stefan removed my shorts and tossed them aside onto the floor before grabbing my ass cheeks into the palms of his hands and hefting me up and then slowly setting me down on his cock.

I gasped as he held me aloft and entered me at the same time.

That's when he began pounding me with unforgiving thrusts that had my ass slapping up against his chiseled thighs.

A startled scream pierced the loud music. For a moment, I thought Stefan had just pinched something, or maybe a couch spring was poking him in the ass.

But when I saw the look of absolute horror on his face, I knew something was wrong. Terribly wrong.

Astonished, I lost control of my arms around his neck and tumbled out of his lap and onto the floor as I turned around to see my mother, Terry, and my grandmother, Emma, standing in the doorway, their faces white with shock.

Hastily, I grabbed a couch cushion to cover myself, feeling idiotic even as I did so.

Terry was the first one to regain his ability to speak. "What in the holy fuck is going on here?" he roared, his face red with rage. He was literally shaking from head to toe as he stomped into our living room.

While Stefan tried to stuff his cock back into his pants, I saw my shorts and grabbed them, along with the rag of a tank top that Stefan had torn off. It had seemed hot at the time, but I kinda wished he hadn't done it now.

Meanwhile, Mom was staring at me with a look that nearly froze my heart.

"It was you two," she said, her voice barely audible over the loud music. "It was you screwing Bella in that video."

Terry did a double-take, and then realization dawned on his face as well as he put the pieces together.

"Explain yourself!" Terry yelled at Stefan, as I stood by, my arms across my chest, my head hung in shame.

My grandmother, who I still couldn't believe was here—just what the hell was she doing here, anyway?—looked the calmest out of everyone as she strolled over to the stereo and shut the music off.

Beside me, Stefan clenched his jaw. I could sense that he was going to be defiant about this to the end, no matter what it cost us.

"How did this happen, Bella?" Terry demanded, turning his gaze toward me.

I couldn't respond, partially due to shock. I couldn't believe Stefan had left the door unlocked and our parents had come along right at the time we were screwing. And partially because I couldn't bear the shame of what my actions had brought.

When I didn't answer, Terry turned his furious gaze back on his son.

"Well?"

Still defiant, Stefan refused to reply.

Terry shook his head, his body visibly shaking with rage. "You went in on me about what I did with that sorority girl, when this whole time, you knew exactly who she was and why she did what she did. This whole time, you've been screwing your own stepsister, Stefan. Your stepsister!"

Terry's tone seemed to break our deadlock, and Stefan growled an answer. "So? Just because we knew her doesn't make what you did okay."

Terry looked incredulous. "So? What the hell is wrong with you, boy? It's not right!"

Stefan laughed in his father's face. "Why should I care what a cheating bastard says is right or wrong?"

"You goddamn son of a bitch!" Terry roared as he rushed forward. They both had always had tempers, and Stefan had been struggling for weeks with trying to stand up for us. Now, he'd just been pushed too far.

"Terry!" Evelyn yelled in unison with my grandmother as her husband collided with my stepbrother.

The two men went down on the floor and began rumbling around the apartment. I watched in shocked horror as Stefan overpowered his dad and wrapped him a chokehold. Terry began beating his hand against the floor, his face red as he struggled to get out of the hold.

"Stop it, Stefan!" I finally managed to cry out.

Stefan didn't listen, and he seemed to tighten his hold on his father.

My mother rushed forward to pull Stefan off Terry, but he fell into her as Terry was still struggling. Mom fell onto the floor. All three of us began to plead with Stefan to stop and let Terry go, but he wasn't letting go, his face twisted in a weird mask of rage.

When Terry seemed to start to struggle to breathe, I made a decision, even though I was sure it would cost me everything.

"I'm pregnant!" I shouted.

* * *

The silence was deafening. Timed slowed to a standstill. The pounding of my heart was so loud that I'm sure everyone in the room could hear it.

Thump, thump. Thump, thump.

In slow motion, I noted everyone's expression. Terry's was one of disbelief, my mother's was one of outrage, and Stefan's was one of fear. Surprisingly, my grandmother seemed the least shocked of all, with a distasteful expression but a calm demeanor overall.

I stood there, taking it all in, my forehead covered in sweat, my hands as clammy as an eel, waiting for the shit to hit the fan.

And it did.

Suddenly, my senses went into overdrive as time rushed forward with everything happening all at once.

Terry pushed Stefan away and climbed to his feet, coughing and grabbing at his throat. Emma walked over to my mom and grabbed her arm as if preparing to hold her back from killing me with her bare hands, and my mother glared absolute fucking murder at me.

"What did you just say?" The frost in my mother's voice was enough to freeze my blood.

I bit my lower lip, nausea threatening to overwhelm me. "I'm pregnant." The words seemed alien to me, as if I'd said them for the first time.

Silence once again overtook the room as my mother stared at me as if I'd stolen her best piece of jewelry out of her charm box.

"Who's the father?" Terry asked finally, breaking the silence. He still didn't get it, even after walking in on

Stefan and me fucking like wild rabbits.

How could he, though? The thought of me and Stefan having a baby together was probably inconceivable to either one of our parents, even after what they'd just witnessed.

They don't know, I thought. *They can't possibly know. But they are about to find out, though it may break them.*

Out of the corner of my eye, I could see Stefan staring at me, his powerful chest heaving from exerting his dominance over his father, silently pleading for me not to reveal the truth. But I no longer wished to hide it. One lie would just lead to another and then another until it all came crashing down—just like now.

It was time to put an end to our secret once and for all.

Unable to face my mother's furious gaze any longer, I lowered my head, filled with unbearable shame. "Stefan."

"Jesus Christ!" Terry yelled with astonishment.

My mother smacked her palm against her forehead and swayed on her feet, causing my grandmother to grab her by the arm to steady her. "Dear God, help us!"

In unison, our parents began yelling at us, gesturing wildly while hurling obscenities at us, demanding to know what, when, where, and how this all happened. I found myself unable to answer, overwhelmed by their furious barrage.

While they went apeshit on us, Stefan stared at me in shocked disbelief.

I can't believe you just did that, his eyes seemed

to say to me.

I averted my gaze from his accusing eyes. In a way, I felt bad for him. The baby was both of ours, and therefore, he had a say in what we should have told our parents, whether we should have kept the last part of our lie going. My admission of guilt robbed him of that.

I was tired of it, though. There was no way I could've had a healthy pregnancy with the stress of all the lies weighing me down.

I just prayed that when it was all over, Stefan didn't hate me for it.

"Cut it out, the both of you!" Emma snapped over our raging parents, quieting them. "All that yelling isn't going to solve a thing. The poor girl is obviously traumatized and in a fragile state." She turned her cool gaze on me, and once again, I was filled with surprise at how calm she was considering the mega-fuck bomb I'd just dropped. In a soothing, calming voice, she asked, "How did this happen, Bella?"

I told them everything—about the sorority contest, the Sacrifice, and the mistaken identity that caused Stefan and me to sleep together, and then, finally, about the school's investigation.

"And that's why we left," I said as I got done. "We'd caused too much trouble on campus with the fight Stefan had with his frat brother, and the rumors were getting too much to bear. A bunch of the frat boys really were harassing me though."

"You have got to be kidding me!" my mother wailed when I was done with my tale, clutching at her hair in despair. "Tell me this is all some kind of sick joke? Please! How in the hell could you and Stefan have not recognized each other?"

The same way you didn't recognize us fucking on the TV screen at the party, I thought. *You didn't want to believe it.*

"I don't know," I said weakly.

"Well you had better fucking find out!" Terry snapped, still rubbing at his throat. His face was livid as he glanced back and forth between me and Stefan. I don't think I could remember a time Terry had ever been this mad at me before. "Because I don't want to believe that either of you knowingly did this."

Shivering, I glanced over at Stefan for help. He had his jaw clenched, a sign that he was about to boil over. I feared that if things kept escalating, he'd wind up back rolling on the floor with Terry, trading blows, and this time, none of us would be able to stop it.

"No, Terry. I can only tell you that I've always loved Stefan," I said, somehow finding strength inside me. Now that I'd revealed our secret, it was like a floodgate had been opened inside me, and I couldn't stop talking, whether they were mad or not. "For a very long time now. I fought against it as hard as I could, but it's true."

My mother's gaze flickered back and forth between her mother and Terry. "Are you guys hearing this?" she demanded incredulously. She looked back at me, a sick look on her face. "Is this some kind of rebellious game you're playing, Bella? Please, please tell me it is, because I can't imagine what I have done to deserve this."

My mother shook her head in denial, and despite the situation, I held in a laugh. My mother spoke as if our actions hurt only her and not Terry too. "You can't really be pregnant. I can't believe it. I can't. Did Bella force all of this on you, Stefan? Is this all some sort of scheme she made up to get back at me?"

Anger welled up within me. I resented the insinuation that all of this was my fault, that I'd somehow seduced Stefan and made him my slave who would do anything I said. As if I really wanted this clusterfuck in my life right now. I mean, who would?

Get over yourself, Mom.

My mother stared at her stepson expectantly, a hopeful look on her face.

Stefan returned her gaze with his arms crossed across his powerful chest, his gaze unflinching.

"Stefan?" Terry asked, finally letting go of his throat. The redness Stefan had caused by choking him was finally going away, but it looked like he was ready to fight again. "Answer your stepmother."

"No," Stefan said finally. "None of this was Bella's idea. I made her lie to you both about everything." He glanced over at me and swallowed. "And I feel the same way about her. I love her. I always have."

All hope in my mother's face died and she doubled over as if she'd been punched in the stomach, twisting slightly to the side. "Good God, Terry, they're killing me."

Fire raged in Terry's eyes as he appraised Stefan and me with fury. "I paid good money to see you both off to college," he growled, his voice low and threatening, "and this is how you repay me? Look at all the mess you two have created for our family!"

Stefan and I exchanged glances, Stefan's of

defiant anger and mine of shame.

Neither of us could offer an answer to Terry. How could we? There was no excuse for what we did.

Stefan and I stood there for the next five minutes, being endlessly berated by Terry, accompanied by an occasional whine from my mother, and we were unable to offer any kind of rebuttal to his furious tirade.

Several times, I attempted to try to speak up in our defense, but Terry would not hear of it. He was on a roll.

Finally, Stefan could take no more. "Will you shut the fuck up already?" he yelled.

Terry froze in his tracks, visibly trembling, eyeing his son with murder. I knew then that we were two seconds away from disaster, and I placed a restraining hand on Stefan's arm.

Stefan swallowed back anger and calmed slightly as he gazed at his dad challengingly. "Look, we already told you everything that happened. Yes, we've always had feelings for each other, but we didn't recognize each other on the first night we had sex. You guys can either believe us or don't, but I'm not going to stand here any longer listening to this bullshit. Yeah, I knocked Bella up. Accept it and move on," Stefan growled, "or get the fuck out of my apartment."

I hoped that his powerful declaration would settle things. Instead, roaring with rage, Terry rushed forward, intent on murdering the insolent Stefan with his bare hands.

Chapter 34
Bella

"Terry, stop!" Emma shouted.

Terry pulled back just before colliding with Stefan as Emma calmly stepped in between them. "No more violence. All you're going to gain is a swift trip to the ER and land Stefan a seat in the local jail cell."

Terry bristled visibly at being told what to do by my grandma, but she stood her ground, unperturbed. Finally, Terry let out a disgusted huff and stepped away, muttering something under his breath about 'meddling old women'.

Though he tried to hide it, I saw relief flash in Stefan's eyes as Terry backed down.

Emma glanced once at Stefan, making sure he wasn't planning any other inflammatory statements. Satisfied, she nodded and turned her gaze on me.

"How far along are you?" she asked me. In her eyes, I saw compassion and understanding and I was almost moved to tears.

I glanced down at my stomach. "About 12 or so weeks."

Relief swept through my grandmother's face. "Good, maybe we can—"

"Get rid of it."

My mother's cold words cut through me like a knife and I stared at her with horror.

"What?" I gasped. Beside me, I felt Stefan stiffen in anger.

My mother's face was emotionless as she returned my stare, as if she'd been shocked into numbness. "Get rid of the baby. The sooner the better."

"How can you say that?" It was hard to draw air into my lungs. The life growing inside me was my mother's soon-to-be-grandchild. I couldn't believe that she could so callously dismiss its potential chance at life just because the father was Stefan.

Her voice was firm and even. "You have your whole life ahead of you. Why throw it all away on a foolish mistake? The love you two claim to feel for each other is not real. It can't be, so stop pretending that it is. You're both just confused."

I couldn't believe it. It was as if our secret had put my mother into total denial. "Come on, now," my mom urged, holding her hand out to me as I stood there in a horrified daze. "I'll take you to the clinic myself."

"Listen to your mother, Bella," Terry added, as if someone asked for his fucking input. "It would be best for you to do it now before it's too late to do anything about it."

I couldn't find the strength for a response, my knees incredibly weak. They wanted to kill my baby—*Our* baby. It wasn't fair.

"Don't you think you two are being just a little too harsh on Bella?" Emma asked.

"No," my parents responded in unison.

Emma gave a pleading look to my mother. "I love Bella dearly, and I want what's best for her just like you do, but she's an adult. She can make her own decision."

My mother scowled at Emma. "How can you defend this? You, most of all, should be outraged by what's happened here!"

"Because it's happened before," Emma replied calmly in the face of Mother's wrath.

No wonder she's been so calm this whole time, I thought. *She's totally used to this.*

That gave Mom pause, a look of bewilderment twisting her features. "What are you talking about?"

Emma nodded gravely. "Your own union with Terry is one such an example. You know, Terry is Baron's nephew . . . my nephew."

Mom rolled her eyes. "Oh please, Mother, that isn't even close to the same thing. Terry and I were grown with children of our own already!"

"Even still, they're not blood related. It may be frowned upon, but it's not that big of a deal, Evelyn."

Mom growled and turned back to me. "Come, Bella. You don't have to make a decision today, but at least let us go talk to a counselor about this. I'll help you through the entire process."

Abortion. The thought sizzled inside my brain like bacon in a frying pan. It was something I'd tried not to think about, but it had loomed in the back of my mind like the boogie man.

Now the boogie man had been let out.

Before I could reply, Stefan stepped in front of me. "Bella isn't going anywhere," he announced flatly. There was none of the insolence, none of the smart mouth that had been in his voice only minutes before. Instead, there was just a rock-solid determination, an unwavering belief in what he was saying, in us and in our baby. In that instant, I watched as Stefan truly became a man. "And you can quit trying to convince her that she should terminate the pregnancy. We're having the baby, and that's final."

"Listen to what you're saying, son," Terry advised. "You want to have a baby with Bella, Stefan? With Bella. Your stepsister."

Stefan nodded. "I do. And?"

Terry hissed with exasperation. "And what do you expect will happen when you have the baby and people find out that you are the father, huh? Do you know what kind of shame that will bring down upon our family? Or the damage it will do my reputation?"

Stefan shrugged to say it didn't matter. "Who cares? It's no one's business but ours," he said quickly when Terry's face grew red with rage. "Bring on the world. I'll tell it the same thing. I love Bella, and I'm glad she's having my baby."

Before Terry could explode, my grandmother saved us all again. "I know how we can keep things safe and secure—for now, at least," she suggested, surprising everyone in the room. "Make sure that Bella's baby is born healthy and in a good home, and that you'll both have futures."

Though my parents looked appalled, Stefan looked intrigued and gave Emma a slight nod. "Go on."

"Let Bella come back with me to the Livingston manor. She can stay there in complete privacy. Meanwhile, you can return to school and resume your sports career, satisfying your father in the process." My grandma gave me a warm smile. "You would so enjoy the estate now. Your grandfather has done several renovations since you last visited."

Memories of playing with Stefan on the estate

grounds with green grass that spanned several acres flashed through my mind, and warmth spread throughout my chest.

At Emma's suggestion, a thoughtful expression showed on at least Terry's face, but Stefan was immediately shaking his head. "Thanks, Grandma Em, but I can't do that. Bella will be staying with me. I'm not going to leave her on her own."

For the first time since I could remember, my mother seemed to grow angry with Stefan. "You promised me, Stefan," she growled, her voice choking with emotion. "You promised me that you would take care of Bella . . . and I trusted you. I believed in you. I thought you really cared about Bella's best interests. Now this?"

Stefan looked ashamed, but still, he was man enough, proud enough to stand up for what he did. "I know, and I'm sorry, Evelyn—"

My mother raised a sharp finger to cut off his reply. "You're not fit to speak for Bella. She doesn't need you controlling her every move at a time like this. What she needs is someone to talk sense into her about the huge mistake she is about to make with her life." My mother turned to me. "Bella, sweetheart, honey, please listen to me. I don't know if Stefan is controlling you, or what is really going on here, but I need you to understand that once you go through with this decision to have the baby, there is no turning back. Please let me take you where we can discuss all the options available to you."

You don't care about my options, I wanted to scream at my mother. *You just want me to kill the baby.*

A black cloud seemed to press down on my chest and it became hard to breathe.

Surprisingly, Emma spoke up on the side of my mother. "Stefan, you must let Bella decide. You're not helping the situation by making life-altering decisions for her. If you really love her as you say, you'll let her have some freedom."

Stefan stared at Emma for a long time before nodding in acceptance and stepped away from me. "You're right. This is Bella's decision here. I'll let Bella decide what she wants to do if that will make you all shut up. Bella?"

He turned to me, his eyes full of hope and love, and a little bit of fear as well, fear that I'd go with my mom, but he knew he had to trust me now. "What do you want to do? Do you want to stay with me or go with them?"

My answer was immediate. Sure, we'd made a lot of mistakes. We should have come clean on this as soon as things started going to hell. But standing there, his eyes shining with new-found maturity and the love they contained, I knew all my worries in the past were phantoms, and I needed to trust him as much as he was trusting me.

"I'm staying with Stefan," I said after I found the spit to moisten my dry mouth. "I don't want to go anywhere or talk to a counselor because I plan on having the baby . . . no matter what."

Stefan let out a sigh of relief, and our parents began laying into me again, trying to make me see reason. Mom was worried about some mythical future, about a social reputation. Terry was thinking about his company and the family name. Neither of them said one thing about Stefan or me. It pissed me off. They were thinking only about themselves.

"That's enough," Stefan said loudly over them after they'd started repeating themselves, and he could see I was about to scream at them. "You heard Bella's decision. She isn't giving up the baby, no matter how hard you browbeat her otherwise. Now that the issue is finally settled, if you can't respect her decision as an adult, you can all just leave."

Our parents resumed yelling, calling Stefan out on how hypocritical he was, but Emma interrupted them.

"You heard Stefan. He wants us to leave. I know it irks you both as their parents to be kicked out, but they are adults and this whole thing is going nowhere." She glanced uneasily between Stefan and Terry. "Lord knows, we don't want another fight to break out."

"You heard Grandma," Stefan reinforced, pointing at the front door. "Go."

Emma walked over to the front door and held it open, motioning to my parents. "Come on, you two. There is nothing left we can do for now."

Mom glared at us both for a long while before throwing up her hands in exasperation. "Fine!"

Shaking her head, she walked out of the apartment, not deigning to throw me a second glance. Grandma, however, paused at the door, giving us an appraising look. I wondered—it had been so long since we'd spent a lot of time together. Just how much wisdom, how much did I miss not going to see her before? She nodded once, and while she didn't smile, she wasn't pissed off, either. She was worried, but still, there was a look of respect in her eyes when she saw Stefan come over and put his arm around my shoulders, and I wrapped my arms around his waist.

"The invitation to come out to the estate is still there. Goodbye for now, you two."

"Bye, Grandma," we said in unison.

Chapter 35
Stefan

"I can't believe what just happened," Bella said quietly when our parents were gone. "That was the most embarrassing thing ever."

Her arms were crossed across her chest, and she stood there in her short shorts and tattered crop top, looking vulnerable. She looked so beautiful to me in that moment, so sweet. I held out my hand, and she clasped it, letting me pull her into an embrace.

"I know it was tough," I whispered, knowing it was the understatement of the century but not wanting to dredge up the bad shit that had just happened. "But in some ways, I'm glad it's finally in the light of day."

"Why didn't you lock the door?" Bella demanded, her voice sharp. "Jesus, Stefan, if we had just locked the damn door!"

The me that I'd been even a few hours before would have gotten pissed off. Hell, maybe I was still pissed off, but I was so over the line that I didn't know it. Instead, I hugged her tighter, holding her close. "Whatever the reason, it doesn't matter. Bella, you don't know how much it meant to me when you said you'd stay."

Bella swallowed, looking down. "I'm sorry."

It wasn't the answer I was expecting. "What do you mean, sorry? Bella, in that one answer, you told me that you loved me, that we're doing the right thing, and that somehow, for all the fuckups I've made, you've still got faith in me. I promise you, when I figure out how we're going to get out of this—"

Bella held up her hand. "Stop right there, Stefan."

I was confused and tilted my head. "Stop what?"

Bella looked up at me with a hint of her old fire, the same light that I'd taken for bitchiness, the same desire for power that she'd only shown flashes of since we found out she was pregnant. "Stefan, I love you. And I've learned over the time we've been together that I like taking care of you. Hell, I like cooking you breakfast and washing your funky ass socks. But I can't just sit back and let you do everything. Now, I understand that you want to work to save me some physical stress, but we can't do it alone anymore. You can't just expect me to sit here on my rapidly expanding ass while you figure things out by yourself! I've got a brain too, you know!"

I stopped, stunned by the determination in her voice and the glint in her eyes. I nodded, licking my lips. "You're right. I haven't respected you sometimes. But I don't want you to be working. Like you said, it's for the baby."

"Then we'll figure something out together," Bella said, still determined. "Stefan, at the Governor's party, you called me your future wife. If you really meant that, if you want me to be your wife, then we need to be a team. No athlete, I don't care how much of a superstar he or she is, wins without a team."

Her eyes were filled with fire, her tiny little fists balled by her side, and I stood in momentary awe at the strength of my Bella. She was so determined, and maybe that was what had been missing from all of our efforts. I'd been trying to do it all by myself, and I even worked to stop Bella every time she tried to help or even to offer an idea. But if I was going to make a life with her, to have a baby with her, it was going to have to be a team effort. Finally, I nodded. "Okay."

She stopped, stunned. "Okay?"

I nodded, smirking. "Would you like a poem or something? You're right. I've been fucking up as much as I've been doing the right things. I need you, and that means all of you."

Silence wrapped around us and my eyes fell to her chest. I could see the swell of her nipple buds pressing against the torn fabric. Blood rushed below, causing my pants to tighten.

Horny as fuck now, I pulled Bella into a passionate kiss.

"What are you doing?" Bella gasped breathlessly when I finally allowed her to breathe. "I mean, I'm happy you're going to listen to me, but—"

I pushed her back onto the couch and tore off her shorts, my mouth watering as I prepared to go down on her with a vengeance.

"I'm going to celebrate by finishing what we started before they came in," I growled. "I'm going to make love with my future wife."

Bella's moan started even before I got to my knees, kissing up her long leg and across the inside of her thigh. I've never had a problem going down on a girl, considering the number of times they've gone down on me, but with Bella, it was different. I loved licking her sweet pussy. There was a heady aroma, a sweetness to the taste that was different.

Or maybe I was just nuts, and it was special

because it was Bella's.

I didn't care as I let my tongue drift over her lips, relishing the texture. Bella didn't totally shave. She kept a little 'landing patch' up top, but her lips themselves were as smooth as silk, sensitive and tender to my touch.

The effect was just what I wanted. Bella gasped, reaching up to pinch her nipples herself while her left hand went to my head, urging me on. "Mmm, Stefan . . ."

"I love you," I mumbled into her pussy, her thighs and soft skin blurring my words, but her fingers tightened in my hair. She got the message.

I ran my tongue up and down her tender lips, teasing Bella a little, just the way she liked it, before I slid my tongue between her wet folds, driving it as deep as I could inside her to feast on the dark tanginess that was her essence. Her hips lifted off the mattress and I grabbed her ass cheeks, loving the extra curves that she'd added. Forget the concern about baby weight. Bella had become thick in all the right places. Holding onto her ass, I didn't let up at all, wiggling my tongue until I couldn't get any deeper.

Bella rewarded me with a deep moan that started in the middle of her chest, her fingers tugging on my hair as I pulled my tongue out to nibble and suck on her clit just the way she liked, running my tongue around it before sucking hard on it. "STEFAN!"

She screamed so loudly that I wondered if our neighbors heard us, but then I realized I didn't give a shit. Let the whole world know. Hell, let Veronica release our sex tape on the six o'clock news. I loved Bella, and if I could make her this happy, who cared?

Bella screamed again, no words but just a deep cry of pleasure as she came, soaking my face in her juices and her hand yanking out a few of my hairs before it tore free to beat against the cushions, tossing her head side to side as she rode it out, delirious.

When it finally passed, Bella collapsed, gasping against the back of the couch. "Holy fuck, you were more amazing than normal."

I stayed on my knees, taking her hand. "You deserve the best I can be."

Bella chuckled and ran her hand through my hair again. "Well, give me a few minutes, and I'll show you the best *I* can be. Have I told you that one of my pregnancy hunger urges is your come?"

I raise an eyebrow, smirking. "No, but now that I know, I can think of great ways to add to breakfast in the mornings."

Chapter 36
Stefan

"Holy shit!" Bella exclaimed from the kitchen, where she'd just gotten off the phone.

It was several days after the explosive argument with our parents and our coming to a new agreement with each other. Since then, while Bella and I were enjoying every new day as we explored our new level of relationship, our parents hadn't called or tried to check on us, but I knew they were planning something. I just didn't know what.

It made me nervous as fuck.

Sitting on the couch, I looked up from my laptop and over at Bella. I'd just sent in yet another application to another company for a job. It was hard finding a decent job without a college degree, and I refused to work a minimum wage job. The type of money I would make flipping burgers was just not enough to support Bella and me. Unfortunately, if I didn't find a steady job soon, that's exactly what I'd be doing.

Maybe I can try my hand at modeling again, I wondered.

The last company had accepted me in less than twenty-four hours. They had really wanted me for the job, stating that I had the looks of a Hollywood movie star and the type of face that could sell millions of magazines. Obviously, if I couldn't use my brains to support Bella, maybe I could use my looks.

"What?" I asked curiously.

"That was Sara Delany who just called."

"Sara?"

"Yeah, the girl I roomed with back at school. Remember?"

"Oh yeah," I said, remembering the girl who had greeted me at Bella's dorm and eyed me like I was a piece of meat. They'd stayed in touch, although Bella and I had both agreed to wait a little longer before making the general public aware of our relationship. There was a chance to rebuild a relationship with our family, so we weren't ready to nuke that bridge just yet. "What'd she say?"

Bella walked out of the kitchen and over into the middle of the living room. She was wearing some of her short shorts that always got me hot under the collar and a light pink top. The shorts hugged her hips and showed off her growing ass. She still wasn't sure I wasn't bullshitting her, but I felt pregnancy had done her body good, filling her out in all the right places, and it was hard to keep my eyes off her. "You're not going to believe it."

"Spit it out already."

"Well, first, she said the school has finally concluded its investigation. Both institutions will remain open. Kappa Beta was hit with probation, but Alpha Gamma basically got off clean, which is not surprising at all." She paused dramatically and her expression became darker. "Second . . . it's Veronica."

My heart jumped in my chest, but I kept my

expression cool as a thousand doomsday thoughts ran through my head, mainly about our sex tape that I knew Veronica still had in her possession.

Had the bitch spread it to the internet now? I might not have cared if people knew that I loved Bella if they found out, but there's a big difference between declaring my love and having my dingus on the Internet for everyone to see. But if she was up to something else, there wasn't shit I could do about it.

"She quit school."

I looked up at Bella with surprise.

"Quit?"

Bella nodded, and I could tell she was trying not to crack up laughing. "Yeah, Sara said that someone in Alpha finally cracked and told everyone in Alpha and Kappa that Veronica had planted the camera. Apparently, she was planning on blackmailing me over the Sacrifice no matter what. Hanna, the Kappa president, found her diary, and Veronica had hated me from first semester, for some damn reason. She wanted to ruin me no matter what and get me to quit school."

"Damn," I muttered. "That's fucked up. Why?"

Bella shook her head. "I don't know for sure, but I think it was even before the stupid damn dildo sucking contest. During one of the Rush Week parties, a guy hit on me. I heard afterward that Veronica had her eyes on him. I didn't fuck him, but neither did Veronica. I'd blown it off. He was a drunken asshole. I guess the bitch didn't." I was taken aback by the hatred burning in Bella's eyes, but I suppose I shouldn't have been surprised. Veronica had done some really fucked up shit to us, and the worst thing about it was, none of it made sense. To try and ruin a girl's life over a drunken idiot hitting on you? Fuck my life.

She got exactly what she deserved as far as I'm concerned, I thought to myself. *And she's lucky she didn't end up with worse. Fucking with people's family is asking for bad shit to happen.*

"She's lucky," I finally said. I shook my head. "We don't like her, but if she had done that to some of the people I know on campus . . . a lot of crazy, messed up dudes have no qualms putting their hands on women. I knew a couple back at Alpha."

Bella's face darkened into a scowl. "Jace being one of them."

I grinned at her. "Yeah, but he got his."

Bella giggled. "And now Veronica is getting hers."

"Yeah. I just hope she learned her lesson, although as long as she stays out of our lives, I don't give a shit anymore."

My phone thrummed inside my pocket, and I quickly snatched it out and answered it without looking at the caller ID, hoping that it was someone calling me back about a job interview.

"Hello?"

"Stefan."

I held back a groan and contemplated hanging up. "What do you want, Dad?" I asked finally.

"I just want to have a real talk with you."

"Didn't I tell you that I'm not going to discuss Bella's and my relationship with you? The answer is still the same."

"Just give me a minute, Stefan."

"No, Dad."

"I'll make it worth your while."

I paused. I could read between the lines. My father was offering money. Considering how I hadn't gotten any job offers yet, I could definitely use some. But there was no way I was going to accept a bribe in exchange for discussing Bella terminating the pregnancy. That subject was finished. Over and done with. The same with me staying with Bella.

"Just hear me out. If you don't like what I have to say, then you can leave and I'll never bother you about the matter again."

"I'll think about it," I said finally, hanging up.

"What did he want?" Bella asked, placing her hands on her hips, unknowingly enticing me with her sexy curves.

I shrugged and sat back against the couch, spreading my legs out. With the stress pressing down on my shoulders, I could've really used a quickie right about now, but I didn't want to ask. Maybe we did have sex every day, but I didn't want her to think that was the extent of our relationship.

"The usual. He wants to talk."

Bella pushed a section of her hair away from her face. Since her pregnancy, her hair had gotten really thick. I liked it. "Mom's been calling me too," she said quietly. "Mostly, when you're asleep or out looking for a job. I ignore her."

"Maybe we need to look at changing that," I said as I stood up.

Bella stared at me in surprise. "Where are you going?"

"I'm going to talk to Dad."

Shock spread across Bella's delicate features. "What's brought on this change of attitude? A few days ago, you didn't want to say shit to them."

I scratched the back of my neck. "I did, but Dad said he had an offer for me. I want to at least see what it is before I ignore him altogether." I walked forward and pulled Bella into my arms, delivering a soft kiss to her lips. "But mainly, I'm going because I want to drive the point home to him that we are going to be a couple for a very long time, and he needs to get used to it. Otherwise, he doesn't have to be in our lives."

Bella drew back, suspicious. "Stefan, you know he's going to try and talk you into breaking up with me. Or talk about terminating our baby."

"Which is exactly why I want to talk to him," I reassure her. "Bella, he said he'd make it worth my while. Now, if he's got his head out of his ass, then maybe there's a way for me to get good work. Health insurance, a decent paycheck—think about it. And it's just to talk. If he's an asshole, I'm out of there."

Bella smiled, though I could see the uncertainty in her eyes. "Good." She returned my kiss, albeit hesitantly, and I resisted the urge to grab and squeeze her ass. I didn't want to get hard before going to see my dad.

"I'll be back as soon as possible," I told her as I broke away and made my way to the door. "Keep those clothes on until I get home." I let the hunger I felt for her sexy body drip into my voice.

"I will," Bella promised, sounding breathless at the promise of what was to come. "And if my mom calls?"

I stop for a second, then turn back, giving her a

grin. "I trust you. Tell her I said hi."

* * *

"I'm offering you a job as my right hand man at the company," my dad offered, sitting back in his office chair with an audible creak.

I was sitting across from him inside a mobile trailer that he often used for a make-shift office whenever he moved between construction sites. Considering the problems that he got up to with his laptop in this office, I wondered why the hell he kept it. But now wasn't the time to focus on that.

His teams of employees were hard at work outside, building some sort of mom and pop motel that was a quarter of the way done. Some of them had greeted me with enthusiasm when I arrived on site, wondering where I'd been. They missed my presence since I'd been such a hard worker and easy to get along with.

I didn't really say why I'd stopped showing up at work, just that I had some things I had to take care of. They got the point that it was something I didn't want to share, and they pointed me to Dad's trailer.

Things hadn't started well. No sooner had I gotten inside than my dad began immediately making offers to me, hoping that I would be desperate enough to accept.

"Or, I can totally forgive the money I wasted on your last semester and pay for you to go back to school, where you can still pursue your sports career."

I shook my head. "I don't need money to go back to school. I already have a scholarship offer from Coach Carter back at South State."

My dad gaped at me incredulously. "You have an

offer like that and you haven't taken it?"

"No."

"What the hell is wrong with you, boy?" my father demanded. "Being a professional athlete has always been your dream. Why would you turn down a second chance?"

I clenched my jaw. "You know why. I might, just maybe, be able to juggle being a father and a college student. There's no way in hell that I can be a good father, a student, and a sports player."

"And? Though I've never seen a future in sports for myself, I knew you were different. I've seen you play. You are absolutely amazing. You could be the next big thing, Stefan."

My dad was totally stroking my ego. On one hand, I dismissed what he was saying outright, but a part of me, my egomaniac side, was sucking up his lavish praise.

Coach Carter's words replayed in my head.

We need you, Stefan. I've never seen a kid play as well as you.

I shifted in my seat and glanced at my dad's cell that he had sitting in front of him. I wondered if it was the same cellphone he used to text Veronica dirty messages. "I just don't see how you can expect me to do what you want. We're talking about your grandchild, for crying out loud."

"I'm looking at the bigger picture, Stefan. You're my primary concern. You guys still have a chance to set things right. I think you should forget about Bella, forget about having a baby. I mean, why is it so hard for you to understand? You two can't be together. I think you are both just young and confused. Give it some time, and you'll see. You'll grow out of it." My dad leaned forward in his chair. "Come work for me or go do the sports thing. I don't care. Just don't have that baby."

My dad had some nerve. What did he expect me to do? Just abandon Bella after I promised her that I would be there for her? If I accepted my dad's offer to work with him, or Coach Carter's, I would be abandoning Bella.

"Stefan, most guys your age would jump at the chance to get out of a situation such as this."

"Most guys my age don't love the girl they have sex with either."

My dad's face twisted with disgust. "You can't really believe what you're saying." My dad paused to take a deep breath. "Look, we're just going in circles here. I'm giving you a way out of this situation. Take it. Convince Bella. Her mother will help her through the entire process."

Anger coursed through me. I was mad because I felt like I was finally standing up and becoming the man they've always said they wanted me to be, and my parents wanted to kill the life Bella and I had created. To kill the man I was becoming.

"Sorry, Dad," I said finally. "I can't—I won't—do it. And this will be the last time we talk about the issue, so don't bother calling me anymore unless it's to give me and Bella your blessing."

My father balled his hand into a fist and slammed it against the table, his face red with rage. "You stubborn little shit!" he yelled. "You're ruining everything that I have worked so hard for!"

I rose to my feet, holding back the violent urge to jump across my dad's desk. "This is the last time we'll discuss this issue," I said with a face blank of emotion, and then I turned and walked out of his office.

The last I heard was my dad yelling, "You're making a mistake, Stefan!"

Maybe. But I'd make a bigger mistake in doing what he wanted.

Chapter 37
Bella

"What did he say?" I asked when Stefan returned later that day.

I was in the midst of dusting the furniture, still dressed in those shorts that always got him going. It helped me deal with the stress of everything, keeping the apartment clean, and I knew Stefan liked it when I cleaned up in skimpy outfits. Besides, his eyes roaming over me reassured me and helped me feel sexy.

"What I expected," he said, walking over and flopping down on the couch. He looked exhausted, and I could understand why. "I'm ruining my life, your life, his and Evelyn's, and I'm going to regret it, blah, blah, blah. That shit."

I set down my duster on the armrest of the love seat and stared at him. There was something he wasn't telling me, and I knew the best way to get him to talk was to just wait him out. Stefan was still getting used to sharing all his thoughts with me, and he shifted around a little before I raised an eyebrow. "And?"

"And he wants to get me to come work at his company again, this time as his right hand man, or return to school to resume my sports career."

Sports career. It was something that had been on my mind too, honestly. "I see."

Stefan slid over on the sofa, pulling me into his arms with a shake of his head and a smile. "Don't worry, I told him no, of course. I mainly went to let him know in no uncertain terms that I'm going to be with you no matter what."

"Okay."

Stefan pulled back and held me at arm's length. "Is something wrong?"

I shrugged, for the first time in a while feeling like I was the one with something to hide. "No, everything is fine."

"Come on, Bella," he growled, obviously frustrated. "Don't give me that. Something is wrong. Now tell me what it is."

I put a hand on my stomach, trying to find the words. "Stefan, you know I love you, and I know you've said that you don't want to go back to sports if it means leaving me—leaving us—but I feel like I'm denying you your chance at greatness. Dammit, Stefan, you're not meant to be some working class schlump! You're Stefan Livingston, goddammit, and that means you're special!"

Stefan blinked, stunned at the heat in my voice, and when he spoke again, it was almost as if he sounded amused. "Special, huh? If there's any reason that I'm special, Bella, it's because of you. Any idiot with good hand-eye coordination and enough dedication can make it to professional lacrosse. It's not like the fucking NBA. If I'm going to be special, though, I want to be a special man. And that means I take care of you, like a man."

"I want you to be both," I whisper, shaking my head. "I want you to have it all."

I let Stefan gather me into his arms, where he kissed my neck tenderly before whispering in my ear. "With you, Bella, I do have it all. We'll make it, I promise you."

"Together?" I asked, and he nodded, his breath tickling my ear and making me hot inside.

"Together. Now, I've got an idea. Would you like to go out to eat?" Stefan asked.

"I thought we were supposed to be conserving money until you got a job?" I asked, trying to keep my mind from just asking him to take me right there on the love seat. Sex is good, but I didn't need to have an orgasm from him every time stress entered my life.

"We are, but you've been in a bad mood lately. Today's been a shitty day with what my dad tried to pull, and I want to do something to lift your spirits. A day out of the house will do you some good."

It was so tempting. We hadn't been getting out of the house much, and I know that some of my stress was because I was going stir crazy. Every phone call from my mother made me jump, even if I wasn't answering. The hypothetical conversations would run around and around in my head for hours afterward instead. And we were getting to the point where I was pinching every penny, checking when we went to the market not for the best tasting foods or the foods that Stefan and I liked, but the foods that we wouldn't hate and would be the cheapest. Basically, it sucked.

Stefan nuzzled my neck, which was about the only reason I wasn't jumping up out of his lap. Let him think I needed a little more convincing. His lips and touch felt damn good. "C'mon, Bella, I can't have you moping around like you have been these past few days. It's starting to bring me down too." He wrapped his arms around my waist, pulling me closer, his breath tickling my ear. "Although, if you want to wait on dinner . . ."

Immediately, I was enveloped by his body heat and I melted into his arms. My pulse began to race in my throat as I felt his cock through his jeans pressed up against my ass.

Stefan lowered his lips to my neck, setting my skin ablaze. My lips parted into a sigh in response. I couldn't believe I'd thought we could stop from jumping each other constantly. He practically oozed sex, but I wanted to not be seen as a slut. But with Stefan, who cared if I was? He was my man, I was his woman, and the way his hand felt as he started rubbing my stomach, I didn't care if I was a slut or not.

"We can even buy a few baby clothes," Stefan whispered in my ear, using his secret weapon, the tip of his tongue tracing the curve of my earlobe before he nibbled gently. He resumed kissing me all over my neck and shoulders, running his hands all over my body, and I felt myself moisten between my legs.

"Okay," I cried when I could take no more. "You win. I'll go."

I turned my head to look into Stefan's grinning face, trying not to laugh as he grinned at me. "I knew you would see it my way. I have ways of bending you to my will."

He slapped me on the ass, making it wiggle a little and making us both laugh. "Now go get ready so we can get back fast. I have another surprise for you."

* * *

"Wasn't that great?" Stefan asked as we walked back into the apartment.

I walked over and set down several shopping bags that were filled with baby outfits and some new stretch sweatpants for me. I knew it was stupid to still feel insecure, especially with all the sex we'd been having, but I hated getting the pants. They were so unflattering and so unsexy, but I was starting to have trouble getting into my normal sized clothes. To even things out, I'd gotten a couple of short shorts that were several sizes bigger than the ones I normally wore. Stefan loved my ass, and if I had a way to show it off, I would for him.

"Yeah, I did," I replied. "And I'm so glad I went." Truthfully, I had the most fun since arriving at the apartment with Stefan. After all the stress I'd gone through—the Sacrifice, the school's investigation, the harassment by the assholes at NSU, and lastly, our parents discovering our secret—it was just what I needed to relieve a bit of stress.

At the restaurant, Stefan had been the perfect gentleman, holding out the seat for me and telling me to order whatever I wanted. Over lunch, we'd reminisced over old times together and talked about our future.

After, we'd gone shopping in the mall. Once again, Stefan told me to buy whatever I wanted. When I resisted, he was adamant that I do it. He wanted me to feel better. He'd just put everything I wanted on credit. I just worried about how he was going to pay for it with dwindling resources and no job.

"I can't remember the last time I had so much fun."

Stefan grinned at me. "I can. The first night we fucked."

I gaped. "Stefan!"

He laughed, shrugging. "Well, it's the truth! I'll never forget that night."

My mind wandered back to the night that started all this mess. "And neither will I," I whispered.

"And now it's time to have more of that fun," Stefan said huskily. He walked over to me and pulled me into his arms. His lips quickly found mine, and he moved his hands over the small of my back, dipping me slightly.

Things were going perfectly when his cell ringtone went off.

Stefan pulled away from me, leaving me breathless, and reached inside his pocket.

"Hello? Oh, hey, Coach Carter."

Hot and bothered, I flopped down on the coach and grabbed a magazine off the coffee table and began fanning myself, trying to get my temperature to go down.

"I don't know, Coach," Stefan said, sending a glance my way. "I don't think I can. Really? That would be wonderful, coach," Stefan said, flashing me a thumbs-up. "I would like that very much. But you know what? I'm busy right now. I'll get back with you about a decision by next week. Okay? Cool. Talk to you then. Bye."

Stefan hung up, turning back to me. "That was just Coach Carter calling again. I swear, that guy is not going to give up." He gave me a look that should have had me ready to climb the walls, but instead, it made me angry. He moved toward me. "Now, where were we—"

"Why don't you just tell him no instead of leading him on all the time?" I cut him off, my tone sounding harsher than I wished.

Stefan froze. "What?"

I swallowed back an angry lump. I was sounding accusatory, but I couldn't help myself. I was filled with fear and anxiety. "Why the hell would you keep telling him that you'll get back with him when you know that you can't?"

Stefan stopped and backed up, raising his hands. "Bella, I was going to wait until after my head's in the right space, but what he said was that I might be able to work something out where I can work and go back to school at the same time. It wouldn't be that hard. In fact, SSU offers programs for students who need work. With my athlete status, it shouldn't be hard getting some help."

"And so all that shit you told me the other day about trying to be a good man and giving up sports—was that just bullshit?" I half yelled, not knowing where it was coming from. My body literally shook with rage. I couldn't believe I was saying these things to Stefan. I had never been so angry with him in my life, and it felt like I was losing control over my emotions. "Were you just playing me this whole time?"

Stefan looked like he'd been struck, his face going pale. "How can you act like this to me? I've done everything I can to help us, and I'll continue. Bella, I just heard the news. I didn't say yes or no, and what the hell's gotten into you? For God's sake, if you tell me you don't want me to go to SSU, I won't go to SSU! I'll go down to the day labor office tomorrow and get a temp job digging ditches if I have to! I just thought it'd be a good idea to try and keep our fucking options open!"

I stood there, my chest heaving, feeling a rainbow of emotions. I didn't know what to do. I wanted to slap, hit, bite, and fuck Stefan all at the same time. But most of all, I had a strong feeling of wanting to escape. Where was this coming from, anyway? "Are you just going to leave me in the lurch if you get a pro offer and I can't follow?"

I didn't wait for an answer. I just I took off down the hallway, sobbing all the way to our bathroom, and slammed the door behind me.

* * *

Stefan

Watching Bella disappear into the bathroom, I stood there, confused and kicking myself. What was going on? I hadn't told her for a thousand reasons. The main one was that I wanted to talk it over calmly with Bella when I was thinking clearly with my brain and not my dick. I was serious. I'd gladly tell Coach Carter to stuff a lax stick up his butt if there was no way I could take care of Bella. But that didn't matter, and yelling at Bella only made things worse, a really stupid thing on my part.

I knocked on her door quietly after a few minutes,

and Bella jerked the door open, her eyes wide with fear. Her shoulders tense, Bella waited as if she was expecting me to start yelling at her again. I realized how much yelling there'd been in our relationship, how much stress and how much difficulty, and I vowed to stop it, right here, right now.

I moved forward and pulled Bella into my arms, where she seemed to collapse with relief against my chest and began to sob. "I'm sorry," I told her with as much conviction and emotion as I could muster. "I'm sorry for everything. For ignoring you, for the stress, for all of it. Bella, all I want is for you to stop being scared, because I'm not going to leave you. Not now, not when you have the baby, not ever. But I only have one thing to ask of you."

Bella pulled back to look up at me, and I took a thumb and wiped away a tear.

"What?"

"Promise me that we keep being open and honest with each other. I can live without lacrosse, without my parents, without money, without being a pro athlete. I can't live without you."

We stood there for a long time, staring at each other, and I could feel Bella's heartbeat against my chest. Each moment that ticked by seemed like an eternity.

When Bella finally answered, her voice had newfound strength within it.

"I promise."

Chapter 38
Bella - Five months later . . .

"The baby looks perfectly healthy," said the sonographer as I lay on the examination table.

I stared at the image on the screen, hardly able to believe what I was seeing, overcome by an array of emotions.

"Look, Stefan," I said, pointing a trembling finger at the image, my eyes filled with tears. "Our baby."

Stefan, who had let his hair grow out past his ears and sported scruffy stubble when he was too busy to shave in the morning, peered at the image, a proud look on his face. "It is."

I placed my hands on either side of my stomach and peered down. I couldn't believe how big I'd gotten. It looked like I had a huge bowling ball stuffed inside my belly.

Despite the difficulties, Stefan was still here, just as he promised.

The most uncomfortable thing about it all was learning how to walk with such a burden. Stefan now jokingly called me "the waddle woman" whenever I had to move. Before, such a joke would have made me question Stefan's love for me, but now, I realized that Stefan truly loved me.

Since that final, dreadful day that I'd accused him of being ready to leave me, our relationship had improved by quite a bit. Through working together and communicating, I'd learned to trust Stefan at his word, and I stopped looking for shadows where there were none. Part of it, I'm sure, was my hormones coming back into balance, but also the two of us learning how to be mature adults. Or at least more mature than we'd been.

On the downside, our parents hadn't talked to us in months. Besides a few 'how are you doing' texts from my mom, I hadn't heard her voice in what seemed like ages. I did worry about her, but there was nothing I could do to make her talk to me.

Grandma Emma had started to call to check on us often, though. When I asked her about my mother, she would reply that our parents were too stubborn to see the truth yet and were still being stiff-necked about our decision to continue on with our relationship and the baby.

When I asked about their marital status, Grandma Emma would say, "Honey, you know about as much as I do about that."

It led me to believe that our parents were still in limbo. I supposed Terry was really fighting to keep my mother's hand. I'd learned to let go of the anger at both of them and wish for the best. For their sake, I hoped they stayed together.

Meanwhile, Stefan had gotten a decent job. It wasn't anything great, working security at a industrial site, but it would be enough for us to get by until I could get a job myself, even if it was part-time.

We'd called Coach Carter at SSU together, Stefan putting him on speaker to deliver the bad news. Carter had taken it well and told Stefan that while he couldn't guarantee him a scholarship, if Stefan did decide to come back to school, he'd get a fair shot as a walk-on, and then a semester after that, there could be a scholarship waiting for him. Past that, there had been no more talk about his sports career. For a while, I was bothered by that. Being a professional athlete had been a life-long dream for Stefan. But Stefan insisted he was happy, and he had even said it was more important that after our baby was born, I go back to school. "You're the one with the real brains, after all," he'd told me. "And I'm cool with that."

So while I wouldn't say we were on Easy Street, life was good. We were looking forward to having our little one, even if no one else was.

"So?" asked the sonographer, who had no idea we were stepbrother and stepsister, looking between us both, "When are you two getting married?"

* * *

Marriage.

The very idea filled me with bliss. I could almost picture it—a beautiful wedding out on a lush green lawn with wine, food, and celebration. I could see myself in a beautiful white gown and Stefan looking GQ in his tux. In the background, our parents smiled happily as we swore our vows and our undying devotion to one another.

Who am I kidding? I thought sourly, interrupting the fluffy thoughts. *No one would come to our wedding.*

The fact of the matter was that no one would ever respect our relationship just because of the taboo aspect.

"Can you stop and get me a plate from that seafood place on James Street before we go home?" I asked Stefan as we pulled out of the hospital parking lot. "I'm craving shrimp, scallops, and oysters like crazy.

Hell, I'm hungry enough to even take on an octopus."

Stefan let out a laugh and then grinned at me. "Sure, if it's tentacles that you want instead of me, I won't stop you. Just let me watch."

I gaped at him and then slapped him on the arm. "Stefan!" I gasped, scandalized. I guess it was another sign of how much he loved me. Even as pregnant as I was, he was still horny for me almost all the time. And any time I did need a little of his 'special juice,' he was always willing. And he'd still reciprocate. "You know I didn't mean it that way, you pervert!"

Stefan laughed again. "You know I'm just joking, babe. I'll get it for you, no problem. Don't want that baby to go hungry." Stefan, who had already treated me well before, had started treating me even more like a princess since that climactic day. Anything I asked, he got it for me, no matter how irritated it made him or even if he didn't feel like it.

I smiled back at him. "We sure don't."

For the rest of the ride to the seafood place, I was filled with thoughts of a happy future with Stefan. A big house, a white picket-fence, and two kids, one boy and one girl. Maybe I was just fantasizing, but fantasies were free, after all. I tried not to think about our parents, who would probably miss out on their grandchildren's lives.

At least they would have Grandma Em, I thought.

I was filled with so much happiness from knowing my baby was healthy and that everything seemed to be going so well that I couldn't contain myself.

"I love you," I blurted suddenly to Stefan, placing my hand on his arm as we approached an intersection.

Stefan looked over at me, and my heart jumped in my chest at the love reflected in his eyes. "And I love you too—"

"Stefan, watch out!" I screamed, my heart going off like a battering ram.

As we entered the intersection, a car came from the side street, running a red light, heading straight toward the driver's side of the car.

"Shit!" Stefan yelled, his veins standing on his neck and biceps as he jerked the steering wheel about violently, with only seconds to react.

Our car went into a violent spin and I became dizzy, but not dizzy enough not to see the car still hurtling toward us.

I let out a blood-curdling scream a moment before impact.

The next thing I heard, as my body was jerked violently against the seatbelt, was screeching metal, shattering glass, and a crunching sound.

And then nothing.

Chapter 39
Bella

My eyes fluttered open. I let out a groan. My body felt sore all over, especially my lower body and my belly. Every second that I was awake, the pain seemed to magnify until I could hardly stand it.

"I'm glad you're finally coming to," said a voice in the background. "You've been out for a while."

I tried to look at whoever spoke, but I was still groggy and the room was just a blur. After several moments of rapid blinking, I could make out a few shapes. A chair there. A white-coated figure there, standing over me.

Where was I? What had happened to me? Why was I in what seemed to be a hospital room?

"We are so lucky to have you with us."

I looked up into a white-haired man's face and then down at the name tag on his white coat. Even with blurred vision, I could make out the words *Dr. Warner*.

A doctor.

Suddenly, everything came back to me and I remembered everything right before the accident.

"My baby," I cried, not caring about what was going to happen to me. I clutched my stomach, feeling all over it, but I immediately pulled my hands back at the sharp pain that greeted me. For the first time since waking up, I felt something beyond the pain. Emptiness. I somehow felt empty inside.

Oh, no.

I was suddenly filled with overpowering dread that made me want to vomit at the doctor's feet.

And what about Stefan?

I didn't want to think about it. We'd been through so much, only to have everything ripped from us by a cruel, tragic twist of fate.

The doctor looked at me gravely, and I swear that I felt like I would die in the hospital bed at that exact moment.

"I am very sorry, Bella," the doctor sad sadly. "But we had to perform emergency surgery. The accident caused you to go into premature labor."

Unable to control myself any longer, I burst into tears.

Stefan

I came awake with a gasp. I felt like shit. My body was sore all over, but as a trained athlete, I was used to aches and pains. I shook off the effects of whatever drug I was under and sat up.

I was in a hospital bed, hooked up to a machine. I was naked, garbed in one of those shitty hospital gowns. There were several wires attached to my bare chest and an IV feed going through my arm.

At the foot of my bed, there was a nurse who had a guilty look on her face, and I realized that I'd been lying with my legs spread and I'd somehow kicked my sheet down. I can guess what she'd been looking at, and while I'd normally be flattered, I didn't have time to worry about that.

"Where am I?" I asked her, shaking my head to try and get the rest of whatever they'd injected me with out of my damn head.

She blushed deeply and quickly said, "St George's Hospital."

"Where is Bella?"

The nurse lowered her eyes. "The woman you were in an accident with is fine, but . . ."

"But?" I demanded, feeling more agitated by the second, my abs clenching from anxiety.

"We had to do surgery."

That was all I needed to hear.

"Sir, what are you doing?" the nursed demanded as I began ripping the wires from my body. The IV hurt like hell coming out, but I didn't give a shit. "You've been in a horrible accident and need rest. I need you to lie back down—"

I shoved the nurse's hands away and hopped out of the bed. I stumbled when I landed, off-balance, pain shooting up my side and dizziness threatening to overtake me.

With great effort, I shrugged it all off. Then, ignoring the nurse's protests, I stumbled out of the room. I half-ran, half-stumbled down the hallway. I had no idea where I was going, but I was determined.

I had to find Bella.

I tried to round a corner and lost my balance, crashing into a food cart and groaning as my side was pierced with pain again, so blinding that I sagged to the tile floor, staring at the linoleum and trying to just breathe.

Someone knelt beside me, and I heard a calming,

gentle voice. "Stefan, I'm Dr. Jackson. I'm your attending. Listen, you've got two cracked ribs. Running into food carts isn't going to help you."

"Don't fucking care," I whispered, the loudest sound I could make. "Where's Bella?"

"You really should go back to bed," Dr. Jackson started, but I pushed his hands away and tried to get to my feet.

"Fuck you, Doc. The woman I love, the mother of my child, just had surgery, and you're telling me to go to bed? Fuck you."

I staggered to my feet, but Dr. Jackson was with me, gesturing with a free hand to someone. "Fine, be that way. I'll help you to her, just . . . sit down in the wheelchair, okay?"

I did, slumping into the chair that was being held by a nurse as Dr. Jackson talked with someone on a intercom phone, then whispered in the nurse's ear. She pushed me to the elevator, taking us up to the ninth floor, which I noticed was listed as *OB/GYN-NICU*. I'd seen enough medical shows to know what NICU was. "What's wrong with Bella?"

"I don't know," the nurse said soothingly. "I just got a room number. Don't worry, it's in the regular OB area. I'll get you to her."

I sagged against the chair, trying not to cry. I was so worried as the elevator seemed to take forever and a day to get us there. When the door opened, we turned right, the nurse pointing out the room to me. "Stop," I said, holding up my hand. "I can walk into the room. I insist."

The nurse looked like she was about to argue, but

she stopped the wheelchair, helping me to my feet. "I'll wait right here if you need assistance."

I nodded gratefully and opened the door. The first sound I heard was sobbing, and my heart stopped in my chest as I saw Bella bent over something, a nightmare flashing through my head in an instant. "Bella? Oh no, baby, what happened?"

Bella looked up, tears streaming down her face, but instead of looking sad, she looked . . . joyous.

It was then that I noticed the doctor and two nurses in there with Bella, and all of them were smiling too.

"Look, Stefan," she cooed, holding out the bundle of joy that she held in her arms. "Isn't he beautiful?"

I stopped, all my pain forgotten as I saw a squirm and then a sleeping little face surrounded by swaddling clothes in her hands. I stepped forward, taking him in my arms and looking into his face. "You mean . . . ?"

Bella nodded, sobbing and laughing for joy. "Say hello to your son, Daddy."

Chapter 40
Bella

"He's gorgeous," my mom murmured, peering down into my arms.

"Little Rylan Livingston," I said proudly from my hospital bed, beaming so hard that it felt like my face would crack.

Just before Stefan had shown up in my hospital room, the nurses had arrived with my baby wrapped up in blankets, and I was shocked to find out that he'd survived the crash. Apparently, the impact had induced labor, but other than that, he was fine. He was a fighter, just like his dad.

The doctors had been forced to perform an emergency C-section on me. I wasn't pleased with the large scar it had left. In fact, my stomach and waist area felt like hell, but they'd given me a shot of something that was taking care of the worst of it. The doctors told me if I was attentive to the area when I left the hospital and put a lot of oils and Vitamin-E on it, it would most likely heal and leave very little scar tissue because of my young age.

My first thought was that I hoped she was right, but then the newer voice, the voice that had been growing inside me since Stefan held me and told me that he loved me no matter what, said that I could live with the scar. After all, it was where the precious bundle in my arms had come from.

Then, shortly after Stefan had shown up, my

parents rushed into the room frantically, worried about our well-being. They received the shock of their life when they saw me, Stefan, and the baby, though.

Not all of it was me and Rylan, although we were getting most of the attention. The car had hit us on Stefan's side, which probably saved our baby's life, as all I got were the effects of a seatbelt being jerked into my body. Still, all the athletic ability in the world couldn't save Stefan from looking like he'd taken a beating. The list was pretty impressive—a broken cheekbone, a broken nose, a dislocated left shoulder with a torn muscle that I didn't know how to pronounce, and two cracked ribs. Guess airbags aren't perfect after all.

My mother tore her eyes from the baby and nodded approvingly. "That's a good name," she complimented. There was the sound of bitter sweetness in her voice. In a way, I knew she was happy that she had a grandbaby, but in another way, she wasn't happy about how he came to be. Also, it sounded like there was a note of regret in her voice. I hoped it was regret for the way she'd been acting. We couldn't rewind the past to let her be a part of my pregnancy, but I hoped she could be part of Rylan's life.

The best thing about it was that I understood where she was coming from. I'd missed her too. And even though I felt like she'd deserted me when I really needed her, I was happy that she'd cared enough to be here with me now.

She brought her eyes back to the bundle. "He looks just like Stefan."

I nodded, smiling, unable to hide my joy, even from my slightly disapproving mother. I think Mom was hoping Rylan had a few more of my features, but they were there. They were just a little deeper. "He does."

"And he'll be an All-Star athlete," Stefan chimed in. "Like me. And he's going to be smart like his mother, just you wait and see."

"I don't doubt it," Terry muttered, eyeing the baby with a stoic expression.

Dressed in an expensive business suit, Terry stood by Stefan, off to the side and just behind Evelyn's shoulder. He'd opted not to hold the baby, and instead chose to view him from afar.

Terry, I thought, was having a harder time accepting it than my mother was, but at least he was here. It showed that he at least cared in some fashion.

After a moment of cooing, my mother looked back to me. "I'm so glad you two are all right." She shook her head, tears showing in her eyes. "My heart nearly stopped when the highway patrolmen showed up at my door."

"I thought we were dead meat," I said, explaining to them exactly what happened.

"Thank God," my mother said when I was done. Tears came to her eyes, and emotion choked her voice as she put a comforting hand on my arm. "I'll never desert you again, no matter what happens or what you do."

I suppose I should have been bitter that it took this to bring her to her senses, but I wasn't. I was just filled with happiness that me, Stefan, and the baby were okay and that my parents were here.

"Thank you, Mom," I said, nearly choking on my tears.

"Your grandmother has offered for you two to stay

at the Livingston manor while you recover from your wounds," Terry said, scratching at the collar of his suit. He seemed uncomfortable by the display of affection between me and my mother and was looking for a way to fill the silence. "She knows that you're going to need a lot of help with the baby while you get back on your feet and wants to help out in any way she can. She said when we called her that she'd be here as soon as she got into town."

It should be you guys offering this, I thought. *And not her.*

But then again, our parents were going through a divorce. Apparently, despite their best efforts, things hadn't been that civil, and the house wasn't a place that was good for a baby right now. That, I could at least understand.

The news had hit me hard, but I couldn't let it get in the way of things. Not with Rylan and not with Stefan, and I promised myself that I wouldn't follow down the same path. I could see in Stefan's eyes that he was thinking the same thing. *Not us. We're not going to make the same mistakes.*

"That's so sweet of her," I replied with a glance at Stefan. "Just so like Grandma Em."

Terry cleared his throat. "And I'd also like to tell you both that even though we are going through a divorce right now, we have decided that we're going to start being more civil . . . for your sake and the baby's. If we would have lost you, we would have never forgiven ourselves. No matter what we're going through, we will be there for you. Stefan, I can see it in your eyes, and you're right, we dropped the ball on all of this. Evelyn,

I'm sorry. For all of it, but most of all . . . I'm sorry that I wasn't the man I promised you I would be."

Stefan and I exchanged surprised glances. It must have taken a lot for Terry to say that.

But nobody seemed more surprised than Mom, who took her hand off my arm and looked like she was about to bite Terry's head off . . . and then she let go of something herself. "Thank you, Terry. I hope . . . I know you'll be a good grandfather, too. I've been so angry that I forgot about the good times as well. But, even if we can't be married any longer, I'd like to still be friendly. For our children's sake. And ours."

Pushing my feelings aside, I beamed at them both to let him know I was extremely pleased with their efforts. "That's all we can hope for."

"Now," Terry said, for the first time a half-smile coming to his face as he stepped forward to come over to the bed, "am I going to get to hold my grandson or what?"

Stefan
Four months later . . .

"That was amazing!" Bella cried, her limbs shuddering from the last of her explosive orgasm, her forehead covered in sweat.

Trembling, she dismounted me and rolled off my still tensed stomach, letting out a contented sigh.

"It was good, wasn't it?" I asked her, playfully twitching my cock under the covers.

After the pregnancy and life-threatening car accident, I thought our sex life would diminish, but surprisingly, it got even more heated. I'm glad I'm a fast healer. My ribs were still aching the first time I woke up in the morning to find Bella hungrily slurping my cock, saying she needed her 'morning protein supplement,' as she started calling it.

Not one to turn down sex, I responded to her advances fiercely, giving her all she wanted and more. While my torn shoulder meant that I couldn't hold her up in the shower, there was nothing wrong with my tongue, and Bella found out she had an inner cowgirl who loved to ride me for hours if we could. I lost count of how many times we had adventurous sex all over the humongous manor. She awakened a hunger in me that knew no bounds.

Like now—despite just draining me, I still could go another round or two. I know what it was, really. After moving into the Livingston manor, we felt not just acceptance but security. Grandma Em and Grandpa Baron had both greeted us warmly. There were no tense conversations and no accusations of ruining the family. Just love.

I guess having an accepting family was the world's best aphrodisiac, and the staff had learned to knock before entering our guest wing or risk walking in on two young lovers doing all sorts of things. Like now, a just after lunch quickie that had come over us while I was supposed to be getting changed for my shoulder rehab workout in the pool. Bella just couldn't resist me once I got down to my underwear, it seemed.

Bella giggled and then kissed me on the lips,

running her hand over my half-hard cock teasingly. "Why, yes. Yes, it was."

I glanced around at the big guest room we were staying in. It reminded of an old bread and breakfast inn room, with fancy curtains and furniture. It had a warm, cozy feel. Across the room, there was a door adjoining a smaller guest room. This is where Rylan slept, though after that crazy sex session, he probably wasn't going to be sleeping for long. Thankfully, babies sleep a lot, and the walls of the manor are thick.

After the accident, Bella and I had graciously accepted our grandparents' offer. With injuries that kept me from being able to do heavy physical labor, I'd been forced to quit my job, and I was willing to set my pride aside if it meant that Bella and Rylan were taken care of. Instead of feeling ashamed, though, Bella had made me feel even more like a man, saying that it was the type of teamwork she had mentioned months before.

So that was good, too. Luckily for me, Grandpa Baron was pretty smart and had gone a step further by offering me a job to work for his company as soon as I was up to task. There were other conditions as well. I suspected he was going to get one or both of us back to college at some point, which to be honest, I wasn't that opposed to. Even if I did like working with my body, that didn't mean that was all I could do, Bella neither. Not that she couldn't work her body too.

And judging by the glorious lovemaking I'd just had with Bella, I'd say we were about fully healed.

I tilted my head toward the adjoining room, listening. By now, Rylan would have been awake by all the noises we had made, bawling his eyes out. The fact that he was quiet suggested that he must have been elsewhere.

"Where is Rylan?" I asked Bella curiously.

"He's downstairs with Grandma Em," she replied. "She's getting him ready for tonight."

With how huge the Livingston estate was, downstairs could mean anywhere.

I raised an eyebrow. "Tonight? What's happening tonight?"

Bella looked surprised. "Didn't I tell you? Our parents are flying in for a gathering. Others in the family are coming too, apparently."

Anxiety twisted my abs. That did not sound good at all. "They are?"

Bella nodded, running a finger over my bare chest, causing electricity to spark where our flesh met. "Everyone already knows about us. They've had time to get over it."

"I don't know about that," I said incredulously. "People in our family can be so difficult."

Bella quirked her lips. "I know. I'm looking at one right now."

I grabbed her finger that she was using to trace circles on my chest and playfully nipped at it with my teeth. "Hey, I haven't been so difficult, have I? Especially when it comes to giving you the . . ." I glanced down and twitched my cock several times, causing Bella to burst out laughing.

"No," she chuckled. "Only when it comes to fucking me harder . . ."

Lust burned through my nether regions. "Trust me, we can remedy that right now," I said, grabbing her and pulling her close.

To my surprise, Bella tore herself out of my arms and rolled out of the bed, naked, and placed her hands on her hips.

"None of that, now," she said as I admired her figure. Once she'd been able to walk without trouble, we started to exercise together. In addition to the swims in the pool for my shoulder, we started taking regular jogs around the manor's huge grounds, slow at first, but increasing in speed as Bella's body bounced back from her C-section even more beautiful than before.

She'd lost a few pounds but still carried some of her baby weight in all the right places. Her scar from her C-section had all but faded away, leaving a light mark, but I hardly paid attention to it. If I did, it was normally just to wonder over the miracle that had grown inside her body and what she meant to me. Simply put, giving birth took an already 'ten' Bella and made her about a 'fifteen' or so. I think that helped with my constant desire for her body, too.

"So get up, Mr. Horn Dog. It's time for me to go figure out what we're going to wear tonight." She half-turned as if to go toward the bathroom, giving me a nice wiggle of her butt, and I felt myself twitch again. She opened the door but stopped, turning back to me with a saucy grin. "Oh, and you're expected to dress up tonight too."

I let out a groan. "Why?"

Bella stuck out her tongue at me. "Because everyone else is, that's why!'

I let out a groan louder than the last. "This is bullshit."

Dammit, I had other plans for tonight. I wanted to make this private. But there's so much about this date that I can't put it off. Ah well, guess I'll be winging shit. I'm good at that, I thought. I rolled out of bed and followed her into the bathroom, where Bella was looking at her scar in the mirror.

"You really don't mind it?" she asked, taking down the bottle of Vitamin E-infused olive oil that she rubbed on the scar twice a day. "My scar?"

"Not at all," I said, hugging her from behind, my cock twitching as it nestled in between her pert, bubbly butt cheeks. "You know I think it's sexy as hell. By the way . . . I was kinda wondering, next time, can we try for a girl?"

Bella laughed, moaning softly as she pushed her hips back against my now fully hard cock. "Well, it's not like we can control that, but I don't mind that at all. You ready for me to blow up like an elephant again?"

"A sexy elephant," I teased, kissing the swan-like curve of Bella's neck. She melted back into my body, and I brought my hands up with two thoughts on my mind—the surprise I was going to have to spring in front of everyone, and the beautiful woman I had in my arms who wanted me to make love with her again before that.

Chapter 41
Bella

I felt sexy, wearing that red dress again. Stefan had wondered why I'd chosen to wear the exact cocktail dress that I'd worn to the governor's party, the same one that had ended so horribly, but I knew why. First, it was a great dress, and I was proud of the hard work I'd put in to get myself able to wear it again. If anything, I thought I looked even hotter in it. I certainly filled out the cups and the ass better.

Secondly, and more importantly, I couldn't let such a great dress only have bad memories attached to it. Sure, it was stupid, but I wanted to 'redeem' the dress. Still, I'd added a black shorty jacket to the ensemble, giving the whole thing sort of a Spanish look, and as I came down the stairs, Stefan, who looked amazing in the classic black tux, his hair slightly gelled and his jawline shaved totally clean, gawked a little.

"My God, how am I supposed to behave myself with you looking like that?" he whispered, putting an arm around my waist. "You look ravishing."

"Why thank you, Mr. Livingston. I feel ravishing too," I reassure him. "And you look positively dashing."

"I see you two have been digging around in the estate's library," Grandma Em said behind us, holding Rylan in her arms as she approached us. "Guess that's a better use for those old leather-bound books than just show. Come on. The guests are arriving, and you know they want to see you guys."

"They want to see Rylan. We're just accessories," Stefan joked, and his joke proved correct as our son became the total center of attention. Cousins, aunts, and uncles that I haven't seen in years all gathered around us, every one of them eager to hold, touch, or at least see the newest member of the family.

Rylan put up with it for a while before he protested, and I stepped in, cutting off the cuddles. "Okay, guys, let's sit down for dinner. It's Stefan's birthday anyway. That's supposed to be the reason we're here."

I glanced over at Mom, who was looking better than she did six months ago, more relieved. The paperwork was done. She and Terry aren't married anymore, but watching them talk to each other, they were being civil. In fact, I saw Mom smile once at a comment Terry made, which I guess was a good sign. We've kept in touch, but I still wasn't sure what the future holds there.

Grandpa Baron took charge of the dinner, sitting at the head of the long formal dining room table, Grandma Em at his right, with Stefan, Rylan, and me on his left. The conversation was lively, and we were on the second course when Grandpa Baron set his soup spoon down, looking at me and Stefan. "So, enjoying the party?"

"It's been a blast, Grandpa," Stefan said. "I'll admit I was a little worried, but everyone's been . . . well, at least everyone's been polite."

Grandpa Baron chuckled. He's one of those types of guys that the media likes to call a 'business mogul,' which basically means that he owns enough companies, or parts of companies, that he's got a bunch of money and nobody can really pin him down in one industry. But all that meant was that he was used to being in charge, and he wasn't a man to mess with. "I should hope so. I made it very clear I would not tolerate any trash talk about you two in my house. By the way, before we get to the speeches, I've got an early gift for you two. I'm kicking you out."

"Say what?" Stefan said, his eyes narrowing. "You've got a funny definition of a gift, Grandpa."

I could see Stefan's hand clench underneath the table, and I reached over, putting my hand on his thigh. "What do you mean, Grandpa?"

Grandpa Baron's eyes narrowed for a minute before Grandma Em slapped him on the arm, unable to hold back her laughter. "Stop it, Baron. You're giving your grandson a stroke. See the vein in his forehead throbbing?"

Grandpa Baron's face broke and he laughed softly. "You're right, Em. When I say kicking you out, I mean that I'm sending you both back to school. I've got a friend at SSU who is holding two slots open for you, and I happen to own an apartment building near campus. Now, it's not going to be a walk in the park. You're still both going to have to put in the sweat work, but here's the deal. I checked with SSU, and they'll let you keep your credits from your one completed semester at NSU. So, I'm giving you both four and a half years, full ride. Of course, you'll apply for scholarships and things, but Em and I will cover your living expenses and any gap. If you can both graduate in that time with at least a 3.0 GPA, I'm offering Stefan, and you, Bella, if you want, a position in my company. I'm not getting younger, and it'd be nice to know that Livingston Investments will stay in the family."

"And if we get a 2.9?" Stefan asked, and Grandpa Baron's smile grew slightly hard.

"Then you'll have to find your own jobs. And if you drop out, you get nothing, of course. Don't give me an answer tonight if you don't want. SSU's application deadline isn't for another few weeks."

I looked at Stefan, who was still looking a little stunned by the generosity of Grandpa's offer. He turned to me and whispered in my ear, "Well?"

"I want to take it," I whispered back. "I'm yours forever, Stefan, but I'd like to have my degree too."

"It'll be hard, taking care of Rylan and being students," he said. "But I'll be there for you."

"I know," I replied, patting his thigh. I looked up at Grandpa Baron and Grandma Em, giving them my best smile. "Thank you, both of you. We don't need to wait. We'll take it. We can talk details later."

"Thank you," Stefan echoed. "It's almost the best birthday gift I could have."

"What could be better?" Grandma Em asks, and Stefan clears his throat, standing up. "Stefan?"

Stefan held his hand up, getting everyone's attention. "Excuse me, everyone? I have a few things I'd like to say. First, thank you all for coming. I know Rylan was the superstar, but it feels good having you all here. Second, I'd like to extend special thanks to Grandpa Baron and Grandma Emily. They've opened their home to us, and their generosity seems to know no bounds. Grandpa Baron offered, and Bella and I just accepted—

we're going to go back to school. So Dad, Evelyn, you guys can relax on that front."

Terry and Mom, seated across from each other, raised their glasses in a toast, and Terry wished us both good luck there in a hearty voice. After we all toasted, Stefan continued. "Now, I just told Grandpa that it was just about the best birthday present that I could get, which of course confused the hell out of Grandma. She wondered what could be better. Well, I'll tell you."

Stefan turned to me, his eyes burning, and I felt my heart catch in my throat as I realized what he was doing. "Bella, we've loved each other for years. And while what brought us together was traumatic, I'd go through it all again to have you by my side. If I'd change anything, it would be to learn from my mistakes and not be so damn hard-headed. Bella, you're the love of my life, the woman I want to spend the rest of my life with. So . . ."

Stefan got down on a knee after moving his chair, and reached into the pocket of his tuxedo jacket, taking out a small diamond ring. He took my hand, his eyes locked on mine. "Bella, would you marry me?"

We'd checked once, casually. Of course, there was nothing against it. We're not blood. Family, but not blood, is just fine. I nodded, tears coming to my eyes. "Of course I will. I love you."

Stefan put the ring on my finger, and of course, it was a perfect fit. We embraced, and his kiss was sweet. Before the applause starts and the family gathers to congratulate us, I whispered in his ear. "You said birthday gift. But I'm the one getting the gift, so what are you getting?"

Stefan chuckled and hugged me tighter. "Every minute with you is a gift. But if you want to give me a special gift, we can talk about that after the party, upstairs."

I laughed and kissed him again. Oh, he didn't know just how much I'd be helping him celebrate his birthday that night. In every way he could ever want.

Actually, it was everything *we* could ever want.

Thank you for reading!

Please check out my website at www.LaurenLandish.com for new releases, updates, and to sign up for my newsletter!

Manufactured by Amazon.ca
Bolton, ON